Read[illegible] raving about Sophie Dunbar's Eclaire mystery series!

Behind Eclaire's Doors

"A bright and breezy excursion through the elegant town houses and sleazy back alleys of the Big Easy. Sophie Dunbar has pulled off a smashing debut."

—*Clarion-Ledger* Jackson, Mississippi

"Makes the pulse pound—for several reasons. May there be many of these ribald, racy romps."

—*Washington Times*

"Delightfully irreverent, slightly wacky, and sizzlingly sexy." —*Sunday Magazine*, Baton Rouge

"A sassy, stylish, slightly trashy debut I hugely enjoyed." —*Booknews* from the Poisoned Pen

"A fast-paced and racey read, with deliciously colorful characters, spicey patois, steamy sex and New Orleans' own peculiar social distinctions." —*The New Mexican*

"Cleverly plotted with quirky characters and a good sense of New Orleans." —*Sun-Sentinel*, Ft. Lauderdale

A Bad Hair Day

"An energetic, sensuous romp that is particularly refreshing." —*L.A. Times*

"Sophie, don't keep us waiting so long for the next one!" —*Washington Times*

"Dunbar makes the Big Easy come alive in sight and sound for armchair tourists." —*The Purloined Letter*

"In Sophie Dunbar's delicious A Bad Hair Day, hairdresser-sleuth Claire Claiborne faces down frazzled hair and macabre murder with aplomb and panache while offering readers a zesty, Cajun-flavored, irresistible New Orleans."

—*Carolyn G. Hart,*
author of the Death on Demand
and Henrie O mysteries

Redneck Riviera

"Mysteries don't get more fun than this." —*L.A. Times*

"A fun romp . . . a steamy sizzler . . . a tale that crosses genre lines while pleasing fans of both."

—*Midwest Book Review*

"What lifts Dunbar's romp above the ordinary are the zest and good humor, not to mention the Cajun cuisine and various hearty appetites." —*Barbara Peters, The Poisoned Pen Bookstore*

A Bad Hair Day

Sophie Dunbar

For information, please contact Intrigue Press, P.O. Box 456, Angel Fire, NM 87710 505-377-3474.

First hardcover printing: St. Martin's Press, March, 1996
First paperback printing: Intrigue Press, September, 1998

ISBN 1-890768-08-1

This book is especially dedicated the The Encouragers:

Sylvan Markman
Neil McGaughey
Janine Coughlin
Earlene Fowler
Terry Baker
Audrey Moore
and to the One who encourages us all.

The author gratefully acknowledges the invaluable assistance of Dr. Michael Garst, the criminally-minded chemist of Orange County, who custom-concocted a lethal potion just for me; Edward J. Coker, music technician, Roland Music Corporation, for plotting a spectacular demise; LaVonne Rae Andrews, for explaining the technical aspects of henna; Marcus Daniels of Umberto's, Beverly Hills, for anecdotes and consistently good hair days; and Barbara Hutnick, who has "processed" me through manuscripts that look more like quilts than anything else, when she gets them. A special *merci* to photographer Louis Sahuc, for graciously consenting to appear as himself, on his own balcony.

Chapter 1

The scream sliced like a razor through the dull roar created by ten working hairdryers, as the woman's freshly permed head lolled lifelessly to one side.

Poor thing, she'd been dead set on going curly, but now all she had was body.

Talk about your bad hair days . . .

Chapter 2

It was the rich, dusky aroma of French roast coffee that first coaxed me from sleep, but the real eyeopener was an appetizing rear shot of a big naked man, shaving at the bathroom sink. Oolala! Hot buns to go with my coffee! A downright divine Sunday morning, so far.

The old pink crackleware pot I'd inherited from *Tante* Jeanette waited on my bedside table, emitting a come-hither curl of steam from its spout. After stretching luxuriously, I filled a matching cup, part of the set which had originally belonged to *Tante* J's *grand-mère* back in Nova Scotia, and savored the coffee's dark, delicious bite. My pleasure was no doubt enhanced by the knowledge that it had been freshly brewed by the naked man.

All at once, I was struck by the paradox of how something so fragile as this very piece of china, from so long ago and far away, could have managed to outlast everyone who had ever drunk from it. I held the cup to the light, and its soft patina glowed with rosy confidence. A lovely thing indeed, but it was somewhat irking to think it might still be around after I was gone. Maybe that's what had driven certain cultures to start shouting and breaking their drinking vessels.

When the naked man shifted his weight to his right hip, I decided that called for a hearty *salut*, if anything did, and drained my cup, resisting a sudden impulse to hurl it into the fireplace.

The telephone rang as I was plumping some feather pillows behind me to maximize my view of the gentleman's splendid backside.

"Claire, you must help me. I am having a bad hair day."

Those fateful words rolled trippingly off the tongue of Marcel Barrineau, who only recently had declared himself to be monumentally bored with that trendy buzzphrase. Because, as he'd argued when we were pondering its etymology, bad hair doesn't just happen, it is committed, whether out of ignorance, incompetence, or malice, by human hands.

"Perhaps it is intended to be witty," he'd complained, "but this term is used with such increasing frequency, one would suppose we were all thrashing helplessly in the grip of a national epidemic." To the director of New Orleans's famous Institut de Beauté, owner of five salons throughout the city, *un jour du cheveux mal* is no laughing matter.

Then, the light bulb had flashed on over Marcel's sleek silver head.

To halt the spread of any epidemic required not just treatment, but education and prevention. What could be more logical than to put together a seminar that answered all the above?

He, who had never endured a personal bad hair day in his whole privileged life, had painlessly birthed the perfect scheme to cash in on everybody else's and called it, A Bad Hair Day!

For a fee of fifty dollars (gratuities not included) BHD-stricken patients could receive emergency repairs at the Urgent Care Hair Clinic, along with styling tips and product samples.

Meanwhile, licensed operators who'd signed up for the innocuous-sounding Technique Adjustment Workshop would quickly discover the term to be but a polite euphemism for twelve grueling hours of merciless retraining.

A Bad Hair Day was an extremely ambitious undertaking to be sure, but Marcel, never one to let moss gather, had already gotten it organized and ready to go. With seemingly no trouble, he'd recruited nineteen of what he considered to be the surrounding area's best stylists for the occasion, assuming he had merely to inform the twentieth—me—when and where.

"Well, I don't know, Marcel," I hedged. "I'm pretty booked up just now. When were you planning to have it?"

My attention was diverted by the naked man, who'd finished shaving and was bending over to rinse lather from his face. *Skoal!* I had to ask Marcel to repeat himself.

"I said, I have arranged to hold it next Monday," he answered with a touch of impatience. "Naturally, I would not expect you to abandon your own clientele to participate."

I am among those in the hair business who still adhere to the old tradition of observing a Monday "sabbath."

Marcel went on to say that newspaper ads would begin running in tomorrow's *Times-Picayune*. Classes, of course, were restricted to professionals only and had already been filled to capacity with unsuspecting participants. Admissions to the clinic would be on a first-come, first-serve basis, starting at seven in the morning and going until we were done, which probably wouldn't be before ten o'clock that night.

I sighed, knowing I really couldn't say no. After all, Marcel and I went back a long way. First he'd been my teacher, then my boss, wanted to become my lover, but became my dear friend instead, during the intervening years before I opened Eclaire, my own small beauty shop on the ground floor of an authentically restored townhouse in the Garden District.

Eclaire—which is short and sweet for my name, Evangeline Claire—doesn't look like a hair salon at all, but a rustic cottage somewhere on a hillside in provincial France; rough terra-cotta tile floors, apricot-washed plaster walls, pine antiques, tapestry, pewter, and a rose garden.

Upstairs are seven spacious, high-ceilinged rooms, two of them opening onto a balcony which affords a pleasant view of St. Charles Avenue, Audubon Park, and a distant slice of the Mississippi River. This is where I live with my second (and first) husband, Dan Louis Claiborne.

An expectant pause was hovering at Marcel's end of the line, and I had to laugh. His enthusiasm for a project always generated such a powerful magnetic force, it just pulled everybody else right along with him. "Oh, all right!" I capitulated. "Where shall I report?"

"Thank you, Claire," replied Marcel briskly. "As Dominica is adamant that the teaching duties should remain under the auspices of our regular faculty, your surgical and color expertise in the hair clinic will be most welcome, and pivotal to its efficaciousness. I, of course, shall divide my presence between the two."

Even though Marcel is descended from one of the original French families who settled New Orleans, English was his first language, but it is his rather endearing affectation to talk as if he'd learned it from old Berlitz tapes.

I yawned and poured myself another cup of coffee. The naked man had disappeared into the shower, so I was able to fully concentrate on what Marcel was saying, feeling myself getting drawn in.

Well, this event would certainly be an interesting test of my mettle, but not nearly as much work as it had sounded at first. Since we surgeons were required to provide ourselves with one intern each, that put forty "hairamedics" on duty. Even if a hundred people (Marcel's top guess) showed up—whose individual needs would vary in the specific categories of color, cut or perm gone wrong—our caseloads would average out to something like five heads apiece. "If my trial bad hair day should prove successful, and I do not anticipate otherwise," Marcel concluded, "it will be the first in a series of such events, at a higher fee, of course. I am, after all, not a non-profit organization. Perhaps I should immediately have Dan trademark the title. Also, I must consult with him about forming a franchise."

"Oh, Marcel. You're just a big old money machine, aren't you? Well, bye-bye for now, *chér*. Enjoy your Sunday."

"And just how do you suggest I accomplish this?" he demanded plaintively. "I have been telephoning the succulent Orange all morning, and there is no answer. Either she is simply not picking up, or she is perhaps having an intimate breakfast somewhere with that unsavory Duke Abbidis."

From the beginning of his incredibly starcrossed romance with Detective Sergeant Nectarine Savoy (whom he'd met while she was investigating the murders of his former girlfriend and illegitimate son) Marcel, when speaking of her, always called Nectarine by the name of every other fruit but her own.

I don't know how he addressed the lady in their private moments, but in my hearing, she had always been, "my dear." Dan's theory was that Marcel had worked himself into a state of superstition that, should he utter her real name, he would be committing himself to something irrevocable.

And therein lay the problem.

At the outset of their relationship, he had rather enjoyed the thrill of flouting society—as only someone absolutely certain of his position in it can—by escorting this stunning octoroon woman with skin the color of cinnamon tea, sapphire eyes, and Medusa ringlets of coppergold to even the most exclusive functions. Tell the truth, New Orleans *ton* was pretty small potatoes compared to the high and mighty international circles Nectarine traveled in as a famous fashion model before she quit to join her hometown police force.

Our city is notoriously schizophrenic about color. While it might conceivably tolerate the idea of Nectarine as Marcel's mistress—because of her beauty and because both their families had been here practically from Day One—accepting her as his wife was another matter entirely.

But Nectarine was not Marcel's mistress. To put this as daintily as possible, their passion remained unrequited, because that lady wasn't about to settle for being somebody's little piece of white chocolate on the side, thank you very much.

As for Marcel, the once infamous and remarkably resilient womanizer now found himself helplessly in love with Nectarine alone, and he knew the clock was running out, mainly because of Duke Abbidis. Handsome Mr. Abbidis, from an old and wealthy New Orleans quadroon family, was a criminal attorney of somewhat shady repute. He'd been pitching woo in a very determined manner to Nectarine lately, and she wasn't exactly going out of her way to avoid him.

I finally got Marcel off the phone by agreeing that yes, perhaps he should just casually drive by Nectarine's cottage over on Camp Street to see if her car was in the driveway.

The naked man walked into the bedroom carrying his empty coffee cup. My husband is around six feet tall, with dark hair, blue eyes, and a strong, wide, furry body that looks even better from the front than it does from the back.

I am a smallish blond who can—and frequently does—stand beneath his chin while wearing high heels (and sometimes not much else) and I adore being overwhelmed.

"Hey, darlin'. You leave me any coffee?" Dan inquired. I said I had, and he leaned past me for the pot, creating a dazzling 3-D effect. He intercepted my gaze and I lowered my lashes demurely, but he wasn't fooled.

"Don't get any ideas, you hussy!" he warned. "The bathroom's all yours. Hurry now, and maybe we'll be on time for once."

Dan and I had very recently, very miraculously, been fished from a runaway boat on the Gulf of Mexico by the next best thing to Jesus in a helicopter. A killer had cut us adrift in the middle of a hurricane. Since then we've devoutly attended Sunday morning services at the little Josephine Street Episcopal Church where we were married the second time. Because our prior churchgoing habits had been so irregular, we still didn't quite have the knack of it yet.

He looked down at me. "Be a good girl and I'll take you to brunch after."

I wrapped my arms around his waist and burrowed my face into his solid stomach. "Fine. I'll have the buffet," I said in a muffled voice.

"Would you settle for Brennan's?" he started to laugh but stopped abruptly. "Claire, darlin' . . . don't . . . you'll make me spill this coffee . . . I'm serious . . . please . . . ohhh, baby!"

"Goodness! Look at the time!" I exclaimed and hopped out of bed, scampering for the bathroom, but Dan easily caught me from behind.

"Thought I told you to behave yourself," he growled.

"Honey. You stand there and swing that thing right in my face, what do you expect?"

Dan gave me a steamy look and murmured he expected I knew what . . .

Chapter 3

Brennan's is just a short walk up Royal Street from the Monteleone Hotel garage where Dan parked, past antique shops filled with priceless treasures of wood and tapestry, jewels and gold, glass, porcelain, bronzes and canvases.

Like many other businesses in the French Quarter, the restaurant's building was originally a beautiful private home with a long, soap opera-ish history of wealth, scandal, and recurring tragedy.

Though New Orleans is a city overflowing with fabulous establishments dishing out exquisite food, sometimes nothing will do but "Breakfast at Brennan's," a tradition which still retains its special clubby morning opulence, even if the management had inexplicably abolished a once onerously rigid dress code.

Hard evidence of the latter was furnished by the group of tourists who burst through Brennan's double doors out onto the sidewalk as we approached, triumphantly brandishing souvenir menus picturing the famous crowing rooster, boasting loudly of having just eaten the "finest fifty-dollar eggs in the world!" They were well-fed, even more well-oiled, and they flaunted with fine abandonment their hairless, varicosed shanks in bermudas, and broad, dimpled bottoms beneath tight polyester leggings.

In our city, where real men wear suits when dining out, the natives try valiantly not to notice all those sweatpants and shorts—and worse—that are just so tacky among the linen tablecloths and crystal chandeliers.

Shortly after we entered the famous pink facade, Dan and I were settled cozily by a window that looked out onto the lush green courtyard, and supplied with a pair of Brennan's rich and justly famous brandy milk punches. He caught my eye and gestured discreetly toward the next table, where a California-type couple frantically checked the menu against their pocketsized fat gram counter.

When they overheard Dan give our order—his was Eggs à la Turk with chicken livers and mushrooms; and for me, a double order of Buster Crabs Béarnaise, a house specialty which must be experienced to be believed—the poor things looked like they might go into cardiac arrest without ever having had the pleasure of getting there!

Studying Dan over the rim of my goblet, I immediately lost interest in West Coast health angst. His brown, Sunday-go-to-meeting suit of lightweight wool, creamy cotton shirt and sedately patterned Italian silk tie, melded into an entrancing alchemy of reverence and masculinity. I was glad the weather had finally, in mid-October, cooled off enough for me to wear the olive and gold gaberdine outfit I'd bought in Paris on our first honeymoon.

As if thinking along the same lines, he raised his glass to me and said, "Claire, I realize Tuesday we will have been remarried two months. But we may as well go ahead and celebrate now, baby, 'cause starting tomorrow, it's crunch time. I don't know how late I'll be working Tuesday night."

After many weeks of delays and continuances, Dan's big case, to do with the legitimate ownership of a patent on some kind of processor for recycling paper, was at last going to trial and it looked like a long haul.

"Well, whatever time it is, there'll be a fire in the fireplace and a bottle of champagne on ice, waiting for you," I promised. No doubt these monthly anniversary observances would taper off eventually, but not for a while. During the last two years, so many strange things had happened to us, we were touchingly proud of every little milestone.

"Always begin with the basics," Dan approved. "And did you also plan to slip into something basically black and clingy?"

I smiled. "Do you really have to ask?" Actually, I had invited our closest friends, Dan's law partner Foley Callant and his fiancée Charlotte Dalton, and Marcel, with or without Nectarine, over for a small surprise gathering. None of them would mind in the least when he straggled in. Also Dan's parents, Dave Louis and Rae Ellen, who were due to return tomorrow from a clinic in Austin, Texas, where D.L. had been undergoing a radical new treatment for degenerative kidney disease.

Whatever the procedure was, it was so hush-hush and controversial he wouldn't even tell us, but Dan and I suspected the Austin place was just a front for some maverick doctor operating out of Mexico. If so, more power to him, since we firmly believe people with life-threatening illnesses should be totally free to pursue any course of treatment they choose. Anyway, D.L. always knew exactly what he was doing.

And judging from how wonderful he'd sounded last Friday night when we'd spoken long distance, the risk had definitely paid off. "Well, hell yes, sugar!" D.L. had bellowed enthusiastically to my hurried, whispered invitation when Dan handed me the cordless phone and went to pick up the kitchen extension. "Wouldn't miss it for nothing! We got us a whole lot of catching up to do."

Since Tuesday looked like a fairly heavy workday for me, Our Blessed Lady of Household Help, Juanita Valle, was going to cook and serve a variety of her special Cuban treats. And later on, when it was time for the basic black, I anticipated Dan's reaction to my new nightie, a long sliver of charmeuse the color of spilled ink, would be basically very satisfying indeed.

The California Couple, having thoroughly interrogated their long-suffering waiter, had finally agreed to yield to temptation, "just this once," and went for doubles on the Eggs Benedict.

Our food arrived quickly, and when we'd transferred portions of our respective dishes to each other's plates, Dan asked, "What did Marcel want so early on a Sunday?"

Because of this and that, I hadn't yet filled Dan in on Marcel's latest inspiration.

"Leave it to Marcel!" he laughed appreciatively, after I gave him the gist. "You know, that's a pretty good idea he had about a franchise, too. Seminars and workshop events are very lucrative and trendy just now. I'd better give him a call first thing in the morning because if he's serious, we need to get that trademark process in the works right away.

Otherwise, if somebody sees the ad tomorrow and decides to do a copycat, conceivably they could beat him to the punch. And speaking of punch!" He motioned for refills.

"I think the only thing Marcel worries somebody might beat him to is around five-eleven, female, blue-eyed and slightly off-white," I sighed.

Dan was unsympathetic. "In that case, he'll have only himself to blame if Duke Abbidis manages to persuade Nectarine to become wife number four. It is clearly, 'or get off the pot' time, wouldn't you say, Claire? Sure, it's a big step and all. But, hell! He knows his real friends will back him up. And I frankly can't see it hurting his business that much, either."

I savored a mouthful of mushroom and egg. "You know what?" I said slowly. "I just realized why Marcel's been carrying on like he has. It's the first time he's ever actually loved. Oh, he's been *in* love a gazillion times. But he knows it's going to cost him everything he's got to keep Nectarine. And I don't mean money."

Dan rested his chin on his hands and looked at me seriously. "So what? If he doesn't pay full price, he'll be sorry every day of his life. We should know."

His words stirred a dry little rustle of remembered pain. Not so very long ago we each, in or own way, had greedily tried to consume as much of the galvanic passion that rocked us without anteing up on the emotional tab. The final bill had been a miscarriage, and our divorce.

Dan was right, Marcel had definitely arrived at a *crise*, and the decision he made now would affect him forever. Not to mention Nectarine.

Very interesting cards, but a tricky hand. How would that old moonlight gambler play it?

I took a pleasurable swallow of milk punch, noting out of the corner of my eye that the Californians had bolted their illicit *oeufs* as if the Tofu Police might arrive at any moment, and were now sneaking furtive glances toward the dessert cart.

"Hey, rascal. You've got a milk mustache," Dan informed me. As I licked it off he added softly, "And by the way, just in case I didn't mention it? Thank you for . . . earlier."

"Oh no, baby. It's me who should say *merci,*" I told him, pulling his hand to my lips. Slowly and deliberately, I began to kiss his palm. "*Tu gout si bon, chér.*"

His voice grew rough around the edges. "Claire, I sincerely hope I'm not called to the phone."

I glanced under the table and said solemnly, "Tsk, tsk. What to do?"

"Darlin'," he said, "you're way too dangerous to be running around without a leash. But I do love to give you your head."

I looked at him. "Hmm, an interesting turn of phrase, Dan Louis."

"Woman, you are so *bad*!" he chuckled, and moved my chair closer to his. We talked trash and played touch beneath the linen tablecloth, the remaining food on our plates forgotten.

"Ah, libidos and eggs. My favorite!" a persnickety voice interrupted an especially titillating suggestion Dan was whispering into my ear.

"Too bad, we got the last dish," I retorted to the tall, bony man with sandy hair and a pale, freckled, foxy face regarding us sardonically.

"Dan, do you remember Lochner Smith?" I asked, as he slid his exploring finger from that highly sensitive spot just behind my knee and half-rose to shake hands with the interloper.

"Sure. You were at our wedding, right?" Dan replied instantly.

I was highly impressed, since a couple hundred other people had also attended that significant occasion, that Dan should be able to recall a brief chat with the owner of the LockSmith hair salons, three convenient locations in Gretna, Metairie, and Uptown. I personally was still writing thank-you notes to names I couldn't have put a face to if my life depended on it.

"Yes, and the melody lingers on, it seems," Lock commented wryly. He peered at us through gold-rimmed spectacles, tapping a rolled-up London *Times* against one stork-like, tweedy leg.

Dan flicked a questioning look at me before inviting Lock to join us.

"Thank you, I thought you'd never ask," Lock said pettishly, folding his angles into a chair. "Not only is my own table not ready, but there is no room to wait in the lobby and read until my guest arrives, because it is filled with a large family from Nebraska, or some other farm state. Not numerous mind you. Merely . . . large."

He opened his newspaper and glanced around the room. "Over here, Claude," he called to a waiter, who hurried in our direction.

"Mr. Smith, I'm afraid it's going to be another ten or fifteen minutes yet. The manager apologizes for the delay, and hopes you will accept a drink with her compliments?"

Lock appeared mollified. "I certainly will. A Bloody Mary, if you please. And I assume that invitation extends to Mr. and Mrs. Claiborne here, who were kind enough to offer me a seat?" Lock could be very generous, as long as he wasn't buying.

With assurances that indeed it did, Claude departed for the bar.

Dan and I prepared to make small talk until the bonus drinks arrived, but we needn't have bothered. Almost at once, Lock became engrossed in his newspaper.

I hadn't seen him since the wedding, and not for several months prior to that. Our paths rarely crossed since he'd tried to hire me away from Marcel a year or so before I married Dan.

Lochner Smith and Marcel Barrineau were contemporaries, had even trained together in Paris under the great Alexandre. But while Marcel emerged as a swashbuckler who took calculated risks, Lock, despite a lengthy stint of expatriatism in swinging England from the sixties to around 1975, somehow managed to cultivate a stuffy conservatism in the face of Mod excesses. He returned to New Orleans with a styling technique that bore few traces of his having been present at one of the most seminal locations during perhaps the most crucial decade in hair history, along with an inordinate passion for tweeds and the London *Times*.

Of course he was quite talented, and his traditional philosophy ensured a comfortable stable of clients, no matter what the latest craze. But it's also why, when Lock offered me a job, I opted to stay with Marcel, identifying with his more emotional, innovative approach to hair, yet knowing there was that firm, classical European foundation beneath me at all times.

However, when it came to their respective private lives, the roles were completely reversed. Marcel's was lustily traditional, while Lock's was complicated and . . . exotic, if the rumors were to be believed.

But were they?

Only Lochner Smith could say, and he revealed very little about himself, quite in contrast to a certain breed of stylist who considers the salon their couch and every client a captive therapist.

As a consequence, deservedly or not, he'd acquired a reputation for discretion, the quintessential hairdresser with a sympathetic ear that women could safely confide their most intimate secrets to.

Claude reappeared with our drinks, and Lock reluctantly put the paper aside, folding it to mark his place.

I noticed the issue was dated three weeks ago, a trifle stale as far as news goes, but fairly typical of ordinary mail service between the UK and here. We have friends who returned from Scotland long before the postcard, of long-haired cattle grazing on a hillside, sent at the very beginning of their tour.

A few restorative sips of Bloody Mary served to remind Lock that he was a temporary guest at our table, so for the next few minutes, he made an effort to be sociable.

As it turned out, he'd participated in a big hair show in London a month or two ago, and regaled us with highlights of the event, which featured the obligatory IRA bomb scare.

"The first chance I've had to get back there in *years,*" he concluded, managing to inject an accusatory note which I remembered was a particularly unattractive little trick of his. If you weren't careful around Lock, you'd wind up apologizing for things you didn't have the remotest responsibility for.

"That trip only served to remind me how much I missed it all," he went on fretfully, taking a deeper pull at his drink. "The theatre, the museums, the fine hotels—"

"The tweeds," I interjected.

Lock's thin lips twisted in an unwilling smile. "You always were a Miss Clever-britches, weren't you, Evangeline?"

Dan asked, "Have you given serious thought to moving back to England on a permanent basis, Lochner?"

"Several times a day," Lock snapped. "But really, the only reason I returned to the States twenty years ago was that it began to cost too bloody much to live there. In the style I wish to, that is," he added frankly. "And it's far, far worse now. What is the point of uprooting myself from a life of comparative luxury merely to subsist in a squalid little bedsitter somewhere unfashionable? No, London is only comfortable when you go top drawer, and then it's very comfortable, indeed."

"So you've given up on the idea then," I said.

"Not at all!" Lock countered. "I shouldn't bank on me remaining mired in this mosquito-infested swamp much longer. As a matter of fact, I'm working on a certain scheme"— he smiled secretly into his depleted glass—"that could well be my ticket to Knightsbridge."

"Fine. But in the meantime, if you get too bored, you can always open another LockSmith's. Maybe over in City Park this time. On, say, Esplanade?" I suggested, teasingly. Esplanade Avenue in City Park is where Marcel's newest and most modern salon is located.

"Very funny, I don't think so, Evangeline Claire," he drawled sourly. "And speaking of Monsieur Barrineau, I suppose he's also managed to rope you into his latest escapade?"

Cranky old anglophile or not, I was glad Lock had signed on for Marcel's Bad Hair Day, too.

"Barbara will be assisting me, of course," he added.

In a way, this event was going to be like a family reunion for me. Literally, in the case of Babs Hooper, since we'd lived on the same street before she had to move away—

Lock stole a glance at his watch, and another at the entrance to the dining room, and huffed impatiently. "So what mischief have you been perpetrating lately, E.C.?" he inquired, trying to sound interested, but his eyes strayed longingly toward the folded London *Times*.

"Oh, for heaven's sake, Lock!" I exclaimed. "Go ahead and read your newspaper. We don't mind."

"Well, if you're sure." Lock's long, skinny hand jerked out and snatched it up. "But do fill me in on your life, won't you? I can read and listen at the same time. And while I'm thinking of it"—he rattled the pages until they fell into proper alignment—"whatever happened to your charming friend, the news reporter? I don't believe I've seen her on television lately."

I informed him he was quite right, that Charlotte Dalton had recently left her job at WDSU as part-time news anchor and field reporter for a much better position at a brand new independent station, WBGZ—"Big Easy TV."

Lock, who'd been intently scanning an item muttered something that sounded like, "Hmph!"

"Well, I think a new television station could be a real good thing for New Orleans," I said defensively, reacting to his apparent skepticism. "At any rate, it's going to be great for Charlotte's career. And Harry Corvus, the station manager says—"

Lock's head lifted slowly from the newsprint and his cordovan eyes focused sharply on me. "I'm sorry, Claire. What were you saying?"

So I had to repeat the whole thing, concluding, "Which only goes to prove you can't read and listen at the same time, Lochner Smith!" I gibed. "What on earth was holding you at such rapt attention, anyway? Has Prince Charles confessed to something we actually didn't already know about?"

Lock laughed shortly. "Hardly! In any case, I doubt that's possible. No, my dear Evangeline, I was perusing the death notices. American newspapers are sadly lacking in the art of obituary writing, but the London *Times* has a way of waxing highly literary over the Departed.

"They often contain enough fascinating and eccentric information to almost make you feel as if you'd known the person."

Dan remarked, "Now, what I think would really be fascinating is if you were reading along and suddenly find you *had* known one of those people and that they'd left their entire fortune to you!"

Lochner paused in the act of carefully refolding his paper and looked at Dan in some amusement. “Perhaps they have done, in a manner of speaking,” he said enigmatically, and pushed his chair back.

“Excuse me, I need to make a phone call,” he added. And in a flurry of tweed, was gone.

Chapter 4

Our own waiter arrived to clear the table and bring coffee. We declined dessert, planning to maybe pick up some coconut ice cream at Broccato's, along with a dozen or so of their luscious mini-cannolis (that let you kid yourself you're really not eating too many of them) to take home for later.

When we were alone again, Dan inquired, "Now, darlin'. Where was I before we were so rudely interrupted? Oh, yes . . ."

His rich, husky voice, as much of an aphrodisiac as the sexy adventure he was proposing, triggered a warm, delicious ache.

"Sounds fascinating," I murmured, "if a bit . . . gymnastic in the demands upon your energy."

"Don't worry, I aim to live up to my billing, baby love." He smiled mischievously. "Why else do you think I consumed all those expensive eggs just now?"

"Why, sir!" I exclaimed, fanning my face with my napkin. "How you do go on!"

He laughed. "That's the general idea."

We finished our coffee and Dan signaled for more, then quickly turned to me. "Claire," he muttered, "don't look now, but isn't that the gal who runs that crazy club you dragged me to for opening night? Named Queenie, or something?"

"Duchess," I corrected, after a discreet glance at the statuesque woman being ushered toward the dining room beyond ours by Brennan's suave mâitre d', who appeared unfazed either by her rococo attire, or the buzz rising from the tables left in their wake.

When she'd vanished through the archway with a final wriggle, the tourists returned happily to their troughs, convinced they were getting their money's worth.

In a city where the outlandish, the eccentric, and the downright bizarre are commonplace, Duchess Crowe's everyday wardrobe could deceive a newcomer into standing on the curb, waiting in vain for the rest of the Mardi Gras parade. Even here, one didn't often encounter exotic, Oriental-African types with very long, straight black hair, poured into tight red satin cheongsams and perched on crimson suede platforms with four-inch heels and anklestraps.

According to fairly reliable hearsay, Duchess had been a young local beautician just starting out, when Beatlemania struck the planet. She'd sold everything but her camera and bought a ticket to London, determined to become a rock and roll star, only to wind up as a groupie who gave haircuts and took snapshots. Perhaps it was some consolation that she slept with, and styled the hair of, many of the very biggest names in rock music.

I wondered if Duchess had bothered to save any of those candid pics. Some of them could be worth a fortune by now.

The closest she ever got to a recording contract was singing backup on several of Teddy Boy Crowe's hits, and that was mainly because the megastar had fallen in love with her.

When Teddy Boy, famous for wearing more rings than Ringo, and playing barefoot to display the ones on his toes, was gruesomely executed onstage by his own malfunctioning electric guitar, Duchess stepped forward and claimed she was his widow, and therefore entitled to his millions.

But she'd reckoned without Teddy's family, who surprisingly turned out to be threadbare nobility and saddled with a damp, draughty, money-gobbling ancestral mansion on the outskirts of London. Teddy Boy had been, in reality, "Sir Theodore."

There were several versions of what happened next. Some said Teddy's family hired ruthless lawyers to pressure Duchess into relinquishing all claims as his widow and accepting a payoff.

After all, if she tried to fight them in court, who would take the word of a notorious rock and roll floozy, over that of the peerage?

Others thought she couldn't produce proof of their marriage, either because there was none to produce, or that it had been stolen or somehow suppressed by Teddy's powerful relatives.

Whatever the case, Duchess temporarily disappeared from sight, only to resurface some months later, on the cover of a British tabloid, triumphantly clutching the arm of Mick Jagger, no less, and calling herself Duchess Crowe.

She spent the ensuing twenty-odd years in Europe, among the entourages of the most famous rock musicians, and was credited with creating several major trendsetting hairstyles.

About a year back, Duchess returned to New Orleans and bought a big, rundown house on Napoleon Boulevard near the River, directly across from Tipitina's, transforming it into a rock and roll nightclub.

Old fantasies die hard, but this one had taken a new twist.

Since her day, hair and rock music had mated to produce an entire counterculture. Duchess simply proposed to carry it one step further, by searching for a band whose members were not simply talented musicians, but talented hairdressers, as well!

The trick, of course, was to discover one special group that would take off like a rocket, a process that required a launching pad. Hence, the Mirror Club.

Not a project to undertake on a tight budget, though, as rocket launches often prove to be duds. Which explained the fairly stiff cover charge and pricy drinks.

Invitations to the opening bash, to which Dan had referred, were costly and ingenious. Satiny black stock, diecut in the shape of a compact, was engraved with the The Mirror Club in gold, and opened to reveal a metallic reflective paper upon which were printed the time, date, location and See You.

Decor was done with mirrors, naturally.

The Looking Glass cocktail lounge took up the entire ground floor and had a Victorian bordello theme. Walls painted a rich, vintage bordeaux were hung top to bottom with antique mirrors of every size, shape and condition. Fat brass cherubs of questionable innocence held electric globes that diffused a soft, red glow, while moody piano music trickled from a baby grand.

There were low walnut tables with elaborately turned legs, surrounded by chairs and sofas which were deep, squashy, covered in grape velvet, and athrob with erotic possibilities.

Upstairs, though, it was futureshock, where Reflections lived up to its name with dizzying vengeance. Every conceivable surface—walls, revolving ceiling, tabletops and even dance floor—was mirrored, while strobe lights flashed and a live band blasted out the equivalent of disco for the Third Millennium. After a drink or two, the effect was quite literally staggering.

The night we were there, Dan and I had wobbled out in the middle of a disturbingly Faustian version of "Funkytown," onto the balcony to gulp in fresh air and wait until the spots faded from our eyes before attempting to grope our way downstairs.

We'd spent the rest of the time satisfactorily sunken into the depths of a purple sofa, drinking wine to match, while by the feeble light emanating from a cluster of glass grapes dangled playfully by a nude, definitely male, bronze figure, I pointed out various luminaries and loonies from the local beauty scene to Dan.

Not the least of these was Duchess Crowe herself, sashaying around in full-on retro Shanghai B-girl drag, waving a long jade cigarette holder and cracking witticisms like, "Hey, Joe. You got nylons?" in a harsh, unpleasant voice, remarkably like a crow's.

Dan and I hadn't set foot in the place since, but despite our absence, the Mirror Club had become quite the hotspot.

From Maison Blanche cosmetic countergirls, to the hautest hairstylists, they all flocked to drink, dance and gossip at the Mirror.

"Excuse me." Claude, Lock's waiter, was hovering uncertainly. "I can't seem to locate Mr. Smith. His table is ready. And his, ah, party has arrived," he finished discreetly.

"He went to make a phone call just a few minutes ago," I told Claude, who thanked me and hurried off.

Dan stirred sugar into his coffee. "Duchess, Duchess," he muttered, a puzzled crease between his dark brows. Suddenly, he clattered the spoon into his saucer. "Claire, you know what? I think your Duchess is Duke Abbidis's sister!"

"What?"

"Well, one of his half-sisters, actually," Dan amended. "Darlin', Duke's daddy was married seven times! That's a few more than his son has yet managed, though he seems to be aspiring."

"And just what happened to all those poor Abbidis wives?" I demanded, feeling my hackles rise.

"They either divorced him, or died on him. In fact, I heard he once met a new bride at the funeral of the previous one! Each one had a baby, too, and he named all seven kids after a title. Let's see, there was Earl, he played quarterback for Grambling. And I know there was a Countess, plus Lady, Sir and Princess."

I laughed. "And Prince thought he was being so original! Okay, I'm convinced he named one of his daughters Duchess, and this is probably she. But I've got to know, Dan Louis. What was Duke's daddy's own name? Besides Bluebeard, I mean."

"Why darlin', I'm surprised at you!" Dan replied with a straight face. "What else could it be, but—King?"

I reached under the tablecloth and pinched the inside of his thigh. "You made that up!" I accused, increasing the pressure. "And I want to tell you what, Dan Louis. I am now going to the powder room to freshen up, during which time you had best apply your mind as to how you are going to atone."

I tossed my napkin onto the table, and he rose and pulled out my chair for me. In the South, gentlemen still do that kind of thing, though to be honest, some of them use the gesture as an opportunity to award a surreptitious pat on the derriere, just like Dan was doing now.

As I stood, he leaned down and whispered, "My mind ain't exactly the article I'm planning to apply, baby."

Riding off to the ladies' room on my romance cloud, I never dreamed that just around the corner, death was lying in wait.

Chapter 5

The powder room attendant offered me a towel when I stepped to the sink to wash my hands, but her fascinated gaze was riveted upon Duchess Crowe, who was running blood-red talons through her long, thick mane. She wore it cut square and straight in the Oriental fashion, a very effective frame for her Bali Hai features.

At my approach, Duchess turned away from the mirror to glance at me in half-recognition, and I got the impression she was upset. The tip of her nose was red, as if she'd been crying, or at least blowing it a lot.

She resumed toying with her hair, then suddenly, bent over and shook her head vigorously, straightened up and shook it again, momentarily causing the tresses to fly out from her skull like she'd just stuck a finger in an electric socket. Studying the effect before it settled down around her shoulders again, she nodded, as if having come to a decision.

I dried my hands and the attendant regretfully withdrew to the anteroom. As I started to leave, Duchess flicked slanted eyes at me. "Hey! Do I know you? You're in the business, right?"

Upon close inspection, Duchess was one of those women who look much better from a distance. Her skin was coarse, rather porous, on the oily side, and obviously several facials behind schedule.

The dark hair plummeted beneath its own weight, and she swirled it out again. "Give me your professional opinion," she cawed, when I revealed my name and admitted that I was indeed, "in the business." "Don't you think I'd look like LaToya Jackson or Diana Ross if I got a perm?"

Uh-huh, from a mile down the road in a bad light, I thought. But why would she even want to? Her own look was bold, unique and infinitely more suited to her persona than curls. It seemed so silly to tamper with success. There was probably a man involved.

Isn't there always?

Or perhaps that old rock and roll itch had flared up again, too strong to scratch by just finding a successful group. Maybe she'd decided the Mirror Club was her party, and she could sing if she wanted to. A radical new coiffure might give her the oomph to go up against other hip-grinding grannies like Tina Turner.

Aloud, I said tactfully, "Well, you've certainly got more hair of your own than both those two ladies you mentioned put together."

Duchess looked pleased, until I added, "But you asked my professional opinion, which is that it's usually a mistake to perm hair like yours. As you must know, it can be very unpredictable, and most formulas are geared to caucasian hairtypes, anyway."

I lifted a heavy strand, rolling it analytically between my fingers. While the stuff was definitely virgin, whichever

Abbidis bride her mama had been had contributed a rough, slippery Asian hair gene, which coated daddy's nappy African to produce what amounted to steel wool, sheathed in silk. That strong Asian element was the X factor. Even with so many new perm products making fantastic claims, the timing was still tricky, and Asian scalps were abnormally sensitive to chemical burns.

"Where do you work?" asked Duchess abruptly.

"Oh, I have my own little place," I replied modestly.

"Does it have a name, or am I supposed to guess?"

"Sorry, I didn't realize you wanted to know specifically. My salon is called, Eclaire."

Duchess looked interested. "Oh, yeah. I hear that's a pretty classy shop. Okay then, Eclaire. I want you to give me a curly permanent this week."

"Wait a minute!" I said hastily. "While I thank you for your confidence, I assure you it's totally misplaced. Polyethnic hair is not my strong point at all. Instead of Miss Ross, you'd probably wind up like Mr. Rastaffa if I did it."

Duchess blew her nose and looked sulky. "Well, I am definitely going to get myself a perm," she croaked. "So if you can't do it, how about recommending somebody who can?"

Quoth the raven, I thought crossly. Maybe that voice was perfect for rock and roll, but it was beginning to get on my nerves.

In all fairness, though, I was obligated to give her a referral, especially since she was contemplating such a drastic change. It required an expert's touch, but I was reluctant to wish this job on anybody I considered a friend. Not only was it a high risk procedure, but that jungle of hers would take at least two solid hours to wrap. They'd never forgive me.

Then I had an idea. "Tell you what. If you've absolutely made up your mind, hold off until next Monday. Marcel Barrineau is having a bunch of stylists come in to the Institut to do hair corrections all day long. Technically you're not correction, you're prevention, but it amounts to the same thing. Be warned, though. You'll have to stay for hours."

"Hmmm, thanks," she said noncommittally, turning back to the mirror and beginning to fluff again.

"Well, anyway." I shrugged, bored with the subject. "That's what I'd do if I were you. The ad's going to be in tomorrow's paper."

Dan was waiting impatiently when I emerged into the dark hallway. "Hell, darlin'," he grumbled. "You fall in, or what?"

I explained I'd gotten stuck giving free hair advice to Duchess.

"Ums sounds a little cranky," I observed, sliding my arm through his as we walked up Royal Street. "Does ums need ums' afternoon nappie?"

Dan looked down at me. "Something like that."

On the way home, we decided to take our bicycles over to the Lakefront and ride around for awhile, but somehow, we never did.

Much later, Dan sliced chunks of cantaloupe, bananas and blackberries into a big bowl, sprinkled them with raw sugar and Grand Marnier, and brought the whole thing back to bed, along with two spoons.

Opting for Tony Curtis in *The Great Imposter* instead of the news, we missed the story about a vandalized beauty shop.

Chapter 6

Ad from October 22 Times-Picayune:

Yes, It's Going To Be A Bad Hair Day!
But October 29 will be the best bad hair day you ever had! Because no matter how terminal your tresses are, we've got the cure. Guaranteed. There's only one place to spend "A Bad Hair Day."
The Marcel Barrineau Institut de Beauté
Carrollton Avenue at Riverbend Park
7:00 A.M.
First come, first served

There followed information about payment, then the names of stylists on duty. I couldn't help but be flattered that Marcel had put me first, until I scanned the list and saw it was alphabetical.

Marcel had already mentioned that Mimi Fontenot of Ms. Tress, Francesca of Bacci, and Vicky Su of Scissor Hands, would be participating. But others came as a surprise.

Now, here was a name I hadn't seen in a while, Vince Platina. Once the Sylvester Stallone of hairstylists, the financial collapse of Vince's luxurious Salon Platina in Metairie was rumored to have been due to gambling debts—everything from ponies to poker. And we just didn't discuss the suspicious nature of the fire that had reduced the place to ashes.

And there was Lock's listing. He'd said he was bringing Babs. I experienced a little twinge of guilt when I realized how long it had been since I'd seen, "Poor Babs," which is how I always thought of her, even though she'd done very well in her career. Not only was she bookkeeper for all the LockSmiths, at the Prytania Street location her following was second only to Lock's own.

By the time I finished reading the ad, I was smiling, truly looking forward to A Bad Hair Day.

I flashed the headline at Renee, who was thrilled to learn she was included in the big doings, especially since Mondays were when she ordinarily performed dull but necessary routine tasks such as banking, or picking up last minute items that hadn't been on our regular supplies order. In the beginning, I'd done those chores myself, but when Renee recently proposed her services at a good rate, I was only too glad to let her take over.

On this particular Monday, Juanita had arrived earlier than usual to clean the apartment, after which she was going to do preliminary food preparation for tomorrow night, so Renee and I were banished to have coffee in the downstairs kitchen. Sections of this morning's *Times-Picayune* were spread out over the pine table between us.

Renee abandoned her halfhearted perusal of a recipe for pecan-roasted chicken in the food section, while I explained our respective roles in Marcel's extravaganza.

"Whew!" she remarked when I finished, "a lot of work there, but I guess it could be interesting. Only Claire, it's hard to imagine having people just walk in off the street and expect us to clean up their hair messes! I mean, we won't have a card on them, or anything!"

"Like working in a trauma center as opposed to seeing private patients," I agreed. Then kiddingly, "Some hair-stylists have to do that every day, Renee. Maybe you're just a tad spoiled, working at a fancy shop like Eclaire?"

"I guess so," she conceded, her animation gone. Lately, Renee had been uncharacteristically pensive and with-drawn. No doubt partially because of some major changes in her life, beginning when she turned down her football player boyfriend's marriage proposal, which would have meant a move to New York.

But right on the heels of that, her older sister Yvonne had gotten married a few weeks ago, and there'd been a wild old Cajun *fais-dodo* wedding in Houma. Having expected to hear all the nuptial details, I'd been surprised when she'd hardly mentioned it at all. I figured Renee might be wrestling with the what-ifs.

And though she hadn't yet brought up the subject, she was now a full-fledged, licensed beautician and I knew we were going to have to re-evaluate her status at Eclaire. Personally, I had to decide whether I wanted to remain a solo act, or let Renee start building her own clientele. Or, have her begin looking for a position elsewhere. No matter what, I couldn't keep her on as my assistant forever, much as I'd love to. The day was fast approaching when I'd have to start breaking in somebody new.

Reluctantly, I realized there was no time like the present to discuss this.

"Renee, *dit moi donc*," I said. Since we rarely spoke Cajun together beyond the odd phrase or two, she immediately knew I was getting ready to say something significant.

Renee glanced up in surprise. "*Quoi tu veut?*" she responded automatically.

I reached over and cupped her chin in my hand. "*Tôt ou tard, chère*, you're going to have to leave the nest. Have you thought about that?"

She nodded, misty brown curls rising and falling with the movement. "*Ça c'est vrai, oui.* But I'm . . . just not ready yet, Claire." She frowned. "You—you haven't already found somebody else?" she questioned anxiously.

"Heavens, no!" I exclaimed, surprised by her reaction. "It's just that I'm starting to feel guilty about keeping you here as an assistant, when we both know very well you're capable of much more. And if it comes to that, I want you to begin your career right here at Eclaire." Until the words came out of my mouth, I hadn't realized I'd already made up my mind. To my astonishment, Renee began to cry.

"Oh, Renee. *Quoi y a?*"

"*Pas rien*," she muttered, sniffling.

"Don't you dare sit there and tell me it's nothing," I ordered. "And why on earth did you think I already replaced you, *couillone*?"

Renee was sobbing in earnest now, and finally the story came out. At Yvonne's wedding, one of the young female guests had arrived escorted by Beaudine Guidry, Renee's former boyfriend, who was also from Houma. Lately I'd spotted telltale signs that Renee had begun dating again, but she'd apparently not invited the new guy to the wedding. Without a date of her own, she was immediately at a psychological disadvantage. And, as if the situation weren't already awkward enough, the other girl was flashing a great big diamond engagement ring, bragging that she and Beau were getting married on Thanksgiving, prattling away about the fabulous Manhattan co-op where she and Beau were going to live, and on and on. The irony was, Renee and Beaudine had only broken up less than a month before!

Hearing all this, I was gladder than ever she hadn't married him, only now more for her sake than mine. No wonder she'd been afraid I'd already picked out a substitute!

I got up from the table and went to tear a few paper towels off the roll. "*Mouche-toi!*" I commanded, and she obediently blew her nose. "Look, Renee. I always secretly thought this but I never said so. Beaudine Guidry is *un vaurein, il est vaut pas la peine!*"

"No, he's not worth it," she agreed, blowing her nose again. "But in a way, that makes it worse because I wasted so much time on such a 'no account man.' "

"If you learned something important, it wasn't a waste of time," I assured her. "It'll just save you some later on. But I'm not so sure you did learn."

Renee jerked her head up to look at me. "What do you mean?" she demanded.

"Judging by your immediate assumption I was not only getting set to dump you, I had already found somebody new. I don't think you've fully realized your own worth," I returned. "First of all, even Beaudine didn't dump you. He asked you to marry him and it was you who said no. That was good. Something told you he wasn't the right man. But then, when he simply turns around and grabs the first ditzy little bimbo who comes along, right away you feel devalued, instead of realizing he's the one who's got a serious values problem."

She nodded thoughtfully, and I sat down again. "Now. In my case, it's because I value you so highly that I was opening the door of your cage, so to speak. You're free to fly away anytime, much as I hate the idea. But you're also free to stay until you feel ready," I added gently, and was rewarded with a big smile.

"Oh, Claire!" Renee dabbed at her eyes with the crumpled paper towels. "You are the best, for true! Okay, I will tell you when I'm ready, I promise."

"Fine, we'll let it ride for now," I said casually, trying not to sound too delighted. "But what about the nail situation?" Ever since Angie Labiche, Eclaire's first and only official manicurist was murdered a few months back, Renee had also been wearing that hat.

At my question, she tensed up again. "I want to keep on doing nails and coming in on Mondays, Claire," she said in a strained voice, nervously twisting the paper towel into a rope. "It's been working out fine so far, hasn't it? I'll let you know if it gets to be too much." She lowered her gaze. "I—can really use the money right now."

A million questions sprang to mind, none of which I asked. Renee's family, while certainly not wealthy was hardly *empauverir*, and I gladly paid her a generous salary. Beyond a hopeless addiction to expensive designer cowboy boots, I'd seen no other evidence of excessive spending.

But I figured we'd gotten up close and personal enough for one day. No doubt she'd tell me when she was ready.

Meanwhile, I felt an overwhelming relief things would remain status quo for the immediate future.

You'd think I'd know better by now.

The swinging door flew open and Juanita Valle marched in with a tray of her special empanadas, piping hot from the oven. "The rest I put already in the freezer," she announced, whipping placemats, napkins and forks onto the table, then plunking down full plates without inquiring whether we wanted anything or not. Juanita simply expects to be obeyed, and she is.

"These are all Señor Dan's favorite ones, *niña*," she said proudly, white teeth gleaming in her broad olive face as she described the cumin and cayenne crust, the fillings of black bean and *verde*, chili con carne, and jalapeño chicken.

In order that Dan's sharp eyes wouldn't spot the numerous airtight containers of onions, beans, chopped meats and fresh pineapple salsa in readiness for assembly, Juanita informed me she would be storing them in the downstairs refrigerator.

I felt a surge of affection for this riddle of a woman, whose overwhelming female form encompassed both peasant and aristocrat. She had slim, satin-smooth legs, eye-popping hairy underarms, wide, solid hips, huge breasts, waistlength hair which she never let me cut, Frieda Kahlo eyebrows and pencil mustache, which she never let me wax. And all this was married to a little guy named Carlos she could probably pick up with one hand and tuck beneath a bushy armpit.

The Eclaire phone rang as Juanita left the kitchen with our empty plates. Forgetting it was Monday and the answering machine would pick up, I absently lifted the extension.

There was a surprised little pause, then the caller said, "Oh. It's your own self, Miz Claiborne. I was 'specting to get your machine. This be Marzie, over to Gino's Emporium?"

"Yes, how are you, Marzie?"

Marzipan Jones was a riddle too, but she and Juanita Valle may as well have been from different planets.

With bobbed hair heavily pomaded and tightly crimped, brows plucked to a whisper-thin arc above slightly protuberant eyes, and full lips never bare of magenta lipstick, Marzie milked her strong resemblance to Josephine Baker for all it was worth.

Despite her high-faluting attitude and her penchant for draping herself in fancy Jessica McClintock lace outfits, Marzie stubbornly affected an atrocious vocabulary which seemed to be devised from equal parts of swamp and "the projects."

She also derived malicious glee from informing new acquaintances that before coming to work at Gino's Emporium, she had been a desairologist. Marzie would savor the blank stare followed by the inevitable question before defining a desairologist as an artiste who does hair and makeup . . . for the dead.

Marzipan Jones must've been the life and soul of the party around the funeral home.

"Miz Claiborne," she was saying, "I'm real sorry but we be way behind today. A couple of our drivers be off sick, plus a truck broke down, so there be nobody here right now to deliver your order. But we'll get it to you by noon tomorrow."

"That doesn't work for me, Marzie," I objected. "There are things I'm going to need for my first appointment in the morning."

"Well, we be givin' five percent off to ever'body want to come over'n pick it up their own selves. S'up to you, Miz Claiborne. But I got me a whole list of calls here so I can't be talkin' on. 'Bye now." Marzie clicked off like the autocrat she was.

If I'd known I'd need the car today, I could've driven Dan to the office. Fortunately, Rene's little wagon was perfect for hauling stuff.

I filled her in on Marzie's call, adding, "Ordinarily I'd take care of it myself when Dan got home since Gino's doesn't close until seven. Only he's burning the midnight oil on this big case of his. Either we can go now, or if you'd rather keep to your regular schedule, we'll wait until six o'clock or so, then I'll take you to dinner after."

Renee acted a little flustered. "Um, well. I guess we better go now, Claire. See, I've already got plans to be at the Mirror Club at six. Shear Madness is playing tonight. They're great!"

"Uh-huh," I said absently, quickly glancing through the Style section and spotting an ad for a La Prairie special purchase. "Is that the blonde girl from Hungary you were telling me about? Works at Rouge Carré?"

"Natasha and her boyfriend Yuri. From Russia," she corrected. "Why don't you and Dan go to the Mirror anymore, Claire? It is so cool!"

Lately the only real interest Renee seemed to take in anything was the Mirror Club. Almost every day she regaled me with tidbits of gossip picked up at the club the night before, or how good the new house band was, or the hot outfit Duchess Crowe had been wearing.

For someone so concerned about money, Renee was certainly doing some highpriced partying, though I suspected whoever she was dating hung out there too. If so, that would explain it.

"Renee," I said, with mock severity, "I know what you need all that extra money for."

Her eyes widened. "How did you—uh—what do you mean, Claire?" she stammered.

I laughed. "You buy a new pair of boots every time you go to the Mirror Club, of course! Listen, *petite*. Dan and I love to dance, but not in that disco inferno! Maybe we're just too old or something, because you obviously adore the joint. Anyway, after meeting the Duchess herself yesterday, I'm less inclined than ever to get involved with that scene. She bothers me, for some reason."

"You mean, you actually met and spoke to Duchess Crowe?" Renee demanded tensely. "Where? How did that happen? What did she say?"

I told her about that odd little episode in the ladies' room at Brennan's concluding, "You're so impressed by her? Well, I think she's coming to Marcel's clinic for a perm. Feel free to assist whoever gets stuck with that job, God help them!"

Renee looked down at the table, fiddling nervously with the newspaper. I admit I was pretty sharp with the girl, but nothing to warrant the way her face suddenly drained of color. Oh, Lord. She couldn't be pregnant, could she? And if she was, the baby would have to be Beau's. Had I inadvertently stumbled upon the reason she was acting so strange?

Speaking more gently I told her, "Come on, *chère*. We'll stop at Gino's first, then the bank. Go ahead now and get the copy of that order you phoned in from the desk drawer, while I run upstairs and let Juanita know we're leaving."

"Okay," she mumbled, giving me a tremulous smile as she went through the swinging door.

I rinsed out our coffee cups in the sink, then began gathering up the scattered sections of newspaper. A small article at the bottom of the front page caught my eye, about a beauty shop out by the Lakefront that had gotten trashed and robbed last night, The Strand. Damage was estimated at around twenty thousand dollars. A substantial loss by any standard.

I felt badly for the unknown owner, but it had nothing to do with me.

That's what I thought.

Chapter 7

Something seductive was bubbling in a big dutch oven when I entered the kitchen. I inhaled deeply, and was rewarded with the expensive, smoky fragrance of saffron. "Juanita! You made *arroz con pollo*!"

She turned from the sink where she was washing up some utensils and beamed. "*Sí, niña!* Señor Dan call to say he will not be home until seven o'clock, and told me he had to stay inside the office and eat a sandwich only for lunch. He say to me, 'Juanita, I'd give anything for a big plateful of your *arroz con pollo*, right now!' "

"And so you decided he shall have it, right?"

Juanita grinned, causing the pencil mustache to stretch and curve around her mouth like an extra upper lip. "But, *sí!* Señor Dan deserves to have whatever he wishes, no?"

I thought about a few of Dan's wishes and felt a little tingle run through me. "Oh, yes. He most certainly does," I agreed, and she chuckled knowingly.

Before I left, Juanita gave me instructions about reheating and displayed the luscious-looking salad she'd assembled from cooked red cabbage, pinto and white beans, carrots and red onion, marinating in balsamic vinegar, mustard and spices.

Presently, Renee and I were zooming up St. Charles Avenue in her white Isuzu with pony patterned upholstery. She had an obscure zydeco band blasting away on the tape deck, deliberately rendering conversation impossible, so I scanned my order list for Gino's, realizing I needed a few more things since then. It was just as well I was making this trip after all.

With a touch of drama, Renee swerved into the parking area fronting an enormous rust brick building with a bulging roof. Somewhere around 1930, a Hollywood producer had taken the notion to open a film studio in New Orleans. To that end he purchased several acres off Tulane Avenue, and optimistically constructed a soundstage, offices, and sundry satellite buildings, completed just in time for the Great Depression.

During WWII, the lot had been used as an armory, then chopped up and sold off haphazardly. All that remained intact of the original structures was the enormous white elephant of a soundstage, which nobody seemed to have the vision or money to tear down and redevelop. Consequently, Gino Gambara had purchased it in the late forties for next to nothing.

Over the decades as his business had grown, he'd never needed either to add on or branch out elsewhere in the city. Even after forty-odd years, there was still plenty of room to accommodate a full-blown wholesale beauty supply outlet, and virtually unlimited warehouse storage space for an inventory which allowed Gino's to ship merchandise across several states. Plus, it was as centrally located as you could possibly get in New Orleans, perfect for pickup and delivery.

"Volare" was gusting from the loudspeaker as we came in.

Renee groaned. "This pasta music always makes me feel like I'm walking into that movie, *Goodfellas*."

Ironically, there was talk that the now-invalid Gino was, or had once been, a big woo in the underworld. Of course they said that about all Italian businessmen.

True or not, the place had been impeccably maintained for nearly a half-century, its authentic Fifties ambience intensified by nonstop vintage pop/rock ballads sung exclusively by Italian entertainers, punctuated with the occasional familiar operatic aria.

And what merchandise!

Eclectic American items like violet-tinged Ambrosia astringent and Marchand's Golden Hairwash shared shelf space with rare European products. And if collectors ever got wind of the valuable old goodies casually mixed in among the contemporary Aveda, Framesi, Goldwell, and such, there would be a stampede.

This might happen sooner than later, because one of the salesladies told me that a set decorator from Los Angeles had wandered in last week to buy shampoo, and nearly ascended to Heaven when she saw the display of Tangee Natural Lipstick, in the same place where it had been since 1952. It turned out Tangee Natural was the only lipstick that ever looked good on her in her life, and she'd been trying to track some down forever. She'd bought all the remaining tubes at thirty-nine cents apiece.

Other near-antiques, like Halo shampoo in original concentric-ringed glass bottles, and squeeze bottles of Veto deodorant, were still for sale at their barely legible original prices, which meant they could be had for from eighty-nine cents and up.

Gino's even boasted an array of "natural remedies," from pepper cream to DMSO, along with assorted herbs, elixirs and teas, including one from some Brazilian tree bark I'd heard was poisonous.

Renee went to the service desk to let them know we were here, while I took a pink shopping cart through the narrow aisles, soothed as always by the rich aromas of potions, lotions, and the myriad concoctions that promised a more beautiful you if only washed with, combed through, slathered on, or applied to, some of them actually delivering on that promise.

I quickly located the special brushes I sought, with thick, molded rubber bristles only three-quarters around a hollow base to prevent tangling. But a beautician on the loose at Gino's is like a kid in a candy store, and I kept waltzing up and down the seemingly endless aisles of fascinating stuff, keeping time to Dean Martin's silky, "That's Amore."

The spell was broken when the song ended, and I braked my pink cart, amazed that it was nearly full. A dose of Dino apparently sent me into a shelf-emptying frenzy. Just what had I intended to do with those four packages of tinted mustache wax, in blonde, brown, black and red, complete with cunning little combs, anyway?

What's more, I was lost. Somewhere along the line I'd taken a wrong turn and landed in a part of the store totally foreign to me, a much narrower space than the main shopping area. Here, the ceiling was lower and the shelves higher, stacked with sealed cardboard cartons instead of loose merchandise.

A heavy-looking door, which reminded me of the kind they use in saunas, was set into the back wall, and the area was redolent with a heavy, cloyingly sweet aroma I couldn't quite identify, mixed with the definite tang of tomato sauce.

I closed my eyes in an effort to visualize Gino's exterior, and was rewarded with a dim memory of a small wing extending from the right, far to the building's rear. That meant if I backed up and turned around, I should be able to retrace my steps, even though I'd thoughtlessly neglected to scatter a trial of crumbs behind me.

Relieved, I made the necessary U-turn, about to head out when I caught an unmistakable whiff of coffee vying with all the other odors. I looked over to my right and saw what appeared to be a booth transplanted from an old-fashioned Italian restaurant. A high-backed semicircular seat in button-tufted burgundy vinyl enveloped a large round table of some ancient dark veneer. Standing in the middle, its red light glowing invitingly, was a tall electric urn, surrounded by a litter of mugs, cups, packets of sugar and artificial sweetener, a jar of Coffee-mate, and the gooey remains of a Mackenzie's Blackout Cake.

Behind the booth, birthday greetings, picture postcards, selected Garfield cartoons, snapshots of kids, and drawings that only proud grandmas could love, were haphazardly thumbtacked to the wall around a group of old black and white photographs that held pride of place in the center.

I knew I was hooked.

My father, Gabriel Jennerette, was a Cajun fisherman whose short (and, I was certain, deliriously happy) marriage to a Danish au pair rapidly produced me. But my mother's past had been forever shrouded in mystery because, soon after I was born, she and Gabriel died together in a violent storm while shrimping on the Gulf of Mexico, leaving me to be raised in New Orleans by Gabriel's much older brother Hebert, and his wife Jeanette, both now deceased.

My parents weren't alive long enough to begin a family album together, though a few candid shots did exist of my father—a wiry, curly-haired man with merry dark eyes and a cigarette permanently attached to his lower lip. There was one of him with my mother, who'd been small and blonde like me, but only one of her alone, standing on a dock and backlit by the setting sun.

I'd once shown it to an antique dealer friend of mine, who immediately remarked upon the inadvertent symbolism of the sunset behind her. "In portraiture, a sunset is deliberately incorporated to indicate that the person is dead," he explained, citing the two-hundred-year-old oil painting of his multiple-great *tante* Celestine which boasted a spectacular *couchée du soleil* in the background.

At times I'd stare at Mother's picture, as if I could literally will it to reveal who she really had been, who I really was.

Consequently, old family photographs held an irresistible attraction for me; all those grandparents, uncles, aunts and cousins there for the taking, imparting a vicarious sense of history.

I gazed in fascination at the faces frozen in time on Gino's wall. At the top presided an oval-framed, stiffly posed formal portrait of a stocky young man with bristly mustache and snapping black eyes, unmistakably an immigrant, circa late 1920s. It was Gino Gambara himself, known to many as Papa. Known to certain others, perhaps, as Godfather?

Fanning out beneath him was a delightful jumble of chubby little boys in short pants, chubby little girls in ringlets and frilly dresses, a group of children in First Communion white, brides and grooms, and a long strip of shots taken in a photo booth, featuring a teenage girl in 1950 *Laverne and Shirley* sweater and chiffon neck scarf. Something about her high forehead and beak nose looked teasingly familiar. But given my hobby, that didn't mean anything; eventually they all started looking familiar to me.

"Lady, you don't believe in signs?"

Although I did manage to bite back a small shriek, I was so startled I literally jumped, whirling in a graceless pirouette to confront the fat man in a hightech wheelchair who had approached soundlessly behind me.

"The sign says Employees Only," he persisted. "Maybe you don't read so good, lady?"

Anyone who thinks Marlon Brando's rendition of Don Coreleone's voice was merely a brilliant figment of imagination should consider the amazing number of Italian men who sound exactly like he did in the movie.

Gino Gambara was one of them, speaking as if his words were being squeezed through a drinking straw, then popping like soap bubbles the moment they hit air, no doubt enhancing the stories about him. I personally found the notion of him as a crime boss impossible to take seriously. If nothing else, his sartorial eccentricities fell so woefully short of that custom-tailored elegance we have come to expect from our really important gangsters.

Today, Gino wore a shapeless baby blue sweater, tan corduroy trousers, and black leather bedroom slippers over sagging argyle socks. An old tan felt porkpie was pushed to the back of his bald, speckled head, and a truly elegant ebony and silver cane, which had long ceased to serve as anything but a decorative accessory, was sort of wedged between his bulging potbelly and spindly shanks.

John Gotti he was not.

My breathing slowed to normal and I said politely, "I'm very sorry to trespass, Mr. Gambara. I didn't see any sign. Frankly, I wasn't paying attention and got lost somehow. Then, when I spotted these old family pictures, I just couldn't resist taking a closer look."

His bushy brows drew together over watery black eyes. "Why are you interested in my family, lady?"

"Not yours in particular, Mr. Gambara," I assured him. "I just love all old family pictures." I added, "You see, my parents died very young, so I don't really have any of my own to look at."

Gino's suspicious glare softened and he gave a sympathetic nod. "I understand," he said surprisingly. "Who's been, who's gone, who was good, who was bad, what they looked like—you don't know."

He glanced over at the wall of photographs, and his frown returned. "Sometimes, it's better not to know," he muttered. Then he caught my eye and abruptly snatched up his cane.

Pointing with it he said, "That way out, lady."

I obediently pushed my laden cart in the direction he'd indicated, unable to pin down the nagging impression that I'd seen something or someone important.

Chapter 8

Back at the service desk, Renee was checking boxes piled onto the trolley against our list, unaware she herself was being checked out by an attractive, muscular young man waiting his turn in line.

As I approached, Connie Francis broke into "Where the Boys Are." Renee looked up and, seeing me, began to roll her eyes at the music, until she noticed the curly-haired admirer standing behind her.

He grinned. "Hey, darlin'. How you doing?"

Seeming puzzled, Renee gazed at him for a second, then her expression cleared. "Oh! You work at the Mirror Club, don't you?" She did a pretty little dip with her long lashes. "I'm sorry. I didn't recognize you at first."

"Well, now, that's understandable, darlin'," he laughed. "It is a tad dark in that lounge." He shoved aside his pink shopping cart and extended a hand to her. "I'm Sal. Sal Romano."

"Renee Vermilion," she responded, shaking the proffered hand, her cheeks suddenly pink. "And this is, um . . ." Renee trailed off vaguely.

"Claire Claiborne," I supplied helpfully.

Sal turned to me. "Nice to meet you," he said politely.

Renee was looking perplexed again. "But . . . aren't you a bartender at the Mirror?"

"Guilty as charged," he agreed cheerfully.

"So, why all this?" she indicated his basket of beauty supplies.

"Oh, hell!" he groaned comically. "Caught in the act! Now you know what we put in those drinks. Nothing like a little Barbicide to jack up the Jack Daniels."

Renee giggled. "No, really."

Sal surveyed her appreciatively, probably thinking how adorable she looked in those red jeans and blue suede cowboy boots. "Okay, really. Boss lady just got a license to operate a salon up on the third floor. Going to call it"—he paused for effect—"Mirror Image."

"Oh, how cool!" breathed Renee.

Well, well. Duchess certainly hadn't given me the slightest hint she was about to open her own place. Quite a concept, a club where you could get a drink and a haircut. A real clip joint, one might even say.

"But how does a bartender come to be transporting beauty supplies?" Renee inquired, in a kittenish voice I'd never heard her use.

Sal spread his hands. "Well, for one thing, they couldn't make deliveries from here today, so I volunteered to pick up the stuff. And for another thing, I'm also a hairdresser."

He laughed at our surprise. "Hey, it's a perfectly logical progression! From mixing haircolors to mixing drinks. It's all chemistry."

His voice lingered suggestively, on the last word, and Renee sparkled. "Or cocktails!" she riposted.

"Where do you work, then?" I asked Sal.

"Oh!" he shrugged. "Lately, I've been doing a lot of freelance type gigs. Housecalls, photo sessions, you know the kind of thing. I don't mind assisting if that's all that's available."

The minute he uttered those words, I knew Sal Romano was definitely not the unambitious, bartending hair gypsy he was making himself out to be. There was too strong an air of confidence and prosperity about him for that.

Nor was this very sexy, smiling guy with midlength dark, curly hair and a well-pumped body fetchingly packed into tight 501s and sweatshirt, as boyish as he'd appeared at first glance.

Not with those eyes. Pale grey and watchful, they added another decade to my original estimate of twenty-four or -five.

Watching them flirt, I sighed inwardly, wondering what Renee was about to get herself into this time. At least she was smiling, which was a big improvement. And Sal Romano, whatever he might or might not be, seemed nice enough. Anyway, I wasn't the girl's mother.

I left them to it and pushed my cart over to stand in another checkout line, but was distracted by a loud, scolding voice.

"No, Voncilla! You went and done it all wrong again!"

In the far righthand corner, a group of Gino's matronly saleswomen attired in uniforms of puckered pink nylon that made them look like school cafeteria lunch ladies, were huddled around a big table presided over by Marzipan Jones, dripping lavender lace.

She was reprimanding a large, redhaired female with powdery basset hound jowls, and those big fussy glasses that look like they've been put on upside down.

"It be shampoo, conditioner, gel, spritz and comb, in that order. Jus' like in this here sample. See?" Marzie thrust a packed vinyl zip bag, pink on one side, clear on the other, with Compliments of Gino's Emporium scripted in black on the pink side, right beneath Voncilla's rather large nose.

Then she dumped the contents of another bag, presumably the one Voncilla had so wrongly arranged, onto the table in front of her. "Jus' try to get it right this time!" Marzie snapped.

Voncilla's glasses caught the light, imparting a sinister appearance as she bent over to fumble with the scattered plastic bottles. An incongruously dainty diamond watch bit sharply into her doughy wrist.

"Hurry up, now!" Marzie prodded, circling the table and peering over shoulders as they assembled the travel kits. "We only got a hunnert to do, for mercy's sakes. Afternoon, Miz Claiborne," she added, noticing me.

"Hey, Marzie. What's all this?" I indicated the boxes of sample size products that had been labelled with Gino's logo.

She waved her demonstration kit. "Seein' as how Mr. Marcel is gonna be usin' our stuff nex' week on folks, I figgered we'd jus' fix up these little fellers for'm to take home as a *lagniappe*, like. Remind'm they can shop here too, jus' like beauticians.

"Looky," she went on, indicating the pink paper strip which lay across the small bottles and was visible beneath the clear vinyl. Have A Good Hair Day! was printed in black. "Jus' got these done over to the Quik Print this mornin'."

"Very smart idea," I told her. "You must've moved pretty fast."

She lowered heavy eyelids complacently. "Got to be fast in this bizness anymore," she replied. "It be every bitch for hurselve."

"What do you—?" I began curiously, but she was looking over my shoulder to watch Gino wheel his chair into the service area. He was nodding graciously to customers and employees, benevolently waving his ebony cane as if imparting a papal blessing.

Marzie abandoned me and took hold of the wheelchair grips. "Now Papa G, lemme show you what we's doin' over here," she said, pushing him toward the makeshift assembly line.

A moment later, she was paged to the telephone over the loudspeaker.

"Mrs. Jones. Lochner Smith on line two."

Marzie returned to a wall extension about ten feet from where I stood, and began to mutter intensely into the receiver.

The only reason I had stayed put was because I wanted to find out what she'd meant by that bizarre remark, so I wasn't really paying any attention to the phone conversation until her voice grew louder and she began to swear like a Scorsese film.

Call me prissy, but I find extremely crude language offensive. Even Dan, earthy as he is, doesn't use the F word unless it's as an imperative verb he's actually engaged in at the moment.

Marzie, however, had no such compunctions, and when her profanity deteriorated into downright blasphemy, I decided to remove myself from the immediate vicinity before a bolt of lightening came down from heaven. But Marzie's sudden screech froze me in my tracks.

"What? Three hundred thousand! Your mama done left you out under the moon too long, boy. Little fellers get hurt plenty bad messing with big folks. I'd be watchin' my back, I was you."

Viciously, she slammed the phone back into its cradle and when she turned around, her already normally protuberant eyes were bulging like those of a rabid pekingese. Goodness, whatever could Lochner Smith have said to Marzie to get her so riled? Her hands were clenched and she was breathing rapidly.

"Marzie, are you all right?"

The peke eyes focused on me, and she seemed to gain control of herself. "Oh, Miz Claiborne. You be needin' any help?" she inquired, with something of her usual hauteur, adjusting a filmy butterfly sleeve.

"I was just going to ask you that same question," I said. "I couldn't help but overhear just now. Lock Smith seems to have upset you very much."

Marzie patted her carefully crimped bob. "Oh, that!" She pursed magenta lips and gave an unconvincing little laugh. "Guess I did fly off the handle some when hoity-toity Mr. Lock be demandin' we jus' drop ever'thin' and deliver his stuff this minute. He don't care we short on trucks. Nuh-uh! He don't care ever'body else wants their stuff, too. Makes no diff'rence to him we gotta get ready for Mr. Marcel's big hooha nex' Monday."

She looked sly. "'Tween you'n me, okay? I think Mr. Lock be major jealous of Mr. Marcel."

I conceded it was indeed a possibility, meanwhile thinking that, though she'd managed to come up with quite a plausible cover story on the spur of the moment, it failed to explain the references to three hundred thousand dollars and people getting badly hurt.

Renee tapped my shoulder. "Claire, Sal here very kindly volunteered to help me load these things in the back of my car."

"Well, thank you," I said to Sal. "Knights are in rather short supply these days."

" 'His strength was as the strength of ten, because his heart was pure,' " Sal quoted.

I looked at him. "Uh-huh."

He winked, then followed Renee out with our loaded trolley.

Gino had lost interest in the sample kits and was looking our way. When I smiled at him, he raised his cane in benediction, then rolled himself over, chuckling windily.

"Voncilla got the zipper stuck on one of those bags," he observed.

Marzie gave an agitated cluck. "Lord, that woman's dumber'n any white person got a right to be! Don't care what you promised your dead cuzzin 'bout lookin' after his widow. She don't know a gnat's ass 'bout the beauty supply bizness."

Gino displayed snaggly yellow teeth in a grin. "Don't forget, Voncilla's got her own special skills," he declared emphatically. "Her marinara sauce"—he kissed his fingertips —"*magnifico*."

"Let her work in the restrunt bizness, then!" Marzie snapped. "Got me enough to do without havin' to babysit that old she-ellyphunt."

Gino replied with a Mediterranean shrug. "That's your problem, lady. Like I told you before, family comes first."

Marzie waved her hands in the air, frosted burgundy nails flickering nearly black beneath the fluorescent lights. "Go ahead, then, Papa G. Hire on your whole damn fambly. I got nothin' else to say about it. Nothin'!"

"That'll be the day, lady!" cackled Gino, and pushed himself off down the shampoo aisle.

Marzie noticed my full basket. "You ready, Miz Claiborne? I can ring you up now."

She went behind the counter and opened a vacant register with the key dangling from a long gold chain around her neck. Her dark, bony fingers flew over the numbers, eliciting little birdlike peeps from the machine, and I realized Marzie was lefthanded.

Not for the first time, I wondered about the plain gold wedding band she always wore. Nobody had ever seen hide nor hair of any Mr. Jones, though there'd once been a vague tale going around that he was serving hard time in Angola. But since no one had yet worked up the nerve to mention this to Marzie, that story remained unverified.

Marzie was still in an ill temper. "Them drivers couldn'a picked a worst time to go and catch thurselves flu, what with trucks breakin' down and Mr. Marcel's thing nex' Monday," she complained. "And *that* one's had ever'body 'round here in a tizzy last coupla weeks. Man gets a bee in his bonnet and turns the whole hive hindside up!"

I laughed. "Tell me about it!"

As she was bagging my purchases in pink plastic, Sal returned to park our now unburdened trolley, accompanied by Renee, who reminded me we'd better hurry and get to the bank before it closed.

"Guess I should thank you for comin' down to pick up your order your ownself, Miz Claiborne," Marzie remarked, grudgingly. "Not like *some*," she added, flashing Sal Romano a malevolent glare. "*Some* thinks they is way too fancy to be comin' down here to pick it up their ownselves. Got to *send* somebody else."

Sal held up his palms in mock surrender. "Hey! I just get my orders from the Duchess, and I obey. After all, she's the boss."

Marzie's only response was to grunt like an angry rhino.

"Oh, Sal." Renee fluttered a delicate hand on his enormous bicep. "I'd better give you that Queen Ida tape you wanted to borrow now, before I forget. It's out in the car."

He looked down at her. "Sure thing.

"Oh, see you, ladies!" he called over his shoulder as he followed Renee out.

Since neither of them had offered to help me with my bags, I was in the process of threading several over each arm, when I noticed Marzie was all buggy-eyed again, and seething so hard she looked fit to explode.

She managed to hold it in until the glass doors had swung shut behind Sal and Renee, then she blew. "Callin' hurselve Duchess and struttin' round got up like some heathen Chineezer," she spat fiercely. "Top of which she think she be so slick she can slide somethin' right by me? No, honey. Got to be gettin' up pretty damn early for that."

Ah, now we were getting to the part I wanted to hear. "She *didn't!*" I murmured, knowing Marzie needed no further encouragement to tell her story.

The upshot was that, early this morning, Duchess Crowe had telephoned in an order for three hundred silver metal compacts and matching combs, as premiums to announce the opening of her Mirror Image Salon.

So far, so good.

But when the shipping clerk who wrote up the purchase informed her they would need two weeks to fill that large an order, Duchess demanded a rush to be put on the first one hundred. She then made the mistake of telling him the compacts must be delivered by Saturday, because they were going to be distributed Monday morning.

I was beginning to see the light.

". . . and then Miss Duchess thing wanted to know if she could get the powder puffs printed up with Always a Good Hair Day at Mirror Image," Marzie finished with a snarl.

Marzie told the shipping clerk that she'd handle the order personally. The first thing she did was cancel the rush, then proceed to come up with her own promotional gimmick, the travel kits.

"But, Marzie," I protested when she'd run out of breath, "I don't understand. I mean, it's not like you're in competition with her, or anything. It's no skin off your nose if she wants to pass out compacts while she's at Marcel's next Monday."

Recharged, Marzie unleashed a string of adjectives and descriptive nouns concerning Duchess which would've shocked me if I hadn't already overheard her ranting at

Lochner Smith. I did experience a flash of real alarm, though. Had Marzie suddenly slipped beyond merely being a "character" into something more ominous?

"Can't stand that bitch with her Yurropeen talk and—" Marzie stopped suddenly.

"You say she goin' to be at Mr. Marcel's hurselve nex' Monday?"

I had started to explain about Duchess telling me she wanted a perm, when a sudden clamor broke out among the pink ladies putting Marzie's kits together. Evidently Voncilla had opened a bottle of conditioner to smell it, only the thing slipped out of her hands and spilled all over the table.

Gun-shy by this time, I cringed inwardly, waiting for Marzie to erupt again. Surprisingly, though, she merely stared hard at Voncilla, almost as if she'd never really looked at her before. Perhaps she hadn't. Under her breath she muttered something that sounded like, "Speshul skills."

When a cleanup operation was underway, Marzie's big eyes turned back to rest on me. "Now, Miz Claiborne. You was sayin' what?"

I summarized what I'd told Duchess, that she shouldn't risk her hair on a perm, but she'd told me flat she absolutely intended to get one, end of discussion.

"And so," I concluded, gathering up my pink plastic bags, "I said if she was that determined, Marcel's event was the safest place to do it."

And I couldn't possibly have been more wrong about *that*.

Chapter 9

At 7:45 on Tuesday evening, Juanita ushered in Foley Callant and relieved him of a bottle of Cristal champagne festively swathed in gold cellophane and curly silver ribbons.

My last appointment had run late, and I'd made the mistake of turning on the local news while I rushed around trying to get ready.

That's how I happened to catch the story about another beauty shop getting trashed. This time it was Ms. Tress, Mimi Fontenot's place, and it had apparently happened late Monday night because she'd discovered the wreckage this morning.

I tried to call her, with no success, thinking it was beginning to sound as if somebody had launched a private vendetta against beauticians.

"I left Danbo about half an hour ago, hunched over a pile of books in the law library," Foley reported when I'd belatedly greeted him. "So, just to keep the boy from nodding off, I told him Charlotte and I might be stopping by for a drink. Don't worry, I didn't even hint I knew it was your anniversary."

"It takes a lawyer to mislead another lawyer," I said admiringly.

He smiled. "Well, I started thinking as to how he might notice our cars parked out front when he pulled into your driveway, so I figured I'd better come up with a good explanation ahead of time."

"Explanation for what?" Charlotte demanded as she entered. "Are you trying to get Claire to help you concoct some tale to deceive me?"

Foley engulfed her in a bear hug. "Not a chance, darlin'," he avowed. "I'd be a fool to try to fool you, my hawk-eyed dove!"

"Oh, you got that right, mister!" laughed Charlotte, turning up her face for a kiss.

Foley and Charlotte were the result of some adroit matchmaking by Dan and me, and they made a striking couple. He was a big, handsome strawberry blonde with blue eyes and ruddy complexion; Charlotte was tall, willowy, chestnut-maned and greeneyed with delicate white skin.

Their kiss had passed beyond the hello stage and seemed to be heading for an in-depth discussion when Foley suddenly exclaimed, "Hell!" and jumped backwards. "What was *that?*"

"Foley, you weenie!" Charlotte jeered. "It's just my pager! I switched it to vibrate instead of deedle." She unhooked the device from her brown leather belt and squinted at the readout. "Shoot, I've got to take this. It's Harry from his car phone."

"But you were just at the station not ten minutes ago!" Foley grumbled. "I don't ever remember WDSU doing this."

WBGZ-TV, with its state-of-the-art equipment and sumptuously decorated facilities that took up two floors of the newly-restored Pontalba building overlooking Jackson Square, was promising to deliver "the best view in New Orleans" when they went on the air December first.

Between now and then, though, there were a million details to be ironed out, and Charlotte, despite her impressive title of Executive News Story Director, was evidently expected to do lots of the ironing.

"Happy anniversary, Claire," Charlotte said, giving me a distracted peck on the cheek. "Can I use your telephone?"

"Help yourself," I offered, and she hurried for the kitchen extension, greeting Juanita, who was coming through the swinging door with a tray holding plates, napkins and silver.

"That's okay, here's my *real* girlfriend!" Foley hollered loudly enough for Charlotte to hear. "*Buenos noches,* Juanita honey, you big fine woman, you!"

"Good evening, Señor Foley," Juanita replied coolly, setting out things on the coffee table for all the world as if she weren't delighted with Foley's blandishments.

She was looking unusually crisp and official in a black dress with elbow length sleeves and white ruffled apron. I was relieved there would be no distracting armpits on display tonight. No matter how often you'd witnessed the phenomenon, Juanita's were a sight impossible to ignore.

As was her bosom, even if she'd been wearing something buttoned to the chin, which she wasn't. Juanita's gigantic breasts swelled and heaved against the lacetrimmed black vee of her bodice like waves crashing against rocks.

I had to bite my lip to keep from giggling out loud at Foley, who was striving manfully not to gape.

The doorbell shrilled and I started to go downstairs, but Juanita stopped me. "You must remember, tonight I am in charge, *niña*," she reproved.

Foley chortled. "Well, she sure told you! Anyway, Claire, you ought to get a buzzer installed so you don't have to go traipsing up and down all the time."

I agreed ruefully. "I know. Dan keeps saying the same thing, but he just hasn't gotten around to it yet."

"Probably because when he's home he's got much better things to do," Foley suggested slyly.

Charlotte returned to the room, a slight frown creasing her forehead.

"What's the matter, baby?" asked Foley.

She shrugged. "Nothing, really. Harry just wanted—"

Foley cut in. "I know what Harry wants. But he doesn't seem to comprehend you're practically a married woman." He picked up her left hand adorned with a chunky ruby and diamond engagement ring and waggled it. "Apparently they don't take such things seriously out there in Avocadoland."

The dazzling Harry Corvus, WBGZ's Station Manager, had originally been imported from his native England to Los Angeles by Pinwheel Broadcast Group, which owned WBGZ. Prior to moving behind the scenes, Harry enjoyed minor notoriety as a reporter for one of the racier tabloid television shows, *Ferret*. Which, Foley Callant observed, was the perfect description of Harry Corvus, since a ferret is a kind of weasel.

To give due credit, Harry, who'd been in town for less than a month, had instantly seen Charlotte's potential and custom tailored a unique top news slot just for her, snapping up her contract when WDSU continued to drag their heels during renegotiations. But beyond that, he'd done nothing to endear himself to Foley, who frequently mentioned he'd like to tear the guy's head off and feed it to the alligators. This sentiment was a direct response to Harry's undisguised overtures to Charlotte.

Now Charlotte laughed. "Attaboy, Foley! You're a tad jealous and I like that in my future husband. Just remember though, I'm a redhead, too." She swirled her glossy shoulder-length bob created by me, adding, "So, I don't want to hear any complaints about my being too possessive."

"Sugar," Foley said earnestly, "I can't hardly *wait* for you to possess me!" They were getting married in Atlanta on Christmas Eve, which was also going to be their authentic Wedding Night. As Foley put it, the biggest present was for Charlotte and it would not be under the tree!

When Juanita returned, she was escorting my inlaws, and Marcel, sans Nectarine. Sergeant Savoy had been called onto a case at the last minute, and sent her felicitations and regrets.

Smelling comfortably of cigars, D.L. embraced me vigorously. "Hey, little girl! You're looking mighty sweet in that pink outfit!" He winked, knowing full well that Rae Ellen had bought me the cashmere sweater and pants right before they'd left for Austin.

"I made sure I got me a mother-in-law with good taste to take me shopping," I told him, pressing my cheek affectionately to Rae Ellen's cool, taut, scented one. She was one of the few women on whom that classic Balmain perfume, Vent Vert, smelled like it was supposed to.

Rae Ellen Claiborne was as different from her intensely physical husband and son as *nuit* from *jour*. Lean, blonde, and wiry as a whippet, she was also somewhat reticent and aloof. But I'd learned early on that slightly glacial facade concealed a reservoir of warmth and strength, both of which she'd lavished on me abundantly during my recuperation from the miscarriage and separation from Dan.

I looked her over. "Oh, Rae Ellen. If I didn't know better, I'd swear while Daddy over there was getting his innards tended to, you sneaked off and had some face work done. You seem at least ten years younger."

"Thank you, dear!" Rae Ellen glowed and squeezed my hands. "Listen, Claire. I can't go into it now, but D.L. and I may have some amazing news for you and Dan."

"What do you mean? You're not pregnant, are you?" I teased.

She arched a fine eyebrow at me. "Now that *would* be amazing, but no. Are you?"

I felt my face grow warm. "Well, since you asked, no ma'am. Frankly, we're still making up for a lot of lost time."

Rae Ellen's eyes sparkled with mischief. "Frankly, so are we!" she retorted and laughed girlishly, scrutinizing her patrician features in the English antique oval mirror that hung from a chain on the dijon-tinted plaster wall.

"Yes." My mother-in-law nodded at her image with justifiable pleasure, then glanced back at me over a shoulder draped in mossgreen wool jersey. "You see, Claire. D.L.'s disease took it's toll . . . elsewhere in his body. Understand?"

"Oh, Rae Ellen." Tears stung my eyes. "How terrible for you both. I had no idea."

"How could you? We made sure nobody knew. D.L. especially didn't want Dan to find out. Male pride, I suppose.

"But, not only did this new treatment cure him, it produced some totally unexpected and thoroughly marvelous . . . side effects, shall we say?"

"What? You mean now he can—?"

"Ssh!" she cautioned with a smile. "Hear me, little girl. I was on . . . I guess you could call it a sugarfree diet for so long, I'd quite forgotten the very best beauty treatment on earth is what's inside that great big old cookie jar, you *do* know what I mean?"

I could only stare and nod.

Rae Ellen gave her Tippi Hedren French twist a final complacent pat in the mirror, then turned around and swept me from head to toe with a penetrating gaze. "Of course you do!" she laughed. "Like father, like son, and Dan's every bit as crazy for you as Dave Louis was for me for forty-five years without missing a beat until he got sick. And now that I so miraculously got my cookie jar back, I fully intend to have me a pigfest!"

We giggled together like naughty schoolgirls, then Rae Ellen grew serious. "Believe me, Claire. I'm in no hurry to become a granny. But don't wait too long, dear. If it's a boy, Dan's going to want to do all that sports stuff and he'll be heading for fifty by Little League time, even if you put one in the oven tonight!"

I managed to find my voice. "Did we just leap into fullblown intimacy in a single bound?"

She looked directly into my eyes. "Well, why not, Claire? Life's way too short as it is. And don't forget, I was raised on a Kentucky horse farm. I think I'm entitled to act a little earthy now and then around the three people I love most in the world. And I do love you, Claire."

I hugged her. "I love you too, Rae Ellen."

"Hey, folks!" Foley called, corkscrew in hand. "Time for a serious question. White or red?" He indicated the bottles of dry Argentinean wine Juanita had selected to go with her menu.

Charlotte, flipping through a stack of CDs opted for white, as did myself and Rae Ellen.

"And that means red for the boys," I said, handing Dave Louis his glass. Even before his mysterious therapy, D.L. had continued to partake in moderation. As the rich strains of Mozart filled the room, I touched my goblet to his in a silent toast, then carried one to where Marcel, in his soft suede shirt and pants the tinge of burnt tobacco crouched, moodily poking at the fire.

"Thank you, Claire," he said morosely, straightening up to take the wine from me. Automatically, he inhaled the bouquet, then sipped cautiously. "Not bad," was his verdict. He took another sip. "From some Latin region no doubt, always with the provision that there are those who are growing something other than the coca plant. If, as the television commercial claims, it is true that Juan Valdez still cultivates coffee beans in Columbia, he is certainly one of the few."

Uncharacteristically, Marcel tossed off the remainder in one gulp, then contemplated the vessel in his hand.

"Is this the part in the movie where there's a closeup of you crushing the glass and blood trickles down your arm?" I inquired sardonically.

Marcel grimaced. "Dear Claire! You are right, of course. I am behaving childishly. Actually, I have more reason to celebrate than previously, for the glorious Cherry had at least consented to allow me to escort her this evening. It was most annoying to have criminal activity intrude upon an occasion I had anticipated would perhaps be a turning point in our relationship."

"Well, she *is* a police officer," I reminded him. "And those annoying old criminals don't exactly plan their business functions around your love schedule."

Foley strolled over, carrying two bottles. "Looks like you need a refill, son!" he observed, generously replenishing Marcel's empty glass, then topping mine off with a splash.

I noticed with concern that Marcel's hand shook slightly as he raised his goblet. "What's wrong, *chér?*" I asked, when Foley marched off in search of more customers.

Marcel started to say something, but just then Juanita wheeled in a loaded serving cart.

"Here, honey. Let me help you with that," offered D.L. "Hot damn, that looks good!"

Juanita laughed richly. "*Sí*, Señor Dave. It is good, and it is damn hot!"

"Claire, you little monkey! So this is what you've been getting up to behind my back, throwing wild parties while I'm working my butt off?" Dan roared from the doorway.

"Happy anniversary!" everybody shouted, and I went to greet him with a glass of red wine.

"I ought to spank your bottom for this," he threatened playfully, taking the wine from me.

"Yes, but not now, darling," I murmured, as I stowed his briefcase in the hall closet.

He narrowed his eyes and caught my wrist, pulling me to him. "Don't think I won't," he warned softly, and I felt a quick little scrape of excitement, like branches brushing against a windowpane.

"Hey, Danbo! Hurry up and get out of that lawyer suit!" Foley commanded. "We got some fine champagne waiting for you!"

"At least let me tell my mama and daddy hello first," Dan protested, embracing D.L. and Rae Ellen. "Damn!" he exclaimed. "You two sure look good!"

"Don't we, though?" Rae Ellen responded vivaciously, snuggling up to Dave Louis.

"Why, thank you for noticing, son!" Grinning, Dave Louis accepted Dan's offer of a cigar. "Yessir, Doctor Jesus sure came through for me!" He looked down at Rae Ellen. "Yes, he did."

The doctor's name was actually Miguel Jesus, pronounced Haysus, but Dave Louis insisted on calling him Dr. Jesus, as in the old blues hymn, "Sweet Doctor Jesus."

Juanita served everyone their first helpings, lingering to receive rave reviews for the black bean fritters with pineapple salsa, and plantain tacos with shredded pork and cilantro.

After polishing off three fritters and another glass of wine, even Marcel began to show signs of revival and was soon animatedly holding forth on his upcoming bad hair day.

Charlotte thought it was hilarious. "See there, Marcel? Like I keep telling Foley, celibacy makes you more creative!"

Foley snorted. "Yeah! Since you can't come up with one thing, you're basically forced to come up with something else or explode!"

"Wait a minute, wait a minute!" Charlotte cut excitedly into the laughter. "I just had the most incredible thought!"

"Sorry folks," drawled Foley. "See, we ain't quite got the timing down on these cerebral orgasms of ours, yet. As usual, I finished first."

"Now doesn't *that* give a girl something special to look forward to on Christmas Eve?" Charlotte shot back.

A loud and mildly ribald interlude followed, then Marcel said, "Charlotte, I am most interested in hearing your idea."

"That's because you're an intelligent man, unlike others in this room," Charlotte told him. "Okay, here it is. How about I bring a camera crew over to this shindig of yours on Monday and get the whole thing on tape?"

Marcel's eyes lit up appreciatively. "My dear Charlotte! What a brilliantly original mind you have. I fail to understand how your previous employers could let you go."

"Oh, they didn't really mean to let her go. I just came along and took her away," a new voice asserted, and Juanita showed Harry Corvus into our midst.

Chapter 10

What with music playing and all the racket we'd been making, we hadn't heard the buzzer.

Foley looked askance at Charlotte, who shrugged, disclaiming responsibility for Harry's presence.

I roused myself to switch into hostess mode. In the South, we know how to deceive an uninvited and unwelcome guest into thinking he's just who we've all been waiting for.

Harry Corvus, however, didn't seem to require such affirmation, which was just as well since I didn't feel inclined to give it. If anything, he appeared maddeningly confident that no gathering was complete until he arrived, and made no apology for his intrusion.

"Hello, Harry. I hadn't expected to see you again quite so soon," I greeted him coolly, referring to our initial encounter a few days ago when Charlotte had been showing me her plush new office, with its fabulous view that encompassed Riverwalk and the Aquarium.

"And this is my husband, Dan . . ." I studied Harry covertly as I completed the introductions, acknowledging that he was certainly an eyecatcher, though too slickly packaged for my taste.

There was something unmistakably decadent about Harry, from thick hair artfully highlighted and expensively cut, to the perfectly draped mocha silk suit, and the large gold ring on his right pinky, its crest featuring a sinister-looking bird with outspread wings and empty raptorial talons, which Foley dubbed, "the hungry buzzard."

Not even the noticeable limp served to dent his Ken Doll perfection. He deprecatingly referred to this affliction as, "a spot of the old arthritis, it comes and goes," but was quick to decry the available American medications as ineffective.

He had, he informed us now, brought along an arsenal of European pharmaceuticals when he'd moved to New Orleans, acquired during his last trip home, among them the allegedly superior arthritis medicine, and a potent roach and vermin poison which was impossible to get in the States.

"I had little use for either in Los Angeles, naturally, but fortunately was forewarned of the roach infestation in New Orleans before I transferred here," Harry applauded himself. "Of course I'm living in the worst possible conditions for all sorts of creepy-crawlies, above a restaurant and near the docks, though the old dump does have a certain moldy charm."

There was no possible reply to this.

The Pontalbas, located in the French Quarter on either side of Jackson Square, are the oldest apartment buildings in America. The State of Louisiana owns one side, the City of New Orleans owns the other, and anybody who lives here knows they could grow old before their name makes it to the top of the waiting list.

It was amazing enough WBGZ was able to lease so much space in one of the buildings. But it was an outright fluke that Harry Corvus had somehow managed to meet and snow the right somebody into pulling strings to get him an apartment in the other.

Why is it that Americans in general are intimidated by hightoned British accents, into humble acceptance of rudeness we wouldn't dream of tolerating from others? I made a mental note to introduce Harry Corvus to Lochner Smith. Those two America bashers deserved each other.

"How goes it, Foley old man?" Harry said easily, and Charlotte braced herself.

But Foley Callant was no slouch in the manners department. "Just great, Harry," he returned affably, leading him over to the side table, politely pacing himself to the other man's limp which seemed to be more pronounced than usual. "Let me pour you a drink, I'm playing bartender tonight. What'll it be, white or red?"

Harry had already spotted the Cristal in the ice bucket. "Oh, I'll just have a splash of champs," he said carelessly, and turned away to speak to Charlotte.

Foley clenched his teeth and was on the verge of saying something we might all regret, when Dan intervened diplomatically.

"We're all going to have champagne in a minute, but I've got to change first." He clapped Foley soothingly on the back. "And thanks to my best man here for bringing it. Cristal '81 has a very special significance to Claire and me."

Foley relaxed and grinned. "Well, why the hell else do you think I went to all the trouble and considerable expense to come up with a bottle? In fact, since Charlotte and I seem to be following in Claire's and your footsteps in other ways (if you know what I mean) I figured we may as well adopt the same love potion for our Wedding Night, too.

"Therefore, I would like to announce I have just purchased an entire case of this stuff for our own private use. I plan for us to open a bottle every Christmas Eve for the next twelve years, darlin'!" he declared, blowing a kiss to his betrothed.

Charlotte blushed becomingly and kissed her fingertips back, while Harry watched sardonically.

Dan laughed. "Way to go, bubba. Excuse me, everybody. I won't be long."

"I'll come with you son, if that's okay," Dave Louis said, and they walked off with their arms around each other's shoulders.

Harry glanced proprietorily at the still virginal bottle of Cristal, and gave an impatient sigh. "So! Which anniversary is it, Claire?" he inquired, with barely veiled boredom.

"Two months," I said.

He paused in the act of helping himself to a black bean fritter on the warming tray. "Surely you jest! All this"— he waved a discreetly manicured hand at the food and wine —"for two months?"

Marcel overheard, and interrupted his conversation with Rae Ellen to observe, "True love should be celebrated by those who have been blessed with it as often as possible. We who were *invited* to share such a celebration with Claire and Dan naturally understand the full import of this occasion."

It took Harry a few beats to work out that he had just been exquisitely insulted by the master. Even then, he remained unscathed. Sensitivity, apparently, was not one of the qualities Pinwheel Broadcast Group required in a station manager.

"Oh, well!" He shrugged with a laugh. "That's why they make red hats and green hats, I suppose!"

Marcel opened his mouth, fully prepared to enlighten Harry further, but Dave Louis's and Dan's return forestalled him.

"Come on over here and stand by your man, sugar!" D.L. directed me, and arranged the others in a circle around us.

Dan called for Juanita to join the group as D.L. popped a perfect cork from the champagne, chilled to liquid gold.

"To my dear son and his beautiful wife," he said solemnly, lifting his glass to us, and I saw his blue eyes were a little teary.

Then everybody else had to make a toast. Marcel's was introspective and verbose; Foley's a tad naughty; Dan raised mystified eyebrows at his mother's reference to "cookie jars"; Charlo's was sentimental; and Juanita's offering was emotional and in Spanish, which nobody but Harry Corvus understood a word of. Of course, he couldn't resist letting us know he'd learned the language while his father, the diplomat, had been stationed in Argentina.

Harry had been more concerned about getting a second glass of champagne than proposing his own toast, but now he rattled off something in machine-gun Spanish which caused Juanita's face and bosom to turn a deep rose, and she retreated hurriedly back to the kitchen.

I noticed the fire was dying down, and went over to put more wood on.

Dan followed me. "I'll do that, darlin'," he said, setting his champagne flute on the mantlepiece. He selected a log from the big brass potful of fragrant applewood which had been a wedding gift from some clients in Washington State.

I watched while he bent over to put it in, then took the poker and squatted down to stir up the flames. Ah, just as I suspected. Beneath the steel-blue cashmere sweatpants—a luxury Marcel had gotten him hooked on—it was very obvious he wasn't wearing any underwear. Just one tug on that drawstring, and . . .

"Pass me one or two of those smaller chunks, will you baby?" he requested.

I found a pair of suitable size and sat down on the teal Kirman hearthrug, watching the tongues of fire lick greedily at the sweet wood until it burst into flame.

Dan looked over at me. "Hey, Evangeline Claire. You are just absolutely luscious in that pink."

"Why, thank you, sir. But wait until you see the black."

His eyes narrowed sensuously. "That sounds mighty alluring. What is the time frame here, do you think?"

I calculated. "Probably another hour or two. That is, if you're not too tired by then."

Dan stood and pulled me to my feet, muttering, "Child, you are just begging for trouble."

"Oh, is that what you're calling him now?" I inquired innocently.

"Hey! No fair telling funny stories unless you share with the whole group!" Foley called, leading Charlotte over to one of the twin palomino suede sofas flanking the fireplace.

"Oh, hush and sit down, Foley," she scolded, patting the cushion next to her. "What makes you think you'd get the punchline anyway? After all, Claire and Dan speak a language of their own."

Foley snorted. "If you can call Braille a language!"

Rae Ellen went off to the kitchen to speak to Juanita, and everyone else drifted over with their full plates to join us. Marcel, Charlo, and Harry began to discuss ideas for next Monday's taping.

The rest of us contributed our two cents from time to time, but as the food disappeared and the concept took shape, it became evident that Charlotte and Harry were in total synch and way ahead of us all.

Foley looked on with a mixture of pride and possessiveness, knowing he had nothing to worry about, but not complacently taking Charlotte for granted, either.

"You know," Harry said finally. "I think this piece is going to be so hot, we can bicycle it over to L.A., and maybe one or two other major markets, as well."

"Certainly, for the appropriate consideration," purred Marcel.

Harry laughed. "Okay then, Barrineau. Let's hear your terms."

Marcel looked austere. "I never discuss such details. You will have to consult my attorney, which should not be difficult as he is your inadvertent host for the evening."

Harry swung his attention to Dan. "All in the family, I see. How convenient, if a little incestuous."

"Oh, well!" Foley chuckled. "You know how close we all like to get down here in Looziana!" And he made a half-witted face that cracked everybody up, even Harry.

Suddenly the buzzer shrilled. "Now who could that be?" Foley wondered. "I thought everybody—and then some—was here already."

"Not quite everybody, Foley-pie," Charlotte amended, watching Marcel's hopeful face.

Juanita emerged from the kitchen to answer the bell, followed by Rae Ellen who came over to perch on the sofa arm next to Dave Louis.

"I got the recipes for the fritters and chicken jalapeño empanadas you wanted, D.L.," she said, resting a slim, bejeweled hand on the back of his neck.

"You can have that stuff now, D.L.? Good for you!" Foley congratulated.

Dave Louis winked at Rae Ellen. "Oh, that ain't nearly the best part, son!"

"Señorita Savoy is here," Juanita announced, showing Nectarine over, and Marcel sprang to his feet like a jack-in-the-box amid the babble of greetings.

Nectarine looked strained, and her eyes were dull. She sank gratefully down onto the sofa.

"May I bring you a selection of this most excellent food and a glass of wine?" Marcel offered solicitously.

She tilted her head back to gaze up at him, and her expression softened. "Thank you, Marcel. I could really use something right about now."

Harry stared at Savoy with delight. "Aren't you—?" he began.

"Yes!" she said abruptly. "Who are you?"

"Pardon my bad manners for neglecting to introduce you to Nectarine Savoy, Harry Corvus," I apologized hastily.

Harry gave her a fatuous smile. "Listen, I have the most incredible poster of you from that notorious *Vogue* shoot in Kenya. There you were, lying on your back on a tree branch in the jungle, wearing nothing but a zebra-skin thong and a pair of black patent leather mules with four-inch heels!"

The mental picture, as my high school English teacher used to say, was terrific.

"One would need quite a remarkable sense of balance to achieve such a pose under those conditions," Marcel commented, as he set Nectarine's wineglass and plate of food on the coffee table, then spread a linen napkin over her lap.

Savoy, who had been looking a little embarrassed, chuckled briefly. "*And* about a gallon of calamine lotion! I was covered head to toe with insect bites the next day."

Since I was sitting the closest to them, I was the only one who overheard Marcel murmur to her, "Those most fortunate insects."

Nectarine made no reply, but her lips twitched in a pleased way.

Dave Louis was feeling a little rowdy and said mischievously, "What nobody's yet mentioned to you Harry, is that the lady has relinquished tree, thong, bugs and patent leather to become Detective Sergeant Nectarine Savoy, of the New Orleans Police Department."

"Surely not!" Harry protested, appalled.

Ignoring him, Nectarine continued to eat steadily until her plate was nearly empty. "Oh, did I need that!" she sighed, leaning back against the cushions. She accepted her wineglass from Marcel's hand with a preoccupied look, and sipped appreciatively before addressing me.

"Claire, even though I already intended to make a point of stopping by your party anyway if it wasn't too late, that's not the only reason I'm here now."

"Well, if you're expecting a shampoo and blowdry at this hour, forget it. Not even for you!" I laughed.

Nectarine shook her head. "In fact, I just came from another fancy beauty shop. Or I should say, what's left of it. The place was wrecked like you wouldn't believe."

"Oh, no! Not another one!" I protested. "I just heard about my friend Mimi's shop on the news earlier. But the police said they had no evidence to connect it with the incident on the Lakefront."

"And that's still the official statement," Nectarine agreed. "But what makes this salon over on Prytania Street different from both of those is that it was also a murder scene. Which of course is why I was brought into the thing."

She paused. "I wanted to be the one to tell you and Marcel about this before you heard it on the news."

There was only one fancy salon on Prytania. Marcel and I glanced at each other apprehensively, then turned back to Nectarine.

As we had feared, the crime scene was the LockSmith's original location, lavishly and expensively art deco as a Busby Berkeley musical, with its authentic cobalt glass, blonde wood, black lacquer and chrome.

And the victim was Lochner Smith himself.

Chapter 11

Dan was stretched out in a big tea and cream striped linen easy chair to one side of the fireplace, singing along with Louis Prima's gravelly voice on "Embraceable You" when I returned to the living room, draped in the promised black lingerie.

All was in darkness but for the glow from a dozen tall beeswax candles and the dying fire. The man knew how to set a scene.

"Come to papa," he repeated softly, when he saw me. He held out his arms and I climbed onto his lap.

Only then did I notice the fresh bottle of Cristal in the ice bucket on the floor beside the chair. "Thank you, darling. I hardly got a drop, earlier."

"Probably because your pal Harry made sure he acquired two and a half helpings for himself," Dan drawled, pouring for us. "What a guy, huh? I personally think he's an alien."

I laughed. "So there *is* life on Mars! Isn't that what you call L.A., Dan Louis?"

"Among other things." He smiled, giving me my glass. After we had touched rims he said, "Claire, I'm real sorry about your friend getting killed."

Sighing, I thought of Lochner Smith, watching the bubbles in my glass fizz to the surface, catching the gleam from a flickering candle before evaporating into nothingness. Like Lock's life.

But to call him my friend was overstating our relationship. I had no idea, for instance, whether he would be amused or offended at me contemplating his passing while sitting on my husband's knee and sipping champagne, because Lock was a man I had known, yet not known at all.

Dan said now, as he refilled our glasses, "Honey, the way he was found is very suggestive, I'd say. I mean, unless it was at gunpoint, to allow himself to be maneuvered into a vulnerable position like that . . . you know what I mean."

"Vulnerable position" was putting it mildly. The manner of Lochner Smith's death seemed to be something very sexually esoteric gone dreadfully wrong, and far transcending even the gamiest gossip I'd ever heard about him.

"Well," I replied, "you heard me tell Nectarine about the rumors he had a taste for 'rough trade.' But frankly, I never understood a word of what they were talking about, although I pretended to."

I certainly did now.

Lochner had been blindfolded, then stripped and bound tightly, hand and foot, with extension cords to one of the classic Koken barber chairs (covered, I recalled with stunning irrelevance, in a fabric to mimic shagreen) tilted back to its extreme position.

He was then tortured with an electric curling iron applied to various areas of his body, including armpits and genitals, while gagged with a mouthful of rolled cotton.

The cotton part was deduced from the preliminary examination, because some charred wisps of stuff were found adhering to the blistered insides of his mouth.

That is, after they finally managed to extricate the blowdryer, which had been fitted with one of those new flexible, narrow airflow directors, so the murderer could shove it down Lock's throat.

Then turn it on high until his esophagus had been burnt completely out.

Even assuming Lock hadn't been meant to die, it was difficult for me to imagine that rather finicky gentleman getting up to such macabre antics. But, as recent events had proven, I was hardly an expert on the subject.

I was, however, firmly convinced that a playful, sexy little spanking like Dan had threatened to administer to my posterior was one thing. Being trussed and roasted like a turkey was another thing entirely.

Nectarine had asked if I knew who any of his current "close personal friends" were, and I was relieved to be able to truthfully deny it. I reflected that, for someone who generated the volume of gossip Lochner did, his alleged accomplices remained curiously faceless.

"The only person I know who could probably help you there is Babs Hooper," I'd told Nectarine. "She's been a stylist at the Prytania LockSmith's for years, and his bookkeeper, so she's bound to have some idea if Lock was uh, seeing anyone special."

What would Babs do, now that Lock was gone? For that matter, what would the rest of his employees do? Hopefully, Lock had made some sort of provision for his business in the event of his demise.

Marcel, profoundly shocked, claimed to know as little as I about Lock's amorous adventures, but did admit he'd recently heard a vague rumor connecting one of his salons with drug use, he wasn't sure which location. "Although I find that extremely unlikely," Marcel cautioned Nectarine as she made a note in her brown leather book. "Even in the seventies, Lochner was notoriously intolerant of marijuana, and enforced a most stringent policy. If activity of that nature was occurring, you can be sure he would have stopped it."

"Unless somebody stopped him first," Savoy said thoughtfully.

Now, as we unsuccessfully tried to make sense of what had happened to Lock, Dan and I were both struck by the irony of how often lately, while just minding our own business, we'd gotten mixed up in murder.

"Well, at least *this* time, whoever killed him, I'm sure it's not anybody we know," I said, finally.

But even as I spoke the words, I wondered.

Only yesterday, Marzie was pitching a hissy fit about something Lock had said or done. Forget that lame tale she'd hastily contrived. Whatever it was involved over three hundred grand and danger. She'd been a woman on the edge if I'd ever seen one. Had she just flipped out completely and trashed his place for revenge, getting the idea from those other vandalized beauty shops?

It wasn't so hard to imagine Lock catching her in the act, and her attacking him. But that wouldn't explain the condition in which he was found. Unless . . . could Marzie also be into—? I reminded myself that she had once made a living dressing and making up corpses for their final public appearances like so many huge dolls. It took a certain jadedness to do that day after day. Mightn't one's outlook become a little skewed? I closed my mind, refusing to follow this frightening train of thought.

Dan refreshed our champagne and I pressed closer to him, the gloom instantly dispelled when Louis and Keely began to belt out their cute, sexy version of "I'm in the Mood for Love."

"Well, are you, baby?" Dan whispered, sliding his lips lightly from my ear down my neck and along one shoulder. "In the mood, I mean."

"Now would that be any wonder?" I breathed, savoring those delicious goosebumps as his mouth continued to explore.

He laughed softly, taking my empty glass away and putting it with his on the floor, as Louis and Keely wailed on.

Chapter 12

It was still dark when Dan pulled up in front of the Marcel Barrineau Institut de Beauté the following Monday morning.

"I think I'm finally onto an idea about this pulp machine business, Claire," he said, letting the engine idle. "But I've got to use the first part of the day to get some other stuff out of the way in a hurry. I might have to run over to Mobile for a few hours this afternoon and check something out at the papermill."

I turned, intending to tell him to drive safely, but the dashboard lights were casting dramatic shadows and soft jazz was playing on the radio, and I got sidetracked.

The navy pinstripe jacket to his three-piece suit was hanging in back, and he looked large, rich and luscious in the matching vest, crisp pale pink shirt, and blue silk tie.

As Dan leaned forward to kiss me goodbye, the tang of his new aftershave, Kipling, tickled my nostrils seductively, and I felt breathless.

I opened my mouth wider, searching for more of his tongue, which tasted deliciously of peppermint toothpaste.

"Hey, now!" he laughed in surprise. "What's all this?"

"Oh, just a little something for you to think about, on the road to Mobile," I murmured, running my lips over his freshly shaven cheek.

"Considerate of you. But that adds up to a pretty long drive both ways, darlin'. Maybe you better give me a little bit more to think about?"

Early as it was, there were already several cars in the parking lot, in addition to the WBGZ utility vehicles. The farthest corner was occupied by a brand new white Cadillac Seville convertible defensively straddling two spots, top up, nose out.

Close in there were Charlotte's tanky old Mercedes, Harry Corvus's showy Jaguar, and a few others.

Among them, I noted with surprise, Renee's Isuzu. Now that was unexpected, considering how her first enthusiasm for A Bad Hair Day had seemed to wane over the past week. Hopefully, her unusually early arrival meant she was starting to get her act together.

At the entrance, I had to step gingerly through a maze of cables taped to the black and white tile floor of the big working classroom where I'd trained in my chosen profession.

The sight of that long row of gleaming black porcelain washbowls facing a corresponding row of mirrored stations across the room, brought back an unexpected flood of memories. For an instant, I was once again that timid little Cajun teenager from the wrong side of the bayou, flinching beneath the lash of Madame Justine's sarcastic French tongue.

In the distance, I could hear Marzie Jones screeching, presumably giving orders to the Gino's people delivering nearly every conceivable hair preparation on the face of the earth to the supply room.

The more I pondered her recent erratic behavior, the more uncomfortable I became. First had been that unnecessary public humiliation of the hapless Voncilla, though for a moment I'd thought if looks could kill, Marzie would've been a gone gosling. And even if I could persuade myself to wink at that nasty little trick she'd played with those silver compacts on Duchess Crowe as a slick piece of business, there had still seemed to me something far more personal and vicious behind her attitude toward the other woman.

Then there was the curse-filled telephone conversation with Lock. I stopped in my tracks. In the shock of learning about his death from Savoy, I hadn't even thought to mention that incident to her. Please God, she'd quickly find the killer, and it would never be necessary.

Impulsively, I decided to go back and talk to Marzie, somehow needing to observe her reaction to the subject of Lock's murder.

But, as I entered the dimly lit passageway, a broad male form loomed suddenly in silhouette.

I gasped.

"Uh, hey! Is that you, Claire? It's just me. I didn't mean to spook you or anything." Sal Romano's voice effectively slowed my rabbity heartbeat.

He had moved closer and I could see him better now. Same lazy, let's-go-beddy-bye grin, same watchful eyes.

"Sal! What in the world are you doing here?" I demanded, as soon as I could catch my breath.

"Working, of course!" He laughed. "Why the hell else would anybody in their right mind be up at this ungodly hour?"

"Certainly not me," I agreed, thinking of where I ordinarily was long about now, in a soft, warm bed, snuggled against a big furry body. At least curb service was better than nothing.

I was still having trouble fitting Sal Romano into the picture here, for some reason. And then I remembered. "Wait a minute. I didn't see your name on the list in the paper," I accused.

"Not surprising, considering it wasn't there," he said readily. "No, I'm just going to be assisting Vinny Platina today. The two *paisanos*, like. Hey, you know Vinny don't you, Claire?"

"Who doesn't?" I agreed evasively. Long ago, I'd gone on one date with Vincent—one had been far too many. "I haven't seen him in ages, though. What's he been up to?"

"Actually, he's been working at the Mirror Club quite some time now. Managing, and all like that." Sal waved a vague arm.

I interpreted this to mean Vince Platina had been employed as a bouncer.

Sal hastened to add, "But remember I told you about the new shop upstairs, Mirror Image? Well, the Duchess is going to let him run it for her."

"Ah!" I commented neutrally, thinking that Vincent Platina's career path had certainly taken a bizarre twist or two.

Abruptly, Sal asked, "Claire, is Renee going to be here today?"

I smiled. "She already is, somewhere, but I haven't run into her yet. And I am frankly surprised you waited all this time to see her again."

"But I didn't!" he protested. "Hey, whaddya think, I'm crazy? We went out to dinner last week, then to the club after. And Claire, we had us a great time. And I mean," he said emphatically, "really great. Until we got to the club. Then she all at once shut down on me. And then, nothing!" Sal looked bewildered. "I called her several times since and she's always got some lame excuse not to see me."

"Well, she hasn't said a word about this to me, Sal," I informed him. Or about anything else, I added to myself. "In fact, it's news to me you'd even gone out."

His face fell. "Oh, I was hoping you knew what was up with her, and all. I mean, we had this wild chemistry kind of thing happening. Next thing I know, boom. She backs off."

I gave his bulging bicep a consoling pat, intended as a prelude to my exit. "Well, us Cajun girls have been known to get a little squirrelly, from time to time."

But this only served to remind him of another grievance.

"And something else, too! She promised to take me to this real, authentic Cajun restaurant, not one of those jive tourist joints."

By the time he finished unloading his love woes onto me, the place was starting to fill up and I never did make it back to talk to Marzie.

It wasn't until he'd finally gone away, shaking his curly head at the mysterious ways of Women, that I realized Sal

Romano had been coming from the supply room himself when I ran into him.

Right after I'd heard Marzie yelling.

Chapter 13

An air of festivity was building in the plush faculty lounge up on the mezzanine, where a buffet breakfast of fresh fruit, yogurt, beignets and muffins was being served to the Bad Hair Day team and WBGZ's production crew.

The decibels inched higher with every new arrival as the hair people attempted to catch up on each other's lives at the same time. I looked around for Renee, but she was nowhere to be seen.

Someone grabbed my arm. "Darling, how are you?" demanded a throaty Italian accent. "I hope your beautiful little shop is still in one piece. Those terrible vandals! We must do something!"

Francesca Bacci's powerful contralto carried to where two women and a gangling youth of around twenty were standing nearby. One of the women I didn't recognize, but the other was Mimi Fontenot, whose Ms. Tress salon had been the second to be trashed, with her assistant David in tow.

Francesca hailed them over, and we commiserated with Mimi. The only good news was that the insurance claim had already been settled.

"If I ever find out who wrecked my place," Mimi finished with a snarl, "I'll kill them!"

"Now, Mimi," David cautioned nervously, plucking at her sleeve.

She brushed his hand away like a dead fly, and repeated, "*I will kill them!*"

"Not if I get to the bastard first!" put in the big, freckled woman with corn-colored hair in a French braid who'd accompanied Mimi and David.

So far, she'd simply listened while chewing thoughtfully on a beignet, heedless of the powdered sugar flying in all directions. Wiping her right hand, she offered it to Francesca and me.

"Faylee Wilkins," she introduced herself. "I own the Strand. Or I did, anyway."

The Strand. The beauty shop out by Lake Pontchartrain that had been trashed a week ago.

Mimi and Faylee told us that up to this point, the police hadn't been able to trace a connection between the two incidents, and both women were finding it very frustrating.

"Hell, anybody with half an eye could see there's got to be *something!*" Faylee declared. "The only question is what? So Mimi here and I decided to put our heads together and try to figure it out."

"And then," Mimi said grimly, "I will kill him!"

Francesca tsk-tsked. "No, *bambina*. If it is a him, I have got a much better idea. We will simply relieve him of his *caglioni!*"

Faylee, who'd just grabbed another beignet from the table, hooted through a spray of sugar. "Way to go, Lorena! Hey! What a great name for a hair place—Bobbitt!"

Francesca chuckled wickedly. "Unisex, of course!"

Even Mimi was smiling now, but poor little David looked faint.

"Hey, Vangie! Were y'at, doilin'?" inquired a greasy voice behind me.

I knew who it was, even before I turned around. Only Vince Platina had ever dared call me Vangie.

"Oh. Good morning, Vincent," I greeted him primly.

"Good morning, Vincent," he mimicked. "Vangie, Vangie! Loosen up! You're talking to a guy from the old 'hood!"

Talking to an old hood was more like it, I thought. He'd grown a beard and put on at least forty pounds since I'd last seen him. He looked exactly like a bouncer. There was something else about him too, but it eluded me.

"How's that cute little shop of yours?" Vince asked.

"Still in one piece, thank God, after what I've been hearing. And is it true you're about to get a cute little shop of your own?"

He laughed selfconsciously. "Temporarily taking care of things for a friend, is all." He lowered his voice. "Meanwhile, I'm working on something very, very big."

His tiny brown eyes searched mine speculatively. "Be nice to me, Vangie, and I might cut you in."

"No, but thank you for thinking of me, Vincent," I said, not caring to contemplate what he meant by "nice." "Incidentally, I'd be careful if I were you. The last person who told me they were working on a very big deal just wound up very dead."

"I guess you mean Lock," he muttered uneasily, shifting his eyes away. "That was pretty damn bad."

Then Vince gave me a startled look. "Wait a minute. Lock told you he was about to score large?"

"Not in those exact words, but that's the general impression I received," I agreed absently, suddenly realizing here was something else I'd forgotten to tell Nectarine, and it could well be connected with his murder.

I didn't like to think what she was going to say when I finally got around to mentioning everything I'd forgotten. Maybe I'd better start keeping a journal or something.

All at once, Vince seemed anxious to change the subject. "You still tight with your fancy old man, Vangie? Or maybe you're getting homesick for your, uh, roots?" He leered suggestively.

I just looked at him, and he shrugged an apology.

"Okay, okay. Listen, you need *anything* to perk him up"— he touched his nose significantly and sniffed—"you let me know and I'll fix you up, huh, Vangie?"

I laughed in his face. "Believe me, Vince, it's hardly necessary. And besides, that's not our scene."

"No shit? No shit! What the hell do you Uptown folks do for fun, then?" he demanded, with real curiosity.

I moved away to say hello to some other people, and was introduced to Natasha and Yuri, the rock-singing Russians who owned Rouge Carré, Renee had been raving about.

Natasha's pale, elegant face was framed by hair bleached dead white, and parted in the middle to emphasize the half-inch regrowth.

So was Yuri's.

They both looked like they slept in boxes of their native earth. The only way to tell the difference between them at first glance was by Yuri's orange-tinted John Lennon glasses.

"I hear you're very good," I said. "When are you playing at the Mirror Club again?"

Natasha glared at me from beneath dramatic ebony eyebrows for a long moment before answering, "When blue pigs are flying backwards. Is true, Yuri?"

Yuri nodded. "Is true."

Natasha's response to a perfectly straight-forward question was as cryptic as something from an old spy novel. I was debating whether to come back with a line like, "Yes, and the crawfish are in the étouffée," just to see her reaction, when I heard my name being called.

"Claire Jennerette! No, it's something else now. Some street name, right?"

"Claiborne, but that's an avenue, not a street, and don't you forget it!" I laughed, exchanging hugs with Babs Hooper.

Marcel had offered to let her off the hook in deference to Lock's death, but she'd insisted on fulfilling her obligation.

"I practically had to beg him to let me come in today!" Babs complained. "Finally I convinced him I'd go crazy if I didn't have something to do besides eat." She patted her pudgy hips ruefully with the hand that wasn't holding a heavily buttered muffin.

"The police have still got Prytania off-limits, and even if they didn't, it's going to take a bulldozer and a bunch of money to get that place in shape again."

The thin white skin of her forehead pleated in a frown. "It was just horrible, Claire," she confided. "They made me go in there to get the books out of the office for the audit."

"Babs, what does all this mean for the other Lock-Smiths?"

She popped the remaining piece of muffin into her mouth.

"Well, if the estimates for reconstructing Prytania Street are too high, I'll have to close up and make Metairie the main shop until I can find another place Uptown. Otherwise, nothing's going to change much, Claire. Except for Lock not being around anymore, I mean. And for that matter, he was getting ready to leave the country for good."

"Somehow, I don't think this was quite the way he had it planned, Babs!" I pointed out, a little sharply.

"Oh, Claire!" She was indignant. "You know I didn't mean it like that. But we'd already worked out a deal where I'd be transferring a percentage of the net into his account every month."

That sounded more like "squalid little bedsitter" money to me. Certainly not enough to put Lock in his coveted "top drawer." No, if his plans had been that immediate, he'd been counting on other funds.

Like three hundred thousand?

"So you're protected legally, then?" A lawyer's wife gets into the habit of asking that kind of question.

"Oh, sure," she replied offhandedly. "Even before this, we had an agreement, if anything ever happened to him, I had the option of taking over as sole owner."

I struggled to keep my thoughts from showing on my face. Babs Hooper had just revealed her own excellent motive for murdering Lochner Smith.

But why trash that beautiful salon as well? If plain old greed was behind Lock's death, wasn't it just downright stupid to destroy equipment and furniture worth many thousands of dollars? With an inward shudder, I wondered how Lock's pride and joy, an original Jean-Michel Frank sofa, had fared.

For the rest, Babs could certainly have been privy enough to Lock's . . . proclivities to create a misleading scenario.

I gave myself a mental shake. Could I really be thinking my old friend had changed to the extent of becoming a cold-blooded killer, and a particularly nasty one at that?

We'd met when I was ten and Babs was a junior in high school. She'd just moved to town from Bastrop, Louisiana, all legs and boobs, topped by big green eyes and curly blonde hair. The girls cattily called her Daisy Mae, and the boys just called her. And called her.

But Babs, for all her hillbilly pulchritude, was not to be swept off her feet by some mere adolescent with raging hormones. No, it had taken a sophisticated older man to do that.

How she'd met him or who he was remained a mystery. The only thing she told me at the time was that he was handsome and very wealthy.

Babs had only discovered he was married after she'd gotten pregnant and had to drop out of school three months before graduation.

And when I'd gone to visit her after the baby was born in Baptist Hospital, I made my own discovery. Her lover, whoever he was, was black.

I remember how she'd glared defiantly at me over the tiny dark head nursing at her breast, daring me to be shocked and offended, to walk away.

While I was certainly shocked—stunned would be a better word—I stayed, and Babs relented at least enough to confide that the father was paying for everything, including the flower-filled private room. And later on, I knew he'd footed the sizeable tuition fees to send her to the Marcel Barrineau Institut de Beauté.

But to this day, I'd never known his name.

Only Babs could say whether Lamont Hooper had been worth giving up a high school diploma, her reputation, most of her friends and all of her family for.

The willowy Lamont, with big green eyes like his mother's, was also a hairdresser, quite talented, really, but by now he'd worked nearly everywhere in New Orleans because his outrageous behavior kept getting him fired.

There were Lamont Hooper stories all over town. The funniest I'd heard was about a client he didn't like and had tried everything to get rid of. Nothing worked until one day when he'd asked the ritual question, "How much can I cut off?"

She gave the ritual answer, "Same as always, Lamont. Just leave enough to cover my boobs."

Lamont had then pointed out, "Have you noticed how your hair just keeps getting longer and longer?"

But other stories, like how he'd keep clients waiting for hours, sometimes not even bothering to show up, weren't so amusing. Then there were the tales about petty thefts, and drugs, and vicious fights over rich old men in fancy gay bars. Babs was constantly having to bail him out of one holding tank or another.

Between gigs, which was often, Lamont flew home to roost at the Prytania LockSmith's, and I suppose Lock had continued to put up with him for Babs's sake. That's where he'd been working for the last month or so before Lock was killed.

When Babs told me Lamont was assisting her today, I figured she'd decided it was the only way she could keep tabs on him.

In that case, she was going to have her hands full, beginning right now, I thought, as Babs jumped when a piercing giggle ricocheted through the room.

The sound had come from a corner in the back where a grinning Vince Platina was holding court amid a handful of younger stylists and assistants. I couldn't hear what Vince said, but it made everybody with him laugh.

Lamont squealed again and started dancing in a circle around Vince, rolling his big eyes. "Ooh! Let's do the grand slam! Take me for a ride in your white Cadillac convertible, you big dago!"

Lamont's description of Vince Platina, while politically incorrect, was literally accurate. With all his extra bulk and that florid complexion, he could easily pass for Pavarotti's evil twin.

Before Lamont fully comprehended what was happening, Babs had moved in, neatly cut him out of the group, and was herding him toward the door with the practiced ease of an Australian sheepdog.

But Lamont recovered quickly and began to wail, "Mommy, Mommy! I'm sorry, Mommy! I'll be a goooood boy!"

Their departure was accompanied by rude remarks from those who knew them, and concerned exclamations from those who didn't.

Mimi and Faylee came up to me, minus David, who seemed to have fallen by the wayside.

"Now that," Faylee said, pointing in the direction Lamont and Babs had gone, "is the only thing Mimi here and I can come up with that we've ever had in common. So far, anyway."

Mimi nodded. "Yes. Lamont Hooper went to work for Faylee right after I fired him."

"Well, I'm relatively new in town," Faylee said defensively. "How was I to know the little twerp was a fruitcake? The fruit part was obvious. It was the nuts and the drugs that bothered me." She shook her head reminiscently. "But he sure can cut hair. And what a hoot to have around."

"*When* he's around, you mean," Mimi put in. "I finally had to can Lamont after he went off in the middle of a perm and left the neutralizer in this woman's hair. I was busy and didn't realize what he'd done, until it was too late.

"She was a redhead, and came out looking exactly like Ronald MacDonald! I'm lucky she didn't sue my bra off!"

"Wait, this is serious!" I told them. "If you're saying Lamont Hooper has been indulging in a big old streak of disgruntled employee behavior, then we can expect every shop in the city to get trashed, because he's been fired from most all of them."

Faylee looked concerned. "Oh, no, Claire. We didn't mean that. Personally, I don't think that idiot child is capable of such a thing."

"No, it's just a coincidence he used to work for both of us," agreed Mimi.

"Nevertheless," I said, "somehow, I can't help being glad he never worked for me."

Now that I thought of it, aside from being a murder scene, the salon where Lochner Smith met his death had also been trashed. And Lamont Hooper had worked there more than anywhere else.

I helped myself to a muffin and chatted with a few more people. By now, the room was rife with wild speculations and theories about the vandalized hair salons. But as if my unspoken consent, not one person mentioned Lochner Smith.

When the wall clock chimed six-thirty, I decided to visit the bathroom before everybody else got the same idea.

The hallway separating the *hommes* from the *femmes* was shadowy and, I thought, deserted.

It wasn't until I was within twenty feet of them that I realized one of those shadows was Vince Platina, who was kissing someone he'd pinned against the wall with extreme roughness, holding their arms high above their head, slim wrists squeezed tightly in his meaty fists.

Feeling sick, I slipped quietly away before either of them had seen me.

No wonder Sal Romano had suddenly run into a brick wall with Renee.

Now I knew what she'd been doing and where she'd been most of the time I was looking for her.

In a white Cadillac convertible parked in the back.

Chapter 14

"A bad hair day is kind of like the weather. We all complain, but there's not much we can do. In fact, 'most anything we might try to make it better, would probably just wind up making it that much worse!"

Charlotte Dalton, looking smashing in brown ribbed sweater and leggings, with hightopped rust suede granny boots, was taping her introduction to *A Bad Hair Day*.

Buddy Gaines, a cameraman who'd defected from WDSU along with Charlotte, had explained to me earlier that after the intro was edited, she would be partly on camera, partly voiceover narrating humorous vignettes.

". . . really, the safest way to survive a bad hair day is to simply stay in bed and pull the covers over our heads. However, few of us have the luxury of that option . . ."

Standing nearby watching Charlotte at work, was Harry Corvus, a tad too dapper in navy cashmere blazer and cream wool pants to suit me. His overbred features registered admiration as well as irritation, and I figured I knew why. Harry wasn't accustomed to ladies who didn't succumb to his aristocratic charms, and Charlotte was proving immune.

No doubt she posed a rare and interesting challenge because she was already engaged to a rich, handsome, successful man. Or could I be judging him too harshly? Maybe his feelings for her went deeper than I gave him credit for?

Not a chance.

Charlotte continued. "Well, today is going to be another bad hair day for a lot of people in New Orleans. But, wait! This time, something's different!"

"We're here at the exclusive Marcel Barrineau Institut de Beauté, where twenty of south Louisiana's premier hair-stylists have been gathered by Mr. Barrineau to hold the first-ever official Bad Hair Day . . ."

There was more about how she'd be following various people through the process, having them tell in their own words what went wrong, while the operators explained and demonstrated steps they were taking to correct it. Each would be shown "before" and "after."

Anyone who objected to having their hair tragedy televised for all the world to see had only to refuse to sign a release. So far, nobody had.

By seven-thirty A Bad Hair Day was already in full cry and, judging by the look of things, not a moment too soon.

The *whump* of wakeup rock and roll punctuated moans of agony throughout the room: ". . . said a *fourth* of an inch, *not* four *inches* . . . followed the directions *exactly*, and just look . . . like Shannen Doherty's, but he didn't . . . *green* when I got out of the Jacuzzi . . ."

Now the girl in my chair, who'd been promised a "Reba McEntire look," added her own wail to the chorus. "But he swore it was no problem to perm over henna!" She clawed in despair at the gummy, rusty orange sea sponge that, until two days ago, had been sleek, shoulder-length hair in a rich shade of auburn.

"He lied," I told her. "Obviously."

Official Bad Hair Day baseball caps had been issued exclusively to all the hair docs—in surgical green to match our scrubs, naturally. No two were identical; mine boasted fat pink foam rollers and perforated metal curlers secured by red rubber fasteners that had to be antiques.

Their utter wackiness was meant to break the ice with anxious patients, and we were going to have plenty of those to deal with; the end of the line of hatted and scarved hair victims shuffling embarrassedly through the entrance was no longer visible.

So far though, my cap had failed to work its magic on Rusty, as I was beginning to think of her. She was still tense and shaking, understandably finding it difficult to relax and trust anybody after what had been done to her. I didn't point out that it could hardly get worse.

I gave her some time to calm down a little and looked around the room. It was quite a sight. Marcel had color-coded us according to function, so there could be no mixups about who was what.

Led by Marcel's formidable lieutenant, Dominica Dolcevita, the faculty members on hand to supervise operations could be easily spotted by their long, white lab coats.

Hair doc assistants were outfitted in hip, baggy blue overalls, over MBIdB T-shirts, distinguishing them from some of Marcel's students, who wore their regular "school uniforms" of burgundy jumpsuits. Armed with brooms and dustpans, the students were going to earn extra hours as volunteers for cleanup detail, plus helping out with shampoos and other menial tasks when things got too busy.

All patients completed faculty interviews, paid fifty dollars, paid for a "before" Polaroid, and were appropriately shrouded in black smocks.

The paperwork was then passed on to Dominica, who would arbitrarily decree which of us twenty was the most suitable for a specific situation. Since we had all been trained here at various times, she knew our individual strengths and weaknesses better than we did ourselves.

That Dominica would assign this poor little disaster to me was the supreme compliment.

"So what do you think?" the child quavered tearfully, desperately seeking hope for her violated hair.

There was none.

The reconstructer had not been invented that could undo the terrible ravages of "henna sponge."

She stared at me uncomprehendingly as I gently attempted to explain what had happened to her. "You see, each individual hair is composed of three parts; the cuticle, the cortex, and the medulla. Henna has a metallic base. You could even say henna 'plates' each hair with a coating of metal.

"But permanents have a thioglycolic acid base, which works from within by penetrating the hair. Or, in your case, *attempted* to penetrate the metal coating on your hair.

"When you put one on top of the other, the chemical reaction literally convulses the rods and cones in the medulla, which totally alters the entire hair structure."

I saw it wasn't registering.

"Let me put it to you this way, honey. Your hair just flat exploded!" I squished an atomic cloud-shaped clump between my fingers to demonstrate. "As you can see, this is not simply broken, or even fried. It's scrambled!"

She began to weep again, but I cut in. "Listen, kid. That's not going to help a bit. I think I'm getting an idea here, but you've got to stop crying."

Swinging the chair around, I took inventory of her features: big, dark eyes, straight nose, twenty-year-old firm jawline, fair teeth and full lips. Yes, it could work for her.

I smiled. "Okay. You ready?"

She gulped. "You mean—you can save my hair?"

"Baby, that hair's been dead for two days. Only Jesus could save it now!" I said bluntly. "What I want to know is, how brave are you?"

She squared her shoulders. "As brave as I have to be."

"Good girl!" I patted her back and turned the chair so she was looking into the mirror again.

"I trust you, Claire," she added in a small voice.

I laughed grimly. "Oh, you will absolutely have to do that."

To distract her from what was about to happen, I asked why she'd wanted to copy Reba in the first place, and she answered because she was just starting out in country music and felt curly red hair would give her an edge.

"Well, I'm afraid Ms. McEntire will continue to stand alone for some time to come," I said. "But—you might think about shooting for a Lorrie Morgan kind of image."

Seeing her sudden flare of interest, I warned hastily, "Not for another couple of months, though! No, you're going to be closer to—ever watch the weight loss infomercial with that wild, buzzcut blonde?"

Her mouth fell open in astonishment as she realized I had already applied whining clippers to the nape of her neck. "Renee!" I yelled. "Color switches over here now!"

Renee trotted up carrying a chain strung with a rainbow of miniature ponytails. There were dark circles under her eyes, and a darker bruise on the inside of her right wrist, which I plainly saw as she began to hold up switches against the girl's cheek.

My stomach knotted.

If what I'd seen earlier was a sample of Vince's usual technique, that explained the bruising.

Obviously, she'd hooked up with yet another lowlife, although I didn't think Beaudine Guidry had ever been physically rough with her. But then, I didn't know he hadn't, either.

At this point, I wouldn't be willing to bet on anything about Renee Vermilion.

No wonder she hadn't been so enthusiastic about working here today! She'd gone and gotten herself between those "two *paisanos*." Though how she could prefer Platina the piggish over Sal the sexy was beyond me. But for that matter, given her talent for picking out men who would damage her in some way, how did I know the poetry-quoting Romano was any better? He did have those eyes . . .

Lord, Renee! What am I going to do with you? I thought irritably, watching her take off to mix the high-lift toner we'd selected which, theoretically, would mellow the girl's awful color into a smoky strawberry.

I was nearly done clipping her now. She was laughing and crying at the same time. I tossed a shorn chunk into her lap, ordering, "Take a real good look. Feel it, too. Like a boiled Brillo pad, right? Hang onto that, just to remind yourself exactly what's coming off your head here. It ain't a pretty sight."

"I th-think Susan P-Powter's cool," she sobbed through chattering teeth, tears streaming down her face, oblivious to the presence of Charlo and Buddy, who had closed in to capture the moment.

As it turned out, I was able to leave her with a bit more hair than I expected, so she emerged looking more like a trendy saucer-eyed waif than Susan Powter.

Renee stepped in and started brushing the toner onto the remains, and I went to meet my next case, a slinky little number who'd managed to get a round, narrow brush hopelessly snarled in her long, baby-fine, overprocessed, white-blonde hair, all the way to the scalp. Exactly why I never, ever, used those brushes. A quart or so of Goldwell's Kerasilk finally dislodged the implement, which brought with it nearly an entire handful of broken hair.

After some argument, we solved that problem with a multi-layered and feathered cut, which left her looking like a seductive egret. I left her preening in front of a mirror while I took a well-earned break.

One of the students thoughtfully brought me a cup of coffee, which I sipped while waiting for Renee to deliver another injured party. Harry Corvus was also having a caffeine fix, but his was an outsize container of cappuccino imported from the Italian restaurant nearby. After one taste, he'd absolutely refused to drink the native brew of coffee and chicory provided by Marcel.

I must confess to an unworthy moment of glee when he suddenly sputtered through a mouthful of his high-priced beverage, and some of it dribbled down his chin. Automatically, Harry whipped out a handkerchief and dabbed at it without taking his eyes from a point behind me.

Curiously, I turned to look and I had to admit—such a vision would probably cause stronger men than he to choke on their coffee.

In skintight purple capri pants, matching off-the-shoulder sweater, poontang tigerskin Spring-o-laters, and cat's-eye sunglasses, Duchess Crowe had arrived.

Chapter 15

Duchess had brought someone along to keep her company, a tall, thin youth in black leather jacket and jeans, with faintly Oriental features emphasized by a drooping Fu Manchu mustache.

His long, black hair was an expertly-crafted tangled mass of spiral curls, and I immediately understood why Duchess was so determined to acquire a kinky mane of her own.

I had been right. It was rock and roll. It was also, technically, a man.

"Oh, that's a toy boy," Renee informed me, when she came over to get instructions about prepping our next casualty, surprised when I didn't right away comprehend she was referring to the Toy Boys, the Mirror's latest house band. The group had derived its name from Tom Toy, their lead singer and Duchess Crowe's own personal toy boy.

I was fascinated. It might almost be worth another trip to the club, just to get a look at the rest of them.

"Hold on, *chère!* What happened to Boris and Natasha?"

Renee threw me a condescending glance. "Natasha and Yuri," she corrected witheringly. "And they're out. The Toy Boys are in."

"One of them is, anyway," I observed, feeling a little sorry for the Russians. Recalling that vampirish duo's attitude toward Duchess, I thought she would be well advised to wear garlic around her neck for awhile.

Duchess Crowe's appearance triggered a chain reaction.

"Yoo-hoo, girlfriend!" shrieked Lamont Hooper, who'd managed to slip his leash while Babs was busy elsewhere.

He sashayed over to Duchess with one strap of his overalls coyly off the shoulder, and he'd confiscated his mother's baseball cap, which had fussy bows and little girl barrettes all over it.

"Love that outfit, but hate that color, Auntie Duchess. You know purple makes me look like a hag." Lamont pouted.

Behind the cat's-eye sunglasses, Duchess's expression was unreadable. "Then you won't be trying to borrow this one, will you, Lamont?" she rasped, causing those within earshot to laugh.

Lamont lifted his strapless shoulder and said huffily, "Who cares? Purple's an old lady color, anyway." He stuck out his tongue at Tom and jeered, "Your old lady wears purple!"

"Try to be cool, Lamont," Tom suggested, shifting the large canvas and leather satchel he was carrying.

"I'm so cool, I'm hot. So hot, I'm cool!" trilled Lamont, fanning himself with a long, slender hand. I noticed he had a perfect French manicure.

By now, customers in the nearest chairs, grateful for any diversion from their own private ordeals, were watching expectantly as the scene unfolded.

Right on cue, Marzipan Jones entered, dressed in black, pleated gauze with a handkerchief hemline and black Louis XIV shoes. She was pushing a pink Gino's Emporium cart filled with the souvenir travel kits, intending to pass them out.

Bringing up the rear came Gino Gambara in his wheelchair. Today the old man sported a shabby snap-brim tweed cap, a burgundy Arnold Palmer sweater riddled with snags, gold sweatpants, and slippersox.

Lamont's gnatlike attention was instantly distracted. "Look everybody! It's Granny Badwitch and her pink basket of poison potions!" His red hightopped sneakers flashed as he darted over to Marzie and grabbed for one of the bags, only to have Gino reach over and knock it out of his hand with the silver-headed cane.

"Ow!" Lamont cried. "You nasty old troll!"

"Shut up!" snarled Gino, waving his cane threateningly.

Just then Babs descended the righthand staircase leading to one corner of the mezzanine, where all the hairdryers were located. She took in the situation at a glance, and collared her son, marching him back down to their station without a word.

"And keep that castrato away from me lady!" Gino wheezed after them, as Marzie attempted to calm him down.

But the real action was only just beginning.

With Lamont out of the way, Marzie found herself face to face with Duchess.

"Well, jus' looky here what the cat couldn't be bothered to drag in!" Marzie sneered. "Her royal lowness hurselve! Well, you only be wastin' ever'body's time, cause ain't no amount of permynunts gonna help your ugly face!"

Tom seemed about to say something, but Duchess spoke first. "You pathetic, popeyed old bitch!" she countered, curling a scornful red lip. "Did you really think I wouldn't find out how you stalled my order for those compacts? So I just made other arrangements."

Duchess nodded at Tom Toy, who began to move down the row of stations to the left, putting square envelopes from the canvas bag into eager, outstretched hands.

"What those are?" Marzie demanded.

"Those," Duchess cawed loudly to the room at large, "are free passes to a wild and crazy party at the Mirror Club to introduce the hottest new rock and roll band in America, the Toy Boys! Free drinks, free hors d'oeuvres, and very special prices on any service at my new beauty salon, Mirror Image, where Vince Platina will be working."

Vince, three chairs down from me, paused in the midst of a haircut and snipped his scissors in the air at the captive audience. His color looked even higher, and I wondered how he felt about Duchess announcing him as a mere employee when he'd been telling people he was just helping her out for awhile. Then again, beggars can't be choosers.

Tom was barely keeping up with the demand for invitations, especially from the women, who had discovered he was Toy Boy in Chief.

"And," Duchess raised her croak another notch, "a valuable coupon entitling you to thirty percent off any purchase at any location of Polly's Beauty Supplies!"

Polly's was Gino's most serious competition.

Marzie's eyes threatened to spring out of her head. "You be a dead woman!" she hissed at Duchess, hurriedly wheeling her pink cart to the stations on the right before Tom had finished with the other side.

Duchess laughed and sneezed suddenly.

"We be givin' fifty percent off at Gino's Emporium," Marzie called out, as the fickle crowd converged to snatch up the pink vinyl kits while Gino tooled along behind her.

It was ludicrous.

Just then Marcel, looking like some woman's fantasy doctor lover in a long white lab coat, having completed his portion of the workshop still in session across the courtyard, entered through the side French doors. Seeing the commotion he hesitated, as if debating whether or not to eject them all.

If only he had.

But while he still delayed, Charlotte and Buddy corralled him into an interview about his inspiration for A Bad Hair Day. Instantly, Marcel was at his most photogenic and eloquent as he began smoothly, "I had grown quite weary of hearing a bad hair day spoken of as if it were a supernatural force over which mortals have no power. "Nonsense! Bad hair is always done by somebody. Therefore, it can be undone by somebody else . . ."

Duchess was given her paperwork and directed to one of the long leather benches in the center of the room to await her turn with Dominica. She picked her way cautiously through the cables on the floor, Spring-o-lators slapping softly against bare heels, followed by a short chorus of wolf whistles.

"Mama-san, baby!" exclaimed Buddy Gaines appreciatively, angling for a rear shot.

Charlotte was at his elbow. "Down, Buddy!" she commanded with affectionate contempt. "Who—or perhaps I should say, what—is that, Claire?" she asked, watching Duchess arrange herself decoratively on a bench. The effect was somewhat spoiled, however, when she pulled a Kleenex from inside a purple knit sleeve and blew her nose gustily.

I told Charlotte what I knew of Duchess' backstory, which, even with the addendum of today's events, took all of ninety seconds.

Charlotte feigned indignation. "You mean you've known about that club all this time and never invited me? I thought we were friends!"

Tom Toy had distributed all his invites and joined Duchess on her bench, bearing a cup of tea. While she sipped, he rummaged in the canvas bag and extracted a prescription bottle with a purple K&B label. She used the remaining tea to wash down a couple of pills.

Harry came up to us, predictably wanting to know about Duchess. When I told him why she was here, his reaction was immediate.

"Splendid! Here we have a somewhat different story from the rest. A woman trying to avoid a bad hair day by coming to the experts first. I want you to focus on her as one of the main subjects, Charlotte," he directed.

"Fine. If she wants to, of course," Charlotte agreed.

"Oh," Harry said, with a smug little smile, "I think I can persuade her."

He approached Duchess and Tom, and engaged them in conversation. By her body language, Duchess gave every evidence of being quite flattered to receive the attentions of this handsome stranger, and nodded affirmatively several times, meanwhile fishing in her big bag for a fresh Kleenex.

"I just hope she's not going to be snuffling like that through the whole thing," Charlotte muttered, making some notes on her clipboard.

I went to check on my country singer, and was dismayed to find that her hair had taken on an ominous mauve glow.

Instructing Renee to shampoo the toner out pronto, I accompanied them across to the nearest shampoo bowl, which happened to be right next to the one where Vince and Sal were working over a prostrate body.

I'd seen Sal try to speak to Renee a couple of times already, but she'd rudely snubbed him at every turn, as she did now.

Watching his gaze linger wistfully on Renee's rigid shoulders as she shampooed, I was sorely tempted to shake that exasperating little coonass by the scruff of her neck till she hollered *noncle*.

Marzie hurried by, her empty pink cart rattling as she pushed it over the cables en route back to the supply room.

Gino trailed behind at a more leisurely pace, deftly navigating his space-age wheelchair through increasing foot traffic.

He darted a sly glance in my direction. "Hey lady. Seen any good pictures, lately?" And the *vieux péteux* sailed off, cackling and tipping his cane.

A sudden crash made me jump, but it sounded worse than it actually was. Renee's elbow had knocked a gargantuan dispenser of conditioner to the floor.

When we'd gotten the girl back in my chair, I braced myself for more tears at the final blow I was about to deal to her Reba dream.

"We're going to have to strip every bit of the red out," I informed her. "And even though I took off the visibly damaged hair, what you've got left is still so weak, I refuse to run the risk of putting red color of any kind back into it."

Then I sent Renee off to mix up a batch of White Lightning, explaining to the singer that it was a water-activated color remover containing yogurt powder and vitamins. "White Lightning's going to turn you into a real hillbilly blonde," I teased.

The girl had recovered enough to practice a few sultry sidelong glances in the mirror at her evolving reflection. "Oh," she replied absently, "cool. I want to go platinum then. Like my first album."

So much for Reba. I left her chattering to Renee about cowboy boots and went back upstairs to the faculty lounge for a bottle of Evian.

I drank it while leaning against the railing of the walkway overlooking the main floor, watching the green, white, blue and burgundy shapes scurrying around below. I couldn't help but experience a little thrill of pride as I observed our "surgical teams" at work.

All of us were volunteering our time and talents today. That flat fifty-dollar fee was for supplies and utilities. Tips were welcome, of course, and if some of today's patients wanted to continue on as clients of the various hairdressers that served them, wonderful.

Let others criticize the relevance of such an enterprise in today's world, where new horrors lurk around every corner, but my simplistic theory is that statistics are only people, when you really think about it, and if improved hair could make some of them feel better about themselves, it had to help the planet a little bit.

A squat, white-clad figure with a beak nose walked into view beneath me: Dominica, who was pointing Duchess toward where the funereal black smocks were being disbursed. I was glad I had alerted her to the possibility that Duchess might show up today and why, and was relieved when she agreed I had given the right advice.

As Duchess started off, her path crossed that of Harry Corvus, and they chatted for a moment or two, until somebody called Harry's name.

It was Lamont, who was Rockette-kicking his way up to him singing, "I'm Just Wild About Harry."

While Harry was still gaping at him in bemusement, the light-fingered Lamont quickly whisked a stolen Bad Hair Day baseball cap from behind his back, and crammed it onto the Englishman's careful coif.

Attached to this particular cap were long, straggly hanks of hair in the Howard Stern mode, and the transformation it wrought in the fastidious Harry's appearance was astonishing.

Lamont clapped his hands delightedly. "Hooray! Teflon Man is dead! Mane Man lives!"

Harry tried to remove the cap, but a giggling Lamont wouldn't let him. "Mane Man! Let's do the grand slam!" he chanted.

Duchess raised her cat's-eye sunglasses, observing their ridiculous tango as if unable to believe what she was seeing.

At last, Harry managed to extricate himself from Lamont. He snatched the cap from his head and turned back to resume his conversation with Duchess, but she gave him a pained look and flipflapped rapidly away.

Harry had that effect on certain women, I thought, remembering how Juanita had fled his presence after he'd addressed her in Spanish.

And no wonder.

Rae Ellen had finally got it out of her that what Harry had said was, the champagne could only taste better if it had come from her breasts!

Possibly, he had paid a similar compliment to Duchess.

I chuckled, thoroughly savoring Harry's foolish expression at being left stranded in the middle of the room.

All in all, things were running very smoothly.

Marzie and Duchess had already had their blowup, and it wasn't nearly as bad as I'd feared.

True, a death threat had been uttered, but that, as Marzie herself in a calmer state of mind, would no doubt put it, was, "Jus' a figger of speesh."

Chapter 16

At noon, Dominica began turning people away at the door. We were already up to nearly a hundred and thirty cases, still a controllable number but substantially more than Marcel had anticipated.

The energy level accelerated as Charlotte dashed Oprah-like from one person to another, urging each to spill her guts, and the muted primal scream of a score of hair dramas was sucked into her microphone while rock and roll music pounded in the background.

Certainly some of these disasters were self-inflicted; folks would insist on playing home beauty parlor. But most had been perpetrated by so-called professionals. There ought to be a way to get their licenses revoked.

Harry Corvus gimped at Charlotte's and Buddy's heels, egging them on. His gold pinky ring flashed in the light as he urgently waved the gaffer over to a darker part of the room where they were headed to talk with a plump, weeping middle-aged woman, victim of a friend who'd given her a black dye job in the kitchen.

Make that a *die* job, because the poor thing looked like she had expired and gone straight to hell without passing Go.

When Renee and I rinsed the White Lightning from the singer's head, we paused, basking in mutual satisfaction at a job well done.

I shaped the remaining wisps in little cherub's curls close to the girl's skull before leading her over to the mirror, and was rewarded with her gasp of pleasure at the transformation.

"Country music won't know what hit it," I promised.

Charlo had spotted us and rushed over. "Now that's what I call a Pure D honkytonk angel!" she exclaimed, waving her mike at the girl.

My baseball cap was starting to make my head itch. Apparently others where having the same problem, because several were lying discarded here and there. I started to remove mine, but Charlotte wanted me to wear it on camera while I explained how I'd solved the henna disaster.

After they'd gone in search of fresh meat, I yanked the thing off and was briskly rubbing my knuckles across my scalp when the next thing happened.

Dominica had summoned the representative of Scissor Hands, Vicky Su (what more perfect name for a Chinese southern belle?) and was escorting her to the bench where Duchess sat waiting with Tom Toy.

But when Vicky realized to whom she was being assigned, she stopped cold and shook her head negatively. The movement caused the abundant corkscrew curls she had not been born with, to bounce beneath her baseball cap, which was adorned with colored plastic combs in all shapes and sizes.

Dominica, not accustomed to being contradicted, wore a mildly astonished expression.

Duchess observed their intense pantomime, smiling slightly as Vicky Su's gestures clearly indicated unwillingness to work on her.

"Tom Toy was Vicky Su's boyfriend until Duchess came along," Renee confided suddenly, as we worked rapidly to correct a horribly bungled bleach weave that had cost its victim a hundred and fifty dollars and left her looking like she was wearing an old spotted rag on her head.

According to Renee, Duchess had lured Tom away from Vicky Su with a Rolex wristwatch and all the trimmings, plus a generous allowance.

"*Aufaité!* That Duchess sure knows how to get what she wants," Renee concluded with something like envy.

"But what will Tom do when it's time for another perm?" I wondered. "Duchess sure can't give him that. In fact, very few people could. Bet the one he's got now is courtesy of Vicky Su."

Renee confirmed this. I also heard that since Duchess had been involved with Tom she'd invested major bucks in the Toy Boys, who were about to go into the studio to record their first album. The plan was for Duchess to sing backup and the occasional duet with Tom.

"Although," Renee revealed, tucking the ends of the final foil securely, "there are those associated with the Mirror Club who have strong objections to the money Duchess is taking out of the profits and pouring into this band. It's like she's gone off the deep end."

I didn't have to ask where Renee had picked up that tidbit.

Tom surfaced from a back issue of *Star* with that heartbreaking cover of O.J. Simpson holding his beautiful children's hands while they ate apples, and looked trapped when he realized what was going on between Dominica and Vicky Su. His eyes locked with Vicky's, then he shrugged.

Despair washed over Vicky Su's delicate golden face as Tom dropped his gaze back to the tabloid.

Dominica's temper was beginning to fray, and she summoned Marcel, who was exercising his chairside manner on a sexy young hair patient.

The next time I looked over, a glowering Vicky Su was stalking back to her station, Duchess Crowe stepping gingerly along behind in her wobbly tigerskin mules.

As she passed, Duchess glanced in my direction. I waved and she stopped, recognizing me.

"So you decided to come after all," I remarked, thinking it was too bad Renee was back in the supply room and would miss her idol.

"Yeah, but I'm not sure it was such a good idea," she said, sniffling.

I said sympathetically, "No, it's not going to be much fun for you, sitting through all that with a cold."

"What?" She looked puzzled. "Oh, you mean my . . . allergies. I was talking about some of the people here. If I'd realized ahead of time . . ."

"You mean Marzie," I finished for her. "Well, I had no way of knowing, or I would never have suggested it, of course. And it's none of my business, but your feud with her sounds very personal."

Duchess gave a short laugh. "It couldn't possibly be more personal. But she's not the only one . . ."

Down at the other end of the room, Vicky Su had realized Duchess was no longer with her, and looked askance in our direction.

Duchess started to go, then turned back. "Listen, Claire. That Harry from the TV station? Do you know his last name?"

"Corvus, and no, he's not married!" I gave her a woman-to-woman laugh, privately thinking it was about time she picked on somebody her own age.

Duchess seemed about to say something else, but Vicky Su intervened. "Could we just get started, please?" she said gruffly, and all but shoved Duchess toward her chair.

Right after that, there was a welcome lull in the action. It was around one-thirty, and even over the chemicals, I detected appetizing smells as takeout food was delivered from nearby restaurants. All at once, I was ravenous, and knew I should have thought to order earlier.

But when I scanned the room for Renee, intending to send her to pick up something, she was already gone. I didn't want to speculate as to where.

"Hey, Claire!" Charlotte was approaching with a grin, carrying a big brown paper bag. "Betcha can't guess what those precious, thoughtful men of ours sent over?"

I snatched at the bag gratefully. "If it's Monday, it's got to be red beans and rice from Liuzza's, God bless them!"

But before we could even get it open for a sniff, Harry Corvus strode up, pulling Buddy with him.

"Charlotte, I thought I told you to follow that Duchess person right from the beginning," he reproved.

"Sure, Harry. But Vicky Su only just this minute came and got her, and they haven't even really started yet. I thought Claire and I could eat first."

"This won't take a second," he insisted. "I just want to make sure we capture this before one thing is done. Then you can follow up on each stage. Come along, then," he commanded, briskly.

Buddy handed Charlotte her microphone. "Come along, then!" he mimicked, sotto voce.

Charlotte elbowed him in the midriff. "Shut up, you." Shoving the Liuzza's bag into my arms she added, "You come too, Claire."

"Ouch!" I yelped. "It's still hot!"

Harry turned. "Whatever do you have there?"

"Arguably the best red beans and rice and hot sausage in town," I told him. "There's plenty. Want to join us?"

He grimaced. "Thank you, no. I can't imagine why you people choose to eat stodge and bangers when there's much finer food available."

Charlotte smiled sweetly. "Are you saying we have no palate, Harry?"

"Not in the least!" he denied hastily. "Only . . . it's just that someone told me of a wonderful little place in the English Channel. I rather hoped you'd join me for a bite. You too, Claire," he added, insincerely.

To keep from laughing in his face, Buddy, Charlotte and I avoided looking at each other, agreeing by unspoken consent to let him find out the hard way it was the Irish Channel he sought, not the English.

Duchess was just settling into Vicky Su's chair when we descended upon them en masse, and I had a feeling Vicky was relieved not to be left alone with her right away.

Harry hovered in the background while Charlotte explained to the ladies what was needed from them.

"It's going to look funny if you don't take off your sunglasses though," Buddy warned Duchess.

"Do I really have to?" she protested, grumpily. "I've got bad allergies and my eyes always get weird."

"We won't do a closeup of your face if you'd rather not," Charlotte promised.

"Oh, all right!" Duchess peevishly slid the glasses off. "But please hurry. I have to go to the bathroom."

Her eyes weren't swollen, as I'd expected, just bloodshot and oddly blurry looking.

Vicky Su spoke grudgingly to Charlotte about the complexities of curling Asian hair, and outlined the procedure she planned to follow.

The whole thing took all of three minutes, and Duchess was released to answer her call of nature.

Back at the reception desk, Buddy zipped his camera into a black nylon bag. "I guess it'll be okay to leave it here," he decided, and started to complain about how it was too late to go to Tujague's as he'd planned, and now he was stuck splitting pizza with some of the crew.

Harry broke into his laments. "Well, I'm off, then!" he announced. "I may go back to the station to check on things after lunch. I can trust you to cover things, of course."

"Of course, Harry," Charlotte agreed blandly. "Ta-ta, and *bon appétit!*"

"Don't fall in the English Channel!" Buddy muttered, to Harry's retreating back, and we all laughed.

Buddy left for his pizza a minute later, and I told Charlotte, "Go stake out that table in the courtyard before somebody else beats us to it. I'm going to run up to the ladies'."

The mezzanine bathroom had seen little traffic today, because 'most everybody had been using the larger and more convenient downstairs facilities. Only one other stall was occupied when I arrived, and a flush announced she was about to depart. By the sniffling and snuffling I deduced it was Duchess Crowe, and a flash of tigerskin as she passed my cubicle on her way out confirmed this.

Ready to leave, I had just opened the door a crack when I noticed a trickle of water running in the nearest sink. Holding onto the doorpull with one hand, I reached over and shut the water off.

That's how I happened to glimpse something through the narrow slat that made me freeze, just as I was about to yank it open. Cautiously, I inched it a little wider so I could see better.

It was like déjà vu of the scene in the dark passageway I'd witnessed hours before, only shot in reverse.

It still starred Vince Platina, but the woman writhing in his arms was not Renee.

No, Renee was standing exactly where I'd stood earlier, watching them.

I wondered how she felt about Duchess Crowe knowing how to get what she wanted now.

Chapter 17

"What on earth ails that child, Claire?" Charlotte demanded, when I'd filled her in on Renee's mysterious behavior, between still-steaming mouthfuls of Liuzza's finest. "That Vince is a mean looking old hog!"

I chased down a bite of spicy sausage with some Dr. Pepper before replying. "Well, she's been like this for a few weeks now. The best I can come up with is that maybe it's about her and Beaudine breaking up and him getting engaged about five minutes after that. Kind of a delayed reaction?" But that explanation didn't begin to satisfy me.

Charlotte nodded sagely. "Some of these men can really warp a girl's personality. Thank God I don't have to worry about that anymore." She smiled mistily. "Got me a good one, finally."

"Second best in the world," I agreed. "But there's a slithery serpent in your garden of love, in case you haven't noticed."

Charlotte snorted. "Listen, Claire. I'll confess Harry is just the kind of guy I used to impale myself on. One of the several kinds, long as we're being honest. But now? Honey, the boy don't have a prayer!"

"I don't think he quite gets that, though," I warned her.

She frowned, toying with a crust of French bread. "Well then, let's just hope it's a passing fancy, Claire. You know, it's because of Harry I got a crack at this dream job. Shoot, WBGZ makes my old station look like something the Little Rascals put together with rusty parts from the town junkyard.

"And while I can truthfully say he's made overtures, there's been nothing I can't handle so far. Although I can see it getting awkward down the road if he's bent on playing carry the torch."

I laughed. "Don't worry, Charlo. If Foley ever spotted Harry carrying a torch for you, he'd rip it out of his hands and set fire to him with it!"

Charlotte looked at me and started giggling.

"What?" I asked, but she just shook her head and pointed to what I'd picked up from my plate and had been waving at her for emphasis.

It was an enormous sausage.

"You're pathetic!" I told her. "We've got to get you married!"

Chapter 18

After lunch, things got so incredibly busy, even with Marcel's students helping out, that all our assistants were playing musical chairs.

At one point, Renee was down at the far end helping Faylee Wilkins correct the kitchen black dye job, and I found myself working closely with Sal Romano, adding lowlights in several different shades to rescue a blond gone wrong.

I marvelled again at Renee's bad taste, picking Vince over Sal. But maybe, after what she'd witnessed today, she would finally come to her senses.

Babs had at last given up trying to keep Lamont under control, but perversely, he seemed to have settled down, at least for the time being, and was working with quiet efficiency.

I had originally surmised it would require over two hours to wrap Duchess Crowe's hair on perm rods, but that proved to be a very conservative estimate, because I hadn't factored in the frequent stops Vicky Su and Ling, her tiny Vietnamese assistant, would have to make to see their other people.

Consequently, they abandoned Duchess for five to ten minutes at a time during various stages of her wrapping.

She was never alone for long, however. Tom Toy, who'd been dispatched earlier to pick up Chinese food at Say Tung's Café (probably to get him out of the way while she trysted with Vince) wore a path between his camp on the leather bench, and Vicky Su's station, ferrying cardboard containers, cups of tea, and magazines.

At about four o'clock, the inevitable happened. Duchess ran out of Kleenex. I heard her tell Tom to run over to the nearest K&B on Louisiana Avenue, and pick up a couple of large boxes of Softique.

"Don't bring back those Puffs!" she warned, as he eagerly took the car keys, no doubt glad for the break. That must've been some allowance he was drawing.

Harry Corvus returned, just as Tom was leaving. Evidently, the television station wasn't the only place he'd been; designer chinos and brown leather bomber jacket betrayed a visit to his apartment closet across the Square, as well.

Harry detained Tom for a moment, and they spoke briefly.

"Next thing, he'll be wanting to put a camera in the car for the Kleenex run," Buddy Gaines snickered to Charlotte.

"Bite your tongue!" she exclaimed in mock alarm. "Don't listen to him Andy," she urged the diminutive Filipino intern who'd been dodging in and out all day with a video camera collecting B-roll footage, when Andy showed signs of taking Buddy at his word.

As the pace grew more frantic, it seemed even less important who had come with whom anymore. We were just a bunch of hair professionals, having us a hair orgy. For instance, at one time or another, Sal, Vince, Renee, Babs and even Marcel himself pitched in to help Vicky Su get Duchess's hair rolled.

So did Lamont for that matter, but he was growing restless again, fretting that his French manicure had gotten all chipped, and declaring it was time to grand slam.

If that was the title of a hit song and the latest dance craze, I was sadly out of touch, because I'd never heard of it before today.

Natasha and Yuri took advantage of Duchess being confined to her chair to have some sort of confrontation with her, but somebody had turned up the music so loud I couldn't hear it, no matter how hard I tried. And I did try.

Finally, at four-thirty, Duchess was completely wrapped. As instructed, Charlo and Buddy were on hand to immortalize the event, while Harry hovered officiously in the background and an unsmiling Vicky Su explained in a monotone to the folks out in television land that the next hurdle was to get the timing perfect. As feared, Duchess indeed had that dreaded Asian combination of curl-resistant hair and acutely sensitive scalp.

I lost track of her progress for awhile, because Renee and I had drawn the Jacuzzi chlorine disaster, and we were talking key lime pie.

Coming up for air, I saw Duchess, sitting with her head full of perm rods tipped back over a washbowl, being spray rinsed free of curling solution by Lamont.

When Gino happened to roll by, he couldn't resist turning the spray onto him, and the old man roared in fury.

Lamont was gleeful, until Gino practically put his chair into a wheelie and charged straight at him, swinging his cane like a war club.

"No! Help me, somebody!" Lamont shrieked, staving Gino off with more blasts from the hose, while Duchess struggled to raise up in order to see what was going on.

Like an enormous hawk, Marzie swooped down from nowhere in a swirl of black lace, and grabbed the wheelchair grips, yanking Gino away from Lamont.

"Jus' one more time, boy, and you be wakin' up in that place where you wish you wouldn't," she hissed at Lamont, as Gino sputtered and futilely swabbed at his face with his wet sweater.

"I'm sorry," Lamont muttered. He didn't look all that sorry, but he did look a little scared.

Marzie snatched a towel from one of the students and handed it to Gino, then rapidly got him out of there.

Tom Toy returned with a couple of purple and white plastic K&B bags. He emptied the contents onto the bench he and Duchess had staked out, three large boxes of Softique tissues as instructed, plus a big package of barbecued Fritos, which he ripped open and began to crunch happily.

A stone-silent Renee and I worked our way through the next batch, during which time Vicky Su neutralized Duchess's perm, and Mimi, David and Faylee helped her remove the rods, which was nearly as big a job as putting them in.

As people began to notice the results, a spatter of sincere applause broke out. Vicky Su had done a magnificent job.

The next step, Vicky Su informed the camera, with the most enthusiasm she'd displayed so far, was to apply a heat-activated conditioner to the freshly curled hair.

After she'd worked it through, Vicky Su led Duchess toward the staircase to park her beneath a dryer for thirty minutes, tracked by Buddy and Charlotte.

More applause broke out as they passed, but Duchess seemed oblivious. Her hair looked absolutely stunning, but her face was somewhat worse for wear, and she appeared rather shaky on her pins. Of course, she'd been sitting for hours, and those ridiculous shoes didn't help.

Duly documented by Andy's whirring camera, Tom Toy at the tail end of the procession struggled to balance the canvas bag, a cup of tea, some magazines and an unopened box of Kleenex.

"I say!" Harry Corvus exclaimed heartily, and I realized that was the first time I'd heard him use the expression. "This calls for a proper British celebration! I propose to run over to a wonderful purveyor of spirits I've discovered nearby for some authentic English ale. On the house!"

This time the applause verged on the thunderous. Ordinarily, probably very few of those present would appreciate the subtleties of the stuff, but this was no ordinary day, it was their Bad Hair Day, and it was alcohol.

Harry beamed, drawing on a pair of showy leather driving gloves.

"Oh, brother!" Buddy muttered, stifling a laugh.

Everybody in the parade was halfway up the stairs, except for Tom Toy, who was still at the bottom, juggling his load.

Harry noticed and reached out to take the bulky box of tissues teetering precariously on top of the stack.

"Hey, thanks," Tom said, and I saw he had a surprisingly sweet smile.

There was a tricky moment when Buddy, who'd stepped on a hair roller somebody had dropped, reeled around to his left, nearly creating a domino effect that would've toppled everybody behind him down the stairs. Fortunately, he caught his balance and the procession continued the ascent with no further mishap, except for an embarrassing indication that someone had broken wind.

In a few minutes, Tom came bounding cheerfully down the stairs, jingling the car keys, and headed for the door. Either he was embarking on another mission, or he'd gotten time off for good behavior.

A little later, I took one of my people upstairs to a dryer, and saw Vicky Su had lifted Duchess' hood to check on her hair, which had been stuffed into a plastic cap so it wouldn't blow around. They were jabbering away in what I assumed was Chinese.

I couldn't tell if they were arguing or not, because at Dan's and my favorite Szechwan place, we can hear the husband and wife owners/cooks out in the kitchen, screaming at each other in their native tongue above the crackle of hot grease. There were times we were positive mayhem was being committed, but then they'd appear at our table, bearing sizzling dishes of deliciousness, faces wreathed in smiles.

When I returned to the mezzanine to retrieve my lady from her dryer, Lamont was bending over Duchess, holding a can of Pepsi.

"Auntie Duchess," he was saying, "I'm sorry. See, I brought you the right one baby, uh-huh, to make up. Come on, take just a teensy-weensy sip for Lamont?"

He raised her hood, then jumped back and screamed in terror.

The soft drink can flew out of his hand, spraying its contents all over the marble floor.

The stench of vomit, and something that smelled like a combination of almonds and cooked cabbage, previously undetected amid all the reeking hair chemicals, filled the dryer area.

Duchess's head lolled and her body sagged to one side. Her feet splayed hideously and fell out of the tigerskin shoes.

Incredibly, Duchess Crowe was dead.

Permanently waived.

Chapter 19

As far away from everyone else as possible, Vicky Su huddled miserably in a chair flanking the courtyard doors, taking no notice of the uniformed cop leaning casually against the jamb.

Her station had been gone over with a fine tooth comb, no pun intended, and everything, including her personal case of tools, had been confiscated.

Out in the alley behind the Institut, a forensic team was rooting through today's trash, bagging up all the empty tubes and jars, Evian bottles, and discarded food and drink containers, because the preliminary medical examination strongly suggested Duchess had been poisoned.

Above our heads, sounds echoed from the mezzanine, where grisly parodies of everyday tasks—dusting, vacuuming, and taking pictures—were being performed.

Up there, yellow police tape roped off the sinister little space that had suddenly taken on a macabre resemblance to an electric chair, the way the dryer hood rose above the backrest.

All that now remained of its occupant was a crude outline in chalk on black leather.

Checking my watch against the big wall clock, I couldn't believe it was only 8:45. Surely eons had elapsed since Lamont had discovered Duchess dead beneath the dryer, instead of a mere two hours or so.

The faculty lounge was chosen as an interrogation room, no doubt because of its close proximity to the murder scene. Detective Leo Wickes assisted by three other plain-clothes officers, had done a remarkably efficient job of taking our individual statements, eliminating more witnesses with each round of questioning and releasing them to go home.

The rest of us were instructed to wait in the classroom downstairs, and not to discuss the case with each other.

The question uppermost in everyone's mind, of course, was the whereabouts of Tom Toy. Nectarine had already put out an all-points bulletin for him, and the license plate number of Duchess's Q45 he was thought to be driving.

I remembered how relieved he'd looked the second time he went out. Had he been making an escape? Tom's seeming devotion to his ladylove, fetching and toting tea and food, might have been the perfect cover.

He could have slipped the poison into any or all of it, at anytime. Nothing easier. And she probably wouldn't have noticed a strange taste, because the allergies had clogged her sinuses.

But then, why would he want to kill his golden goose? Duchess was not only providing financial support to him personally, she was backing him to become a big star.

Recalling again the eager expression his face had worn as he'd hurried away to the rhythm of jingling car keys, I wondered if he'd been singing a silent song of "free at last, free at last."

I surveyed my fellow inmates dispersed around the room. Besides Vicky Su and myself, they were Dominica, Marcel, Marzie, Gino, Vince, Sal, Charlotte, Buddy, Babs and Lamont Hooper, Natasha and Yuri, and Harry Corvus.

The reason I'd been detained was because I'd made two or three trips to the dryer area during the crucial time period after Duchess was taken upstairs, and was present when Lamont had discovered her body.

Wickes had been disgusted with me though, because I'd been so busy during that roughly twenty-minute period, all I could remember were hazy impressions of various-colored figures going up and down the stairs.

Harry, who had returned with a trunkful—excuse me, *bootful* of British ale on ice from the liquor store, walked in seeking a couple of able bodies to help him carry it inside, only to find chaos surrounding a very disabled body.

He had immediately dashed up the stairs, but there was nothing he could do, of course.

Savoy and Wickes were hoping that he, along with Buddy and Charlotte, who had close recurring contact with the victim throughout the day, might have noticed something important. All three would have had to stay late anyway, to oversee the dismantling of lights and cables.

Clearly though, poor little Vicky Su was a major suspect.

Gossip and beauty shops go hand in hand, and quite a few people knew the story of how Duchess had snitched Tom right out from under Vicky Su's nose. Now the police did, too.

Vince Platina and Sal Romano were there because they'd worked for Duchess, and might conceivably have had separate or corporate motives.

Of the two of them, my money would be on Vince, but from what I'd accidentally witnessed, they'd seemed to be on exceptionally good terms. Then again, a personal involvement with the victim might only enhance his candidacy.

I couldn't help hoping Renee had mentioned seeing them together.

Nectarine, however, seemed more hostile to Sal Romano, and I couldn't think why. As far as I could tell, about the only opportunity he would have had was when he was helping Vicky Su wrap Duchess's hair. Unless, (very iffy) he injected something into her sensitive scalp and nobody had noticed, including Duchess.

Anyway, quite a few other people participated in that monumental undertaking, and most of them had been allowed to go home.

Natasha and Yuri had admitted to having a fight with Duchess. They stood near the courtyard doors on the opposite side of Vicky Su's chair, chain-smoking disdainfully and flicking ashes outside past the uniformed sentry.

Yuri had removed his orange granny glasses, exposing pale eyes with thick white lashes, which I thought were probably bleached.

Lamont Hooper hadn't recovered from the shock of finding Duchess. His eyes looked glazed, and he remained totally mute, scarcely seeming to breathe.

Babs stood protectively behind the shampoo chair where he had collapsed, a roly-poly she-bear guarding her young.

I looked over at Marzie, perched regally in an elevated client's chair with Gino's wheels parked beside it. The old man's skin was stretched so tightly over his skull, it could have passed for a death's-head, if not for those big, burning black eyes.

Sergeant Savoy, seeing no reason to keep the fragile old man waiting around, had urged him to let an officer drive him home, but he'd refused.

Gino's Emporium was indeed the source of any number of potentially toxic substances, and anybody with a slight knowledge of chemistry could easily have concocted something lethal.

But it was Marzie who'd had that very public fight with Duchess.

Representing the Institut was Dominica Dolcevita, bright of eye and tough as old Gucci boots.

Marcel sat on a tall stool in front of the reception counter, where Nectarine stood scribbling furiously in an elegant brown leather notebook with a gold pen.

I wondered if she was really making notes to herself, or simply trying to shut out Marcel, who, for the second time in their turbulent relationship, was caught up in one of her murder cases.

Nectarine glanced up and stated crisply, "I'll have to confiscate all the tape you shot today, Mr. Corvus."

At the sound of his name, Harry jerked to attention, somewhat intimidated by Sergeant Savoy on the case. With her ebullient hair raked back into a bun, and that severe navy blue suit, which, though a Valentino, made her look every inch the police officer, she was a far cry from that seminude jungle queen of his prized poster.

He nodded speechlessly, causing Buddy Gaines to send an exasperated glare in his direction.

Charlotte quickly intervened.

"Sergeant Savoy," she addressed Nectarine formally, as if the two of them didn't have lunch or dinner together at least once a week, schedules permitting. "We need the original master tape so we can start cutting to meet our deadline. But Buddy here can run you off a duplicate and it'll be waiting on your desk by the time you're ready to look at it."

Savoy turned to Buddy. "Right away?"

"Soon as I can get back to the station," Buddy confirmed, with a relieved grin at Charlotte.

"Then get there, now," Savoy directed, and called out to one of the uniformed officers, "Cates!"

A tall, Nordic blonde woman loped over. "Yes, Sergeant?" she asked eagerly.

"Mr. Gaines, this is Officer Cates," Savoy informed Buddy. "Officer Cates will escort you to your destination, remaining in the same room with you while you duplicate the tapes, three-quarter inch, please. You will then give her the cassettes, which she will deliver directly to my office."

Buddy and Officer Cates eyed each other with a mixture of interest and resentment. On Cates's part, I felt she was very ambitious and therefore reluctant to leave the crime scene.

Buddy just plain didn't like people looking over his shoulder while he worked, not even beautiful young blond ones.

"Yes, ma'am," Cates saluted smartly. "Do you also want me to return Mr. Gaines to this location?"

Savoy shook her head. "That won't be necessary, Officer. I know where to get hold of Mr. Gaines if I need to. But, when you've dropped off the tapes at my office, you come on back here."

Cates looked happier. "Yes, ma'am." She turned to Buddy. "If you'll just come along with me, sir?"

"Words I'd just love to hear you say under other circumstances. Except the 'sir' part," Buddy drawled, grabbing his equipment and hurrying to keep pace with Cates's lanky stride.

At long last, Wickes came downstairs, and engaged Savoy in a muttered conversation.

Then the Sergeant raised her eyes to take in the room.

"Okay, everybody. Listen up," she ordered. "Officer Wickes and I have put together a very rough sequence of events leading up to the discovery that Ms. Crowe had . . . expired underneath the dryer."

Her blue gaze flicked around the room to gauge our reactions.

"I'm just going to go over it once, and if you hear anything that doesn't track with your personal recollection, sing out. And when we're done with that, you can go on home. For now. We know where to contact you. And I can guarantee, you haven't seen the last of us yet by a longshot, ladies and gentlemen."

There were stirrings and murmurs of relief. It was getting late, none of us had had dinner, and *some* of us were going to have to get up very early in the morning. Again.

When the police had arrived and secured the crime scene, we were allowed to finish the clients we'd been working on, but there were still twenty or so more paid-up hair patients who'd been waiting their turns when Duchess was found. We were going to have to take care of them tomorrow, which meant rescheduling some of my Eclaire business, but it couldn't be helped.

This room would, of course, be off-limits, so we'd be using the big Carrollton Salon de Marcel on the other side of the Institut campus.

The cops had already chased away several reporters tonight. One had even tried to sneak inside with a Palmcorder. Poor Marcel! I could already hear the headlines about bad hair days.

And here was Charlotte, who'd been innocently shooting a puff piece only to find herself in the middle of the kind of story careers were made of, but with no air to run it on!

Earlier, with Nectarine's permission, I tried to reach Dan, but he hadn't gotten back from Mobile yet.

Charlotte eventually tracked down Foley, who was watching a football game in Toulouse's Sports Bar. He promised to go lie in wait for Dan at the house, and assured Charlotte they'd both be here as soon as possible, grumbling, "See, if Danbo had a fancy carphone like old Harry's, I could stay here until halftime."

Nectarine Savoy shuffled some papers on the counter and cleared her throat.

"Here we go folks," she announced, and began to read.

Chapter 20

"The deceased arrived at approximately nine o'clock this morning, accompanied by a Mr. Tom Toy. Mr. Toy," Nectarine added grimly, "should be joining us any moment now."

She continued. "The deceased was initially interviewed by Jules Columbier, a member of Mr. Barrineau's faculty. She signed a release form provided by WBGZ-TV, giving them permission to broadcast her image and likeness on national television, then joined Mr. Toy in a waiting area.

"Subsequently, Mrs. Dolcevita, also of Mr. Barrineau's staff, conducted a discussion with the deceased, agreeing that, in her particular case, she had been wise to accept a hair professional's recommendation that she attend the hair clinic for the express purpose of obtaining a permanent wave. That professional was Claire Claiborne.

"Is this correct, Mrs. Claiborne?" Savoy demanded impersonally, and Marcel swiveled his head to stare at me in amazement.

"Yes," I agreed, suddenly convinced that, however unwittingly, I'd set Duchess Crowe up for murder!

Charlotte, sensing my distress, reached over and squeezed my hand. "No, Claire!" she whispered, shaking her head emphatically.

Savoy went on. "Mrs. Dolcevita then decided that Ms. Vicky Su was the appropriate operator to undertake this specialized procedure upon the deceased, but Ms. Su refuted that decision for personal and private reasons."

She gave Vicky Su a piercing blue glance that made her shrink even farther into her chair. "Personal and private reasons," Savoy repeated, "which Ms. Su declined to disclose to Mrs. Dolcevita.

"It was Mrs. Dolcevita's contention, however, that because Ms. Su was the only operator present specifically qualified to perform the service, professionalism must supersede the personal. When Ms. Su continued to resist, Mrs. Dolcevita called upon Mr. Barrineau to intervene.

"Mr. Barrineau's judgment concurred with Mrs. Dolcevita's, and Ms. Su was directed to proceed immediately."

Savoy paused and inquired, "That sound about right to everybody, so far?" There were various murmurs of assent.

She began to read again, and I closed my eyes to listen. If nothing else, this no-frills summary was serving to put the chaos of my own day into perspective.

I was surprised at the clarity of images that clicked across my mind, like slides projected to match her narrative: The nasty fight between Duchess and Marzie; all the different people pitching in to get Duchess's hair wrapped; the argument with Natasha and Yuri; Tom Toy's step-and-fetchit service, where he could have delivered poison along with food, drink, magazines and Kleenex; the triumphal procession upstairs to the dryers; Duchess a little wobbly, even then; talking intense Chinese to Vicky Su; Lamont's shriek . . .

"Obviously, this is not a precise timetable," Savoy concluded. "We probably won't have that until late tomorrow afternoon. Now. Does anybody have something to add?"

Unexpectedly, Harry Corvus spoke up. "Well, I'm afraid she got rather upset with me when I mentioned I thought we'd met a year or two ago in Hong Kong. Apparently she took it as if I was giving her the old don't-I-know-you-from-somewhere? line, and flounced off in a snit," he finished with boyish chagrin.

"Uh-huh," Savoy said tonelessly. She made a brief note with her gold pen, then tapped it against the countertop expectantly.

"I want to say something!" Natasha proclaimed dramatically. "Yuri and I were very angry with Duchess Crowe because she had dropped our band, Shear Madness, for the Toy Boys.

"This was not good, but—okay, what can you do? But when we tell her our management contract with her is over, she says oh no, we have signed exclusive and for seven years. She will not do nothing for us until she feels like, but something happens with our music, big or small, she still gets twenty percent!"

She turned to her partner and demanded, "Is true, Yuri?"

"Is true," Yuri concurred, blinking his white lashes.

"But!" Natasha blared. "We not kill the bitch! Is true, Yuri?"

"Is true."

Savoy, who had managed to keep up with all this, nevertheless seemed a little breathless when she braked her pen. "Thank you for your honesty, Ms. Kavinsky. Anybody else?"

Marzie, who'd been uncharacteristically brooding in silence, slowly came to life. "Yes, I do."

Savoy scanned the list. "Oh? And you are . . . that's right, Mrs. Marzipan Jones." Her lips curved.

"Don't you be so quick to go laughin' at *my* name, Miss Thing!" Marzie flashed angrily.

Savoy's smile broadened. "Actually, I was just thinking how much we have in common, Mrs. Jones," she soothed. "Now, what did you want to tell me?"

Marzie straightened up and arranged her flounces. "At one time, I be married to the daddy of . . . Duchess."

"You mean, Duchess Crowe was your stepdaughter?" Nectarine asked calmly, but the telltale tremor in her voice betrayed she was getting a whole lot more than she bargained for.

So were we all.

Now I finally understood why the two women had seemed to hate each other so. Duchess had actually told me it couldn't have been more personal.

I had no difficulty envisioning Marzie as the classic wicked stepmother. No wonder Duchess had run away from home!

"Oh, Auntie Duchess! I didn't mean to do it! I'm sorry, I'm so, so, sorry!" Lamont Hooper wailed suddenly, nearly scaring everybody out of their wits.

Babs jumped as if she'd been shot, and grabbed him by the shoulders. "Lamont, honey! What's wrong? Tell Mama."

With tears streaming down his cheeks, Lamont gasped out that he pilfered two pills from the medicine bottle in Duchess's bag and plopped them into her tea.

That allergy medication I'd seen her take, I thought, but Savoy nodded at Officer Wickes. "The 'ludes," she said, sotto voce.

"I was so mad at her!" he sobbed. "But I didn't mean to kill her. I swear!"

Babs crouched by her son's chair. "Hush, baby!" she desperately commanded Lamont, rocking him back and forth.

She glared over at Savoy. "Don't pay any attention to him," she pleaded. "Can't you see, he doesn't know what he's saying?"

"Oh, I think he does, Ms. Hooper," Savoy replied. "And this is very important information. But for what it's worth, the victim did not die from an overdose of Quaaludes.

"However," Savoy added kindly, "the boy is probably going to need a lawyer, no matter what."

Babs nodded in a distraught way.

Then Marzie rose majestically from her chair and walked over to Lamont and Babs. Sinking to her knees amid a picturesque splash of black lace, she put an arm around each of them and began to croon, "Don't cry, little feller. Granny's here."

So Lamont had been being perfectly literal when he'd addressed Duchess as his aunt, and Marzie as his grandmother.

While all this was going on, a commotion erupted in the doorway, and two uniformed officers came through, dragging Tom Toy between them.

He was clutching two dozen roses wrapped in green paper in one hand, and a bottle of Moët White Star champagne in the other.

Vicky Su's face lit up with joy. Leaping from her chair, she bounded across the room to him like a gazelle, but the officers wouldn't let her touch him, as one of them read him his rights.

"What the hell's going on here?" Tom demanded wildly, looking around the room.

"And where's my mother?"

Chapter 21

Foley Callant pulled up at Marcel's in his red Saab convertible with Dan riding shotgun, just after Savoy and Wickes had decided they'd squeezed everybody dry as they could for one evening.

It was nearly midnight, but Charlotte and I were too wired and too hungry to go straight home, so we walked diagonally across Carrollton Avenue to Billy's, an eclectic dive featuring active pool tables, Beers of the World, and a jukebox from which blasted all seventies motorcycle rock, all the time.

The Billy's logo—a raunchy-looking goat in a black leather jacket astride a Harley—prevailed over all, and the bathrooms were designated "Billy" and "Billy Jean."

We crowded comfortably into a high-backed wooden booth carved with names, dates, initials and rude messages, and shouted our sandwich orders to the waiter over the thundering of "Magic Carpet Ride."

"Got any Orangeboom tonight?" Dan bellowed.

"We got everything but Bass ale," the waiter roared back. "Some limey came in and bought us out this afternoon."

So Harry's so-called wonderful purveyor of spirits was none other than Billy's. Hardly a trip that required driving gloves. What a jerk!

When our food was delivered, we fell on it like a pack of wolves.

Dan's strong, thick fingers kneaded the back of my neck, and some of the tension began to ebb away. I finished half of my "Billy Jack" chicken sandwich (on French with Monterey Jack cheese) and leaned gratefully on his broad shoulder, not minding the slight scratchiness of his red and black buffalo-check wool shirt against my cheek.

Between us, Charlotte and I were managing to deliver a fairly accurate account of the day's events, up to the point where Tom Toy had made his dramatic reappearance.

"And then what happened?" Foley asked in fascination.

Charlo took a reflective slug from his bottle of Gila Monster. "Well, let's see," she mused. "A better question would be, what didn't happen?"

"The diamond ring," I prompted.

Charlo laughed richly. "Oh, now that was really the icing on the cake of Nectarine's day!"

Savoy was completely unprepared for Tom Toy's revelation that Duchess Crowe had been his mother.

Though he was raised out in Jefferson Parish by Mr. and Mrs. Sam Toy, a Hawaiian-Chinese couple who'd been good friends of Duchess's mother, Duchess had kept close tabs on Tom.

Tom explained that, about a year ago, when his mother came to visit and discovered him and some friends just messing around with a couple of used electric guitars and a keyboard, she'd been ecstatic.

Before Tom quite knew what was happening, Duchess had yanked him out of Delgado Community College, and insisted he take voice and guitar lessons full time. She'd even bought brand new equipment for everybody, and a hot sound system.

The only catch was, he had to totally concentrate on his music, to the exclusion of everything else, because Duchess guaranteed that when his band was ready to debut, it would get immediate international attention, and she wanted Tom to be completely prepared.

Then she demanded that Tom break off his very serious relationship with Vicky Su, with no explanations.

When he balked at this, Duchess revealed what he had never known, that his father was the legendary Teddy Boy Crowe. She told Tom she was working on a major plan that would absolutely blow a whole lot of people out of the water, but it required total secrecy.

Duchess had always insisted he tell no one she was his mother. The only people who knew were the Toys. Tom had never known why, but he'd obeyed, even to the extent of not confiding in Vicky Su.

Nor did she repeal her orders, or even allow him to explain to Vicky Su what Duchess really was to him. Though certainly she knew what not only his girlfriend, but everybody else, would think about their relationship.

Tom and Duchess had finally agreed on a compromise, that he could tell Vicky he had found a serious financial backer for his music, and they would have to put their relationship on hold for the time being.

This had come as a total shock, as Vicky had thought they would soon be getting married. Naturally, she believed that Tom had fallen into the clutches of an older woman, and there was nothing he could do to enlighten her. He had given Duchess his word.

They were almost ready to go into the studio to record their first album, which would consist entirely of Tom's own new arrangements of Teddy Boy Crowe hits. It was going to be called, *Teddy Boy's Boy.*

Tom said Duchess had already laid down some backup tracks and confessed he'd been pleasantly surprised to find out how good she was.

"She was going to announce our relationship the night we debuted at the Mirror," he said sadly. "She had a bunch of jokes made up about us and the Judds. That's why she wanted to get her hair done like mine."

Tom flushed, and shook his curly locks self-consciously.

But something had happened to upset Duchess during the past two or three weeks, Tom didn't know what.

And suddenly, today, she completely released Tom from his vow of silence to Vicky Su.

"The last time I saw her, when she went upstairs," Tom finished, his jaw working with emotion, "she told me to go for it! So I did, before she could change her mind again."

He looked down at the incongruously festive roses and champagne in his hands, then at Vicky Su. "I got these for you, baby," he told her.

Nectarine found her voice. "Does it usually take you several hours to buy flowers and wine, Mr. Toy?" she inquired, harshly. "Had you planned on just leaving your mother to wait around until you showed up in your own good time? Or did you know there would be no reason to rush back because she wasn't going to be going anywhere?"

Tom stared at her in horror. "What? You don't think I—? Oh, boy. I need to sit down," he said suddenly.

Wickes nodded at the two officers to release his arms, and Tom automatically turned toward the same bench where he'd spent most of the day.

Nobody tried to stop Vicky Su when she marched defiantly over and plopped herself down next to him.

Tom gave her a wan smile, tentatively offering the gifts, which she accepted with alacrity.

After a pause, Tom asked in a low voice, "How did it—was it the drugs?"

Savoy and Wickes exchanged glances.

"You knew your mother took drugs?" Wickes barked at him.

Tom nodded. "Yeah. She claimed it was just some kind of tranqs she'd been taking since the sixties, or something, but I knew better. Lots of times she was awfully juiced. And when I tried to talk to her, she'd just laugh and tell me she was a big girl, she could handle herself, and for me to do as she said, not as she did." He looked disgusted. "Like I really would. Drugs are just totally uncool."

"You still haven't explained your schedule, Mr. Toy," Nectarine reminded him. "Where did you go after you left here, and why did you just now get back?"

Tom frowned. "Mom told me to take my time, because after she was done, she was planning to meet somebody. I think it was a guy, because she said maybe they'd go to dinner, but I don't know for sure. She dated a lot, but she kept that part of her life strictly off-limits to me.

how many?—three beauty shops trashed. And now, two murders." He stopped and grinned. "A real crime wave!"

Charlotte elbowed him. "You just had to say it, didn't you? Well, my big love cake, you will be chagrined to hear that your friend Harry Corvus thought of that very angle himself, only wait'll you hear the spin he put on it."

Dan flagged the waiter down for more beer, and Foley grunted, "Okay, go on. Dazzle us with his lordship's brilliant deductions."

Charlotte shook her head. "You're not going to believe it!" she warned. "Because Claire and I were there, and we don't."

"Anyway, remember, all this soap opera stuff had been going on—Duchess Crowe turning out to be Tom Toy's mother, and Marzie Jones admitting she's Lamont Hooper's grandma, although nobody mentioned if she had been Duchess Crowe's stepmother, that would also make her Tom's step-grandma, plus cousins out of Lamont and Tom, sort of, and Vicky Su and Tom Toy, the starcrossed lovers getting engaged in the middle of a murder investigation.

"Suddenly, practically everybody in the room was either related, or about to be. I was starting to feel real left out and nearly suggested to Claire we should compare navels to see if we'd been separated at birth, when Harry stood up and announced to Savoy he had vital information to impart.

"He then told her that she was making a serious mistake, in trying to assign such small, parochial motives for the murder of Duchess Crowe.

"Savoy's storm flags started flying, but she very calmly and politely suggested that Mr. Corvus would perhaps care to enlighten the woefully parochial NOPD as to the enormous scope they were missing?"

Unfortunately, Harry took Nectarine's sarcastic comment literally, and launched into a patronizing account of an old *Sixty Minutes* segment about rumors that Chinese triads operating out of Hong Kong were scrambling to liquidate operations and transfer assets to points west, before the mainland Communists took over the Crown colony in 1997.

According to Harry, this alleged migration of the Hong Kong drug lords had already caused wars to break out between rival triads, and between the triads and the Mafia, in San Francisco, Los Angeles and New York. Could, he wondered rhetorically, New Orleans be far behind? After all, he reminded us, New Orleans is a city originally designed *by* a smuggler, *for* smuggling.

"Not bad!" Dan observed, putting his arm around me. "He managed to offend two ethnic groups present in that room, and drag in the Communists, practically in the same breath."

"And how did Harry suggest this smuggling was being carried out?" Foley began, then said, "No, don't tell me! Beauty supplies, right?"

"My brilliant boy!" Charlo approved, rewarding him with a kiss.

"Hell!" Foley commented, in reluctant admiration. "I gotta admit, it's tailor-made. Those poor dope-sniffing hounds at Customs would be thrown into total confusion by all those smells."

"It gets even better," I promised. "Harry then declared his conviction that not only Duchess's murder, but also the murder of Lochner Smith, plus those three trashed beauty shops, are all connected to a local Hong Kong triad/Mafia power struggle."

This, of course, had caused instant pandemonium. Gino, Vince and Sal all started yelling at Harry in Italian, and Vicky angrily singsonged Chinese to Tom until he got up and walked over to Harry.

"We're Americans!" he shouted, right in Harry's face.

Harry smirked. "Mongrel!" he retorted, pleasantly.

Wickes had had to dive to yank Tom away before he could take a swing at Harry, while the two uniformed officers stationed themselves between the Englishman and the Italians, just in case.

They hadn't reckoned with Natasha and Yuri though, who thought Harry was accusing them of being Communists.

Dan whistled. "And just how did our sergeant respond?"

Charlotte laughed. "Well, by then, it was too late to do much in the way of damage control, but she kept her cool. She said Mr. Corvus's theory was highly intriguing, and perhaps she should accompany him to the FBI headquarters tomorrow so he could tell his story?"

"I bet that shut him up!" Foley chortled in satisfaction.

Indeed it had. Harry suddenly backpedalled, acting all huffy and offended, saying he'd just been trying to help, but if that was the attitude they wanted to take, well.

"I take it no arrests were made," Dan remarked, pulling me closer.

"Short of locking all of us up, what could she do?" Charlotte pointed out. "By then, Policewoman was so disgusted, she just ordered us to keep ourselves available for further questioning, then as good as threw everybody out."

She yawned. "Thank goodness Buddy showed up and said he'd take care of the wrap. Foley, precious. I'm going to leave my car at Marcel's and ride home with you. I can hardly keep my eyes open."

Neither could I. I relaxed against Dan and let myself drift off amid a sea of faces. The coarsely attractive features of Duchess, suffused with the darkness of death . . . Tom Toy, released from his pledge . . . Vicky Su's joy . . . Harry's smugness . . . Gino's death's-head . . . Lamont's shock . . . Babs's terror . . . Marzie's sudden softness . . . Renee . . . Vince . . . Sal . . . Dominica . . . Nectarine . . . everybody related . . . compare navels . . .

The images shifted and dissolved and merged into faces that were trying to tell me something unspoken. I strained to see, to hear, but then there was nothing but the sweet, soft darkness and the warmth of Dan's solid body and a chilly breeze blowing up from the River as Foley drove us home in the backseat of his convertible.

Chapter 22

As I expected, the newswriters had fully availed themselves of this rare opportunity to indulge in some fancy wordplay. After gnawing "bad hair day" to the bone, they moved on to "curl up and die," "hairy-kiri," and "body wave."

While Dan channel surfed to see if there'd been any new developments overnight, I scanned the sparse account wedged in at the bottom of the *Times-Picayune* front page.

It merely stated that local businesswoman Duchess Crowe had died under mysterious circumstances while participating in A Bad Hair Day, sponsored by the Marcel Barrineau Institut de Beauté, and that Detective Sergeant Nectarine Savoy declined to comment on the case.

"Hey, Claire. Look at this," Dan called my attention to the television screen. Some doggedly determined reporter had ambushed Nectarine as she was leaving the crime scene, freezing her in the flash of camera lights like a deer on a dark road.

Savoy glared aristocratically into the lens, growling that the cause of death was as yet undetermined, and there were no particular suspects at this time.

Dan flicked off the set and went into the bathroom to shave. I snuggled back under the down comforter, still drowsy and reluctant to leave its warmth just yet.

"When did Marcel want you over there today?" Dan called.

"Well, I told him I couldn't make it until after eight-thirty because I've got to wait for Renee to come in," I replied. "I need to talk to her about what she's going to have to take care of since I won't be here. If you want to leave earlier though, go ahead. I can just hop the streetcar."

"No, it's okay, baby. Anyway, I've got some preliminary franchise forms he should fill out this morning."

"You mean," I raised my voice above the running water, "you actually think he's still going to want to follow through, after everything that's happened?"

Dan shut off the tap and dried his face. "Listen. Marcel is the world's foremost pragmatist, as we very well know, and the whole concept about holding official bad hair days is basically brilliant.

"It's hardly likely," he continued, "that customers are going to get bumped off at one of these things every time. So why let somebody else snatch his great idea right out from under his nose?"

I acknowledged sleepily that he had a point.

"Don't go back to sleep now, Claire," he warned, as he stepped into the shower. "I thought we'd stop and grab a bite at Camelia Grill on the way over to Marcel's."

"Okay," I grumbled, kicking back the covers.

I rummaged through my closet, trying to come up with something simple, yet stylish enough for Marcel's exalted premises, wishing I could stay on my own cozy turf today, but *c'est la vie*. No make that *c'est la mort*.

Finally I spotted the toffee-colored angora tunic and stirrup pants I'd bought last year but never had a chance to wear. Perfect!

Dan's own closet was conveniently located on the other side of the bathroom. He came out wearing nothing but a pale blue shirt and carrying his charcoal gaberdine suit on a hanger.

Holding up a red silk, white pindot tie against the jacket, he asked, "This one go all right, darlin'?"

"Of course it does," I assured him. "You've got fabulous taste, Dan. I particularly like what you're wearing below that shirt, in fact."

He arched an eyebrow. "Now that's real brassy talk, coming from the woman who literally went to sleep on me last night. I'll have you know, my arm was plumb numb."

"Oh, I'm sorry, baby," I murmured, sliding my hands under the shirt and down that wide, gorgeous bare ass. "I was just so tired, and your chest felt so comfortable. Like a big mink pillow."

"Too comfortable, eh?" Dan inquired, laying the suit carefully across the back of a chair and tossing the tie on top. "Well, I can fix that, right now."

"Whatever do you mean?" I wondered, backing away, until he had me pinned against the dresser.

Without a word, he lifted me onto the top of it, heedless of the numerous framed photographs and ornaments scattering around me.

"Really, Dan!" I giggled. "The dresser. Isn't that a cliché?"

"Oh, yeah? And just how often have you been made love to on a dresser, Evangeline Claire?" he inquired, sliding my nightgown up my thighs. "I'd be real interested to hear this."

"Well, never," I admitted, feeling my blood starting to fizz. Actually, before Dan, I'd never really been made love to anywhere at all, having experienced only two previous and highly unimpressive encounters.

"Me neither, baby. Until now, that is." He caught his breath sharply. "Oh, you are a luscious little thing. You know what they say about clichés, don't you, honey?"

"Ummm?" I was rapidly growing incoherent.

"They only . . . get to be . . . clichés . . . because . . . they're true . . ."

Renee arrived while I was still dressing, so Dan went down to let her in. When he came back to the bedroom, he was frowning.

"Claire, what's the matter with Renee?" he asked. "She's pale as a ghost and acting kind of spooky to boot."

I pulled on a pair of tan Donna Karan silk and cotton socks, and laced up my leopard-print suede oxfords before replying, uncertain how much to say. If Dan found out about Vince, he was liable to march straight over and sling him off the Lake Pontchartrain Causeway.

"Ah, she hasn't been feeling too well, lately," I hedged.

"I'd say that's putting it mildly," he grunted, preparing to knot his tie in the mirror. "That girl looks like death warmed over and cooled off again."

He looked at me sharply. "You don't think she could be doing drugs, do you?"

My heart gave a sickening little lurch. Oh, Lord. Maybe *that* was it, the reason she'd been acting so jumpy and strange, instead of being pregnant. I remembered she'd said she needed money. Either way, Renee was definitely in some kind of trouble, and in deep.

Or, was her behavior just symptomatic of that abusive relationship with Vince? How could I simply stand by and let this go on until something terrible happened? I knew I had to find a way to help her, whether she wanted me to or not.

I came to a decision.

"Dan, I honestly don't know Renee's whole story," I said. "But some things have happened lately you'd better hear about. I'll tell you on the way to Marcel's, though. Right now, I need to give her instructions about how to handle things here today."

"Okay, honey," he said soberly.

Renee wasn't waiting in the main part of the shop when I came downstairs, but I could hear her moving around in the nail salon. Probably getting ready for an early appointment, I thought.

It was completely without premeditation that I didn't call her name or knock, but simply opened the door and walked in.

The nail salon, bright and lovely with French windows overlooking the rose garden, had originally been a combination breakfast room/informal dining area. A previous owner had installed a myriad of built-in drawers, cubicles and cabinets designed to hold china, linen and such. This feature reincarnated perfectly into convenient storage for beauty supplies.

There was even a sliding panel beneath the windowseat that concealed more space. This now stood open, and Renee was kneeling before it, shoving something into the cavern, totally unaware of my presence.

"Renee, hi!" I greeted her, and she nearly jumped out of her skin.

Springing to her feet she quickly banged the panel shut, but not before I'd seen several tan cardboard cartons stamped with a neon pink and black Gino's logo.

"Oh, I'm sorry, *chère*," I told her, "I didn't mean to startle you. I thought you heard me come in."

Renee pressed a slim had to her throat. "Oh!" she gasped. "That's okay, Claire," she said, attempting to catch her breath. "I was just putting some things away," she waved vaguely.

"Uh-huh. Well, Dan's driving me over to Marcel's in a minute, but first, you and I need to decide how we're going to deal with today's workload."

During my speech Renee had been unobtrusively herding me toward the door, and before I knew it, we were back in the shop.

Once away from the nail salon, some of her old efficiency returned. She strode rapidly to the reception desk, her latest pair of cowboy boots (green lizard with black suede inserts) tapping briskly across the terra-cotta tiles. Seating herself behind the desk, she donned Day-Glo orange reading glasses and consulted the appointment book, covered in Gillaud's Poire et Grappe silk tapestry to match the draperies and furniture.

"Okay," Renee said, running a finger down the page. "This morning there's Mrs. Slaughter, Mrs. Gentry, Ashley

Bowles, and that woman from the Nicaraguan consulate whose name I can't pronounce."

"Hmmm. And for this afternoon?"

Renee scanned the entries and wrinkled her nose. "Oh, those three old biddies who always come together, and Mrs. Shelby Bell."

I perched on the edge of the desk and studied her face. No wonder Dan had been so concerned. He hadn't seen her for nearly a week anyway, so no matter what, he was bound to get a shock. But this morning, she looked even worse than last night. Her normally roses-and-cream complexion was pasty and marbleized with a tracing of fine blue veins, and the circles under her eyes seemed to grow darker with every passing day.

Yes, drugs would probably explain it. But then, so would fear.

"All right, Renee," I said. "We'll do this one of two ways, it's your choice. Either you phone these people, tell them I've been called away on a minor emergency, apologize for the inconvenience, and offer to reschedule. Imply there'll be a discount of some type, but don't get specific."

I watched her scribble notes to herself. "Or," I went on, "make the same calls, make the same offer, but give some of them the option of keeping their appointments today."

She looked quizzically up at me, not understanding, and I elaborated, "Meaning, you can substitute for me today if you want to, Renee. I know you've got nails to do, and you certainly can't take them all on by yourself, but—this could be that perfect opportunity we were talking about to test your wings, *petite*."

For a few moments, she was transformed back into the old Renee and her face flushed with pleasure. "Oh, Claire!" she exclaimed. "Do you really mean it? Maybe you were right, after all. Maybe I'm more ready to try this than I thought." She jumped up and ran over to give me a hug and I felt the alarming thinness of her shoulders.

I experienced a surge of trepidation. Was I crazy, to go off and leave her in charge of my precious little beauty parlor? After all, she was mixed up in who knew what. But to see a real smile on her face again, and those big brown eyes dancing instead of rolling like a frightened mare's made me feel it was worth taking the risk. I just hoped Dan would agree, after I told him everything I knew.

The smile grew even wider when I added, "Oh, yes. Don't bother to make that optional offer to Mrs. Shelby Bell."

Rich and stingy Mrs. Shelby "Tinker" Bell was a regular and difficult client, who had recently manipulated Dan and me into an extremely dangerous situation. It wouldn't hurt her a bit to be inconvenienced. "Just tell her she's canceled."

Renee's smile became a grin. "It will be my pleasure," she said.

Chapter 23

The Eclaire phone rang just as Dan and I were coming downstairs.

I heard Renee answer, then say, "Oh, here she is now. Hold on, please."

When we rounded the curve, she was standing below, waving the portable handset in the air at me. Now what?

Dan tapped his watch meaningfully as I took the phone from Renee, who whispered, "It's Babs Hooper."

"Babs, hey. What's going on? I'm kind of in a hurry," I said.

"This won't take a minute, Claire. I just wanted to let you know, Lock's um, remains, have been released, and he's going to be cremated this afternoon."

Oh, Lord. What with everything else, the thought of Lochner's funeral hadn't even crossed my mind. I'd never attended a cremation ceremony before, but Charlotte did once, and described it as absolutely bizarre.

After the minister finished speaking, hidden machinery had revved up and the coffin suddenly started moving slowly away all by itself until finally disappearing behind purple velvet curtains and into the furnace.

Considering how Lochner had died, I personally didn't think cremation the most tasteful choice.

"That's what he specified in his will," she hastened to add, correctly divining my thoughts.

Well, I thought, the least I could do was be there for him. Marcel would understand if I left early.

"What time, and where?" I asked Babs.

She gave a nervous little laugh. "Oh, I'm sorry, Claire! I didn't mean you should come. In fact, he also specified no formal service. But Lock does want you to come to what he calls a 'memorial bash' at his house tomorrow night. You know where it is, right?"

"Yes, though I've never been inside. On Burgundy—wait a minute! What do you mean, Lock wants us to come, Babs?"

"He included a guest list, and you're both on it," she answered simply. "And now, I have to notify everybody else he invited, plus call the caterers and give them the signal. Apparently he had planned a menu, and they've already been paid."

I told her I thought Lochner had gone a little over the top with the preplanning.

"In a way, yes," Babs agreed. "But it sure takes a load off of me. There isn't anybody else, you know."

Her voice grew anxious. "You will come, won't you Claire? I—I need to talk to you about something."

I didn't particularly care for the sound of that, especially since I suspected it involved Lamont. Nevertheless, I assured her I would be there, and she sounded relieved.

"What was that all about?" Dan asked, as he bundled me into the car.

I filled him in and said, "I have to show up, but you'll come with me, won't you, Dan Louis? I don't know . . . somehow I feel weird about going there by myself."

"Sure, honey." He turned right onto St. Charles, and then chuckled.

"What?"

He stopped for a light, then looked over at me. "I just realized why you're getting a case of the creeps about tomorrow evening, Claire. Tell me, did Lochner's ever-so-specific will also specify how the mourners should dress, should the sad occasion fall on any particular holiday?"

For a second, I didn't understand what he was getting at, and then it hit me. Of course! Lochner Smith's memorial service was set for Halloween night!

Chapter 24

As often as I'd witnessed the phenomenon, Marcel Barrineau's physical resiliency never ceased to amaze me. Even on the heels of a fourteen-hour workday that had segued directly into a murder investigation lasting several hours more, he was looking fresh and fit.

Only the slight tremor of his well-manicured hand suggested he may have partaken too freely of the caffeine this morning. Or, more likely, betrayed that he was on edge about Nectarine's scheduled ten-thirty appointment which, she'd informed him, she intended to keep despite the circumstances. Nectarine was nothing if not practical, and she badly need her hair done.

However, she'd warned Marcel his client would most definitely be Detective Sergeant Savoy, whom he should regard as in the process of conducting a murder investigation and behave accordingly. With emphasis on the "behave."

"I am most grateful that you could see your way to lending your priceless assistance, yet again, Claire," Marcel told me. "One would have supposed that after yesterday's—unfortunate event, those individuals remaining would have preferred to receive their reimbursements instead of returning to the scene of the crime as it were.

"However"—an appreciative flare lit his green eyes—"precisely the opposite is the case, for when Dominica arrived this morning, she discovered them all, without exception, waiting at the door!" He gave a French shrug. "What is more, the telephone has continued to ring with people clamoring for appointments."

"Well, there's nothing like a murder to boost business," I observed, speaking from firsthand experience. "But one of those clamoring customers is liable to be Mrs. Shelby Bell since I had Renee cancel her because I needed to come back here today. And I expect you to do the right thing, *chér!*"

Marcel grimaced, but conceded, "For you, even that, Claire." As well he might, considering the way he'd slyly unloaded her onto me in the first place.

"You may," he sighed, "inform Dominica, who is, in fact, now awaiting you in her office, that if Tinker Bell calls today, she is to be given priority."

I took the hint, and stood on tiptoe to kiss Dan goodbye. Unlike Marcel, after a hard night of anything—be it work, partying or loving, you can always tell exactly what he's been up to the next day. No doubt, when Dan reaches Marcel's age he will show his miles a little more obviously, but equally undoubtedly, all vital parts will still be in perfect working order.

"See you later, you great . . . dresser," I murmured.

He smiled wickedly. "Your cliché or mine?"

Marcel cleared his throat and eyed his elegant wristwatch. "You mentioned papers, Dan?" And swept him into his sumptuous office, the ornately carved Portuguese door thudding heavily shut behind them as I waved goodbye.

The muted whir of telephones and click of computer keys emanated from smallish rooms along the hallway, where Marcel's numerous and impressive awards, interspersed with beautifully framed photographs of himself and celebrities, politicians, and even a couple of crowned heads, lined the mahogany panelled walls.

At the other end of a magnificent rose and blue Turkish runner lay the Sigñora's domain, which was slightly larger than Marcel's own office. Her door also sported rich carving, but the workmanship here was Florentine rather than Portuguese. It stood partially open and I tapped, using the inside of my wedding band as a knocker, because on that heavy old chestnut, mere knuckles were ineffectual and wound up bruised.

"Come!" Dominica bellowed from within.

As I entered, she gestured for me to close the door, then resumed her end of a telephone conversation in progress, muttering into the weighty ivory and gold mouthpiece.

I seated myself on a fringed pouf covered with crimson brocade stretched like a tight skirt over a fat lady's bottom, and looked around. Though years had passed since I'd visited this office, it still seemed the same, which is to say opulent.

Dark, glowing walnut furnishings and warm hues of wine, gold and green created a medieval tapestry effect. Old-rose damask draped the long windows behind Dominica's desk, which looked out onto the Mississippi.

From this vantage point, one could always count on catching an interesting glimpse of river traffic. At the moment, faint strains of calliope music were echoing upward from the *Cotton Blossom*, carrying the day's first load of sightseers downriver.

Dominica frowned at whatever she was hearing, and her highbacked swivel chair, constructed along the lines of a de Medici throne, creaked impatiently as she shifted her stocky figure. The only thing that didn't quite fit in with the rest of the decor was the green oval glasstopped desk.

Ricky Gomez, who'd been in my class, had cattily suggested the glass was because she was so vain about her feet, which were tiny, elegant, and invariably Ferragamo-shod, that she wanted to be able to see them at all times. Ricky had also been the one who'd dubbed Dominica the Sigñora, a title which pleased her no end.

Now she replaced the receiver in its antique cradle with exaggerated restraint, but then forcefully whacked her ring laden hands down onto the desktop, heedless of the fragile surface. The Sigñora in action.

Dominica Dolcevita, being short and squatty, sensibly styled herself along the lines of another similarly built doyenne, Helena Rubenstein; midnight black hair hauled straight back into a fat, shiny chignon, beak-nosed face dramatically made up, big showy rings on several Vienna-sausagelike fingers.

She proceeded to light a cigarette without inquiring whether I minded (whose office was it, anyway?) and exhaled gustily. At least she smoked only Gauloises, which I can tolerate better than American brands.

"So!" she boomed, studying me with those hooded hawk's eyes that missed nothing. "You have arrived at last.

You will soon be needed on the floor—I have already made the assignments. But I wanted to talk with you first."

I smiled sweetly. "And a good morning to you, too, Sigñora."

She gave a gruff bark of laughter. "You never were afraid of me, were you Clara *bella?*"

"Certainly not!" I retorted. "Terrified would be the correct word!"

"*Bene!*" Dominica nodded in a gratified way. "You will have some of this delicious espresso of course."

"Apparently so," I agreed, accepting the tiny steaming cup she filled from the copper machine on a credenza to one side of her desk.

She sipped delicately from her own cup, then said, "Now. We will quickly speak of many things. That," Dominica indicated the archaic European telephone with a sour expression, "was the lawyer who represents this Institut. He had just received a call from a man who stated that his client is seriously considering filing a wrongful death action against us."

"How can that be?" I protested. "It's not the Institut's fault, or Marcel's fault, that somebody picked this place to eliminate Duchess."

Dominica tossed off her espresso. "Bah! They will charge negligence in security, or some such thing. Never mind, it is being handled.

"Meanwhile, who do you suppose the client is?"

"Well, it would have to be Tom Toy, wouldn't it?"

Dominica nodded. "Just so. Although I doubt the youngster is aware of this threatened action on his so-called behalf. But there is another plaintiff as well, the man who is acting as Tom Toy's attorney, whose own claim is based on the fact that Ms. Crowe was his sister."

I stared at her. "You don't mean Duke Abbidis!"

She fixed me with a frank gaze. "The plot, as they say, thickens. And yes, I am well aware of his rivalry with Marcello for the . . . favors, shall we say? of Miss Savoy."

The potential ramifications of such a ploy on Duke's part were breathtaking.

First of all, it would put Nectarine in an impossible position. She might even feel obligated to withdraw from the case. In fact, how could she function, caught in the middle like that?

Was Duke's move directed against Marcel personally, or was it greed, or both? I had to agree with Dominica. Tom Toy most likely didn't have a clue what his dear old Uncle Duke was up to.

But there was one crucial element the oily attorney had failed to factor in, and that was, anyone who messed with "Marcello" must stand before the judgment seat of Dominica Dolcevita.

For example, when Marcel had reached an impasse with Nectarine a little over two months back now, he'd selected Dolly Murphy, a large, handsome, brunette student some years older than the others, for his coveted three-month apprenticeship training program.

Admittedly in the past, Marcel often ended up having brief *affaires* with those who were willing, and was indeed viewing Dolly as a possible candidate. But in no way was compliance prerequisite for the job.

I know this for a fact, because I was once Marcel's apprentice.

Dolly, however, turned out to be a dark horse, an extremely militant feminist with a lesbian lover who happened to be an attorney. And the pair of them went gunning to embroil Marcel in a costly sexual harassment lawsuit!

Fortunately, Dominica discovered their plot and alerted Marcel, who over the ensuing weeks made unusually frequent business trips out of the city.

When he was in town, Dominica managed to keep Dolly under her eagle eye and very busy, never leaving her alone with Marcel for a minute.

Dolly, who failed to realize Marcel and Dominica had caught onto the scheme she and her lover were hatching, found herself blocked at every turn. But by then, she had become so obssessed with the notion of pulling off a grand sexual harassment coup, that she lost her grip on reality.

Came the day, as she was blowdrying one of Marcel's clients, an extremely wealthy, blueblooded gentlemen, she saw that his hands were moving rapidly and suggestively beneath the cape covering the front of his body.

Immediately, she screamed at the top of her lungs that he was masturbating while watching her in the mirror, and whacked him hard upside the head with the dryer.

The man had simply been cleaning his three-hundred-dollar Matsuda sunglasses, which were broken during the struggle.

Dolly was fired on the spot, in front of at least twenty witnesses who had seen exactly what happened, and her partner was now defending her against assault and battery charges, plus damages, including replacement of the Matsudas.

Dominica Dolcevita had vigilantly watched over her quarry, patiently biding her time until the moment was right.

Duke Abbidis had best watch his treasured behind.

Now she drummed strong red nails upon the desk. "Marcello may be guilty of many foolish things, but his heart is good and I will not allow this"— she spat out an Italian word I had no difficulty in translating,—"to carry out his campaign against him."

I believed her.

"Dominica," I began carefully, "what do you think happened to Duchess Crowe?"

Her features grew bleak. "God only knows!" she exclaimed, crossing herself. "I am praying they find she had a heart attack, and nothing more."

"I don't think prayer works in reverse," I said. "So let's be realistic. Have you remembered anything new since last night? One little move just the least bit out of order? Maybe even somebody who was somewhere they shouldn't have been?"

She crushed out the cigarette in a Venetian glass ashtray, and shook her head negatively.

"Well, then, Sigñora," I said, even more cautiously, "I have one last question. What is Gino Gambara to you?"

Dominica regarded her minuscule feet through the desktop, then rose abruptly.

"Come, Clara *bella,*" she commanded. "It is time for you to go."

Chapter 25

The subliminal relationship between a woman and her hairdresser is strangely akin to that of a woman and her gynecologist. Both require her to assume a vulnerable position, either lying spreadeagled, or sitting jacked up several feet from the floor, with nothing between her and the one about to do something to her body but a flimsy gown.

In burgundy smock, with wet hair and no makeup, even the bold and confident Nectarine Savoy looked touchingly defenseless.

That Savoy should allow Marcel to see her in such dishabille told me that on a deeper level than she was perhaps willing to admit, she felt comfortable and secure with him. It was highly unlikely that the debonair Duke Abbidis had ever been permitted so much as a glimpse of the Nectarine peeled, so to speak.

I turned my attention back to my own client, a stout, pink young matron in spectacles who'd been talked into paying big bucks for a curly perm, but gotten a mishmash that was kinky at the roots, with the bottom half coming out straight, frayed and bushy. The poor dear looked like Mrs. Potato Head in a tan yarn wig.

My morning's work had gone smoothly so far, thanks to Jennifer, the student assistant I'd commandeered from the bullpen. This wasn't my first experience with her; Marcel had brought Jennifer along to Biloxi to help out in a beauty pageant crisis last month, and she'd done very well, indeed. I reminded myself to put dibs on her with Marcel, just in case Renee decided to move on up to operator.

Thinking of Renee, I frowned. There was something else going on with my talented little protégée besides a bent affair, of that I was certain. For instance, why had she been so anxious to get me out of the nail salon?

At first I'd thought she was trying to keep me from noticing those Gino's boxes stowed beneath the windowseat. But that couldn't have been it, because no matter which drawer, cabinet, or cupboard you opened in that room, you were bound to find any number of Gino's boxes.

And I'd gotten a good enough look to see there was nothing unusual about these, which appeared to be the shallow style that contained a dozen bottles of nail polish.

So there must have been something else. I grimaced, realizing I was probably going to have to snoop around in there behind Renee's back. I hated the idea, but if something fishy was afoot, I needed to find out what.

And I never did fill Dan in on the Renee situation after all. Everything else had taken a back seat to Babs Hooper's telephone invitation to Lochner's trick-or-treat sendoff to the Great Beyond.

Between us, Jennifer and I worked a minor miracle on Mrs. Potato Head, sticking her under the dryer after drenching the yarn wig with buckets of a special conditioner that hardens onto the hair when exposed to heat. Then, after major surgery to the damaged portions, followed by a flattering shaping, we'd repermed with gentle solution on enormous rollers.

Now she was back under the dryer for more conditioning, and I was going to suggest some bronze highlights. Also a lowfat diet and contacts, if I could work up the nerve.

I told Jennifer to take a break, and ambled over to Marcel's station, where he was giving more attention to each of Nectarine's individual curls than many hairdressers awarded a client's entire head.

Through it all, Nectarine sat placidly, those many years as a high fashion model having inured her to the tedium of beautification.

"Dan requested that I tell you he intends to call you later, Claire," Marcel said, without turning from his work.

Nectarine inspected my reflection. "Good morning, Claire. Back at your post, I see."

"Yes, and can't you just see that big old neon halo flashing above my head?" I remarked, lounging against one side of the tall mirror.

Marcel's station was set slightly apart from the rank and file, and constructed entirely out of marble, prompting Ricky Gomez to call it the temple.

And how apt, I thought, watching Marcel's sure hands minister to Nectarine's hair like a high priest to his goddess. I was visited by a distinct sensation of déjà vu, almost as if I were still his eager acolyte, as if I had never left this Salon de Marcel where I'd spent my entire career up until opening Eclaire.

"So you chose to keep your hair appointment over spending a stimulating session with Harry Corvus and the FBI," I remarked blandly.

Nectarine rolled her eyes in exasperation. "Our Mr. Corvus is a pompous piece of work!" she said, with an irritated laugh. "Can you believe that convoluted scenario he came up with last night? According to him, between the Chinese gangs and the Mafia, this country is liable to break out any minute in drug turf wars like nothing since Prohibition!"

"The resulting chaos and distraction affording Great Britain the opportunity to launch a naval invasion upon America, thereby reclaiming the Colonies as part of the British Empire," Marcel added, keeping a straight face.

"In his dreams!" Savoy chuckled. "And I thought I detected a tad of hostility between the French and English the other night at Claire's and Dan's house!"

I rose to Marcel's defense. "Well, Harry has this strange way of bringing out the worst in everybody."

The sergeant concurred. "But then, all those Brits were born knowing how to yank us Yanks around. For instance, when I was getting fitted for a *Harper's Bazaar* shoot that was featuring some British designer they were pushing, every time I'd make a suggestion, he'd just peer down his nose at me and drawl, 'Ew? Dew yew reely think sew?'

"Of course that made me start to doubt my own instincts, as was intended. By then I'd be too confused to push for my idea, and would just let the whole thing drop."

"Thereby enabling the British to move in and reclaim the territory," I paraphrased Marcel.

Marcel remarked it was indeed a useful technique, and perhaps one Nectarine should consider including in her own professional arsenal.

"Good point," she conceded ruefully, "but I'm not sure I would have used it to stop Corvus from his wild ramblings last night. I must admit, I briefly succumbed to a certain horrified fascination."

I laughed. "Charlo and I were wondering about you! It was pretty farfetched."

"Well, yes and no," was Nectarine's surprising rejoinder. "Oh, certainly the part about Duchess Crowe and Lochner Smith getting caught in the drug war crossfire between the Asian and Italian mobs, is ridiculous. No, despite Mr. Corvus's charge of parochialism, we've got to look much closer to home for a motive.

"Although I will be filing his little idea about beauty supplies being the perfect cover for drug dealing in the back of my mind for future reference.

"The odd thing is, Duchess had been using huge quantities of a very new, very lethal, and exorbitantly expensive drug."

"Wait, didn't you say she was poisoned?" I interjected. "Of course I guess enough of something like that is poison, all right."

"Yes, but that's not what killed her, Claire," Savoy said. "We won't be getting the official autopsy report until next week, but take my word, Duchess Crowe did not blissfully drift from this world into the next on a soft, feathery cloud of grand slam."

I felt the room begin to waver. "What?"

"And where I went when I left here was Adlers over on Canal Street. It took me a long time to pick this out."

He started to reach into the pocket of his jacket, and almost jumped out of his skin when the officers pulled out their Magnums and shouted, "Freeze!"

"You gotta be kidding!" he croaked in disbelief, sounding not unlike his late mother. "It's just an engagement ring, for God's sake!"

Upon hearing this Dan chuckled. "Well, there's a proposal the lucky lady will remember for the rest of her life!"

"Very romantic, in a *Twilight Zone* kind of way," Charlotte acknowledged, "but I think Savoy's measuring her for a ball and chain of another kind entirely. The woman scorned, and all."

"Vicky Su already knew!" I exclaimed. "Duchess told her, right after Tom left. I saw and heard them myself."

"You saw and heard two women yammering in Chinese, Claire," Charlotte corrected me. "You don't know what they were saying. And maybe by then, she'd already slipped her the poison, and it was already too late."

I argued that poison required at least some premeditation, that Vicky Su would have to have known ahead of time that Duchess might be there in order to make arrangements.

"Who said she didn't know?" Charlotte demanded. "Duchess could've told a bunch of people she was planning on coming to Marcel's, and any of them could've relayed that to Vicky Su."

Foley spoke up. "But she wouldn't necessarily have needed to know ahead of time," he pointed out. "Hell, your Vicky Su had quite a selection of lethal substances right at her dainty fingertips, when and if she got the notion. For that matter, so did a lot of other folks."

I had known Vicky Su for years; we'd graduated from the Institut in the same class. She was shy until you got to know her, but extremely talented and very sweet.

She'd done my hair many times, and I could still recall her gentle, skillful hands at work. One of the guys had teased that she was such a softie, she even hated to cut the dead ends from somebody's hair. Could those same hands have turned to murder?

Dan paused in the act of raising his bottle of Orangeboom. "Now you just brought up an interesting train of thought, Foley," he commented. "Duchess Crowe ran a nightclub that catered almost exclusively to the beauty business, and could've theoretically had contact with everybody in that room at some time or other. Which means one or more of them besides Tom Toy or Vicky Su might have a motive. Am I right, or am I right?"

That made me feel a little better. "You usually are right, Dan Louis," I told him.

"I am, huh?" he drawled, pressing the rim of the beer bottle to his full lips.

Beer is not a beverage I care for, but I do love the way it flavors Dan's mouth after he's been drinking it. I could almost taste it now, on his tongue . . . absently, my hand traveled like a homing pigeon up his solid thigh, encased in tight, faded denim.

"Hey!" Foley rapped his knuckles on the table to get our attention. "What's really interesting when you think of it, is how all at once so much criminal activity seems to be centered around your profession, Claire. There've been—

"Grand slam," Nectarine repeated. "That's what they found right away. There were traces around her nostrils, on her fingers, and a little bit left in a bottle in that big bag she brought.

"As I mentioned, it's the newest thing. So new, in fact, hardly anyone's heard of it yet. It's a very specific ratio of cocaine to heroin to opium in an amyl nitrate base. I am told all it takes is a kitchen stove, a few pots and pans, and an enormous amount of finesse to refine all the above elements into a crystalline substance that can either be sniffed or smoked, or liquified and injected."

"Such an individual would need to master both the fundamentals of gourmet cuisine, and the rudiments of chemistry," observed Marcel, who had finally worked his way down to the curls at the nape of Savoy's neck.

Something about that rang a bell with me, but I was still reeling from hearing what grand slam was, to pay much attention.

"I thought he was talking about some new dance craze," I muttered.

"What's that?" Savoy's blue eyes darted to capture mine in the mirror, and I reluctantly explained how Lamont had been dancing around chanting, "Everybody grand slam."

"Poor little boll weevil," she said, unexpectedly. "He's definitely mixed up in all this somehow. And that mother of his isn't helping him, either."

"But Lamont told you what he did," I reminded her. "He put those tranquilizers in her tea."

"Because he was mad at her, I know," Savoy retorted. "But in my sad experience, people often confess to the lesser thing they've done in order to avoid taking responsibility for something worse. We'll see."

I said, "Well, there are plenty of other possibilities."

"Yes," Nectarine agreed. "Technically, both Marcel and yourself could be considered suspects, Claire. As well as any of those who were present at the time of death."

Marcel had remained uncharacteristically silent throughout our conversation. Now he lifted his scissors as if he were taking up a baton to conduct the orchestra, and began the overall shaping of Savoy's hair. "It was not Vicky Su," he declared, adjusting her head to an angle and observing the mirrored effect.

Without stirring so much as a fraction from the position Marcel had arranged her in, Savoy demanded, "Oh, really? And just what makes you so sure about that, Inspector?"

He sighed. "I have known this child for a long time. She is simply incapable of committing such an act."

"That *child*, as you call her, Marcel, is almost thirty years old!" Nectarine responded acidly. "And one of the very first things I learned about the enormous culture gap that exists between East and West was from a stunningly beautiful Vietnamese model I worked with. She was in great demand and highly successful, but her family considered her a shame and disgrace because she was thirty-one and still unmarried."

Marcel swiveled her chair slightly to the left and made no comment.

Nectarine went on. "Another thing I learned from her was how even the most trivial incident is magnified into a very serious thing called 'losing face.'

"Don't forget, your dear little Vicky Su thought she'd lost her official boyfriend to an even older, less attractive Asian woman. It doesn't matter if she seduced and bribed him into her bed or not. No, the very fact that Vicky Su was unable to hold him, despite all Duchess Crowe's lures, had caused her an incredible loss of face in the Chinese community she might never have lived down, if Duchess hadn't turned out to be his mother. Unless . . ."

Nectarine deliberately trailed off, waiting for us to fill in the blank.

"Surely," Marcel expostulated, shaking a comb at her, "you are not implying that the only way Vicky Su could regain 'face' would be to eliminate her rival!"

"That's just too crazy," I argued.

"To you and me, maybe," said Nectarine.

"But Duchess told Vicky Su the truth," I pointed out.

Nectarine shrugged. "So she says."

Marcel decided to take an enlightened, populist view. "One can discern the necessity to retrieve one's honor, when one has had it stolen. But to suspect Vicky Su of pursuing such a convoluted course of reasoning to the point of murder is to me unthinkable.

"Shake your head," he added to Savoy, who obediently complied.

"Motive, means, opportunity," she recited. "Vicky Su had them all."

"I refuse to believe it," Marcel said stubbornly.

I checked my watch. Mrs. Potato Head was nearly done baking. "Well, let's see. Who's left? Not Tom Toy, since he was counting on Mommy Dearest to help him produce his big rock and roll album.

"And since I know you're an equal opportunity employer when it comes to suspects, what about Wicked Stepmother, Marzipan Jones? She hated Duchess like, well, poison. Plus, she had constant access to any number of lethal substances in the supply room."

"Mmm," Nectarine replied, either to my theory or to the way Marcel was massaging a moisturizing conditioner into her scalp.

"Nor should we overlook Natasha and Yuri, the Dracula twins," I reminded her. "Duchess had them locked into a ironclad contract. They couldn't play with her, or without her. That's a pretty strong motive, I think."

Marcel's thumbs were expertly kneading Nectarine's forehead, and she didn't even bother to acknowledge what I'd said.

I wound up, "And last, but not least, there's the Italian contingent."

"Not, perhaps, overly concerned with saving face, but certainly dedicated to the fine art of revenge," Marcel ruminated, applying a touch of shiatsu to Savoy's temples.

An image of Duchess and Vince in a lustlock as I'd witnessed them yesterday, appeared in my mind's eye. Could it be that Vince also hadn't known Tom's true relationship to Duchess? Perhaps she'd planned to keep teasing him with it a little longer, but he'd lost his temper and things backfired.

I'd already told Savoy of Vince's offer to supply me with something to "perk Dan up," but she hadn't seemed too interested.

"Did he actually name a substance?" she asked.

"Well, no. But—"

Savoy couldn't conceal a smile. "I think he was suggesting an aphrodisiac, Claire."

"Yes, but he touched his nostrils!" I told her, but she merely said he could have been scratching his nose.

Now I thought of Sal Romano, and the penny dropped. Marcel's mention of chemistry had reminded me of something, and it was Sal's flirtatious remark to Renee, that mixing drinks was the same as mixing haircolor—they both required chemistry, after a fashion.

I brought this up to Nectarine, who was loath to talk at all, because Marcel was presently working on her neck and shoulders with slow, sensuous strokes. Was it just my imagination, or had I seen his fingers flicker, ever so lightly, just inside the vee of the smock, against the golden skin on her upper décolleté? The hand is quicker than the eye, especially when it's Marcel's.

"Don't worry, Claire," Nectarine purred slowly, without opening her eyes. "I'm keeping tabs on Mr. Romano." She yawned, deliberately displaying plenty of pink tongue to Marcel, who gazed hungrily down into her open mouth.

This was no place for a third wheel.

"Well, I've got to go take my potato out of the oven now. No, please. Don't bother to get up. I can find my own way out. See you at the party tomorrow night, Marcel."

Nectarine's mouth closed and her eyes opened wide. "What party?" she demanded.

When Marcel and I had filled her in on the hairdresser's sendoff Lochner was throwing for himself, she smiled.

"How interesting! And I take it you're going?" she asked Marcel.

"But, certainly! I knew this man for over half my life," Marcel replied.

Nectarine tilted her head back and looked up at him. "How would you like a date?" she inquired.

It was almost heartbreaking to see the expression of delighted amazement dawn upon Marcel's handsome face.

"My dear, I would be only too pleased to escort you!" he breathed.

"Oh," Savoy teased. "It's not going to be me, exactly. I'm going undercover for the evening. Your date is with a slightly trashy, very flashy, and oh-so-sweet party girl, a beautician from, let's make it Baton Rouge. That's far enough away so nobody will wonder why they've never heard of me. I mean her."

Marcel laughed. "And what is this adorable creature's name, may I ask?"

"Well, I think it should be something as trashy, flashy and sweet as she is," Nectarine mused.

"How about Honey Love?" I suggested.

"That's it, exactly, Claire!" she squealed excitedly, and I stared at her in astonishment. She was already evolving into her new character.

"Honey Love," Marcel's voice trailed over the words like a caress. "Most appropriate."

"Hey, this may be a murder investigation, but there's no law says I can't have some fun!" Savoy declared. "Now come on, Daddy. We've got to figure out what this chick is going to look like!"

Chapter 26

The exterior of Lochner Smith's French Quarter home, located on a relatively sedate block of upper Burgundy Street, bore an uncanny resemblance to himself: tall, narrow, bony, and the color of pale orange sand.

And like its recently departed owner, this house also had plenty of unexpected things going on inside.

Following Babs Hooper's direction, instead of approaching the front door, Dan and I rang the bell by a solid metal gate set into a high brick wall to the right of the building, which most effectively frustrated the slightest glimpse of what lay beyond.

We were buzzed inside, and followed the brick walkway toward the faint thump of music, until we'd passed under an archway around which were knotted fragrant muscadine vines, laden with ripening fruit.

Simultaneously, the music swelled and the terra-cotta tiled courtyard fanned out suddenly before us, lit by strings of tiny white lights woven through the branches of sweet myrtles in stone planters, which were set along the curves flanking French doors that led inside. In the center of the courtyard bubbled a stone fountain, which looked as if it had been excavated from an ancient Roman bathhouse.

Many of the people in the courtyard looked as if they'd been excavated themselves, some from bath houses not so ancient.

It was the costumes, of course. They explained they had come dressed to attend various Halloween parties afterward, but I suspected that few of Lock's invitees would have been unable to resist the opportunity in any case. Traditionally, Halloween is the favorite holiday of the beauty trade in general.

Not mine, though.

When the British deported the Acadians from Nova Scotia back in 1755, they were too anxious to get rid of them by then to make any distinctions between Protestant and Catholic, so my Jennerette ancestors, though of the Huguenot minority, were swept into exile along with everybody else. They'd had to fight hard to retain their identity along the way, and *N'oncle* Hebert had inherited a strong streak of anti-papism from his forebearers.

Consequently, I was raised with a push-pull attitude toward All Hallows' Eve. First, there was the old Huguenot contention that the Catholic hierarchy had committed blasphemy, condoning a popular celebration with indisputable roots in demonic paganism by calling it a religious holiday, and that they were perpetuating heresy by implying that departed souls have the power to return from the dead on this one night and drag the living to hell.

From this arose the superstition that wearing a disguise would prevent the spirits from recognizing you, but it had always seemed to me, if they were all that powerful, they would be able to see right through my Little Red Riding Hood costume.

But I was also exposed to the warm, fuzzy, Americana side of Halloween. Jack o'lanterns, trick or treat, and my favorite, candy corn.

Nevertheless, I had always experienced an underlying apprehension about the holiday, even before our country lost its remaining innocence, before people started sticking needles and razor blades into apples, and a daddy poisoned his little boy's trick or treat candy to collect the insurance.

Tonight was no exception, although I knew my natural discomfort was enhanced by the actual occasion of Lochner Smith's bon voyage party.

One of the first recognizeable denizens amoung the Elvises, witches, and assorted androgynes, was Lamont, in a long-sleeved black leotard and tights, which formed the basis of his cat costume.

He was sporting a set of pointy feline ears attached to a wide, black velvet Hillary headband, long metallic eyelashes, pink lipstick on lips and nose, and sequined whiskers glued to his cheeks.

In one hand he twirled his very long tail, which turned out to be a braided horsewhip, and around his neck was fastened a studded black leather collar from which dangled a large red heart inscribed Pussywhip.

A waiter approached us. "Good evening, folks. May I bring you a drink?"

"Now that's a tough one," Dan said. "What do you think, Claire? Will a drink make all this"—he gestured around the courtyard—"seem better, or worse?"

The waiter followed his gaze. "That all depends on your point of view, sir. My personal recommendation would be a little something to dull the edge, without completely relaxing your guard."

Dan grinned. "I predict you'll go far, young man! Tell me, how are your martinis?"

"Crystalline, sir."

Dan turned to me. "How's that sound, darlin'?"

I nodded, thinking a medicinal nip of gin might be just what the doctor ordered. Certainly it's what the "doctor" sitting over there on the edge of the fountain, his stethescope pressed into the heaving cleavage of his "nurse," would order for himself.

"Okay," Dan told the waiter. "Listen carefully. I want you to find a couple of those double oldfashioned glasses, put in plenty of rocks, pour us two dry Bombay martinis, and plop in about three olives apiece. That way, we can carry the same drink around all night, if need be. And vice versa."

"An admirable solution, sir," the waiter nodded approvingly, and with a flash of green deftly appropriated the bill that had somehow appeared in Dan's hand.

"Well, Claire!" Dan laughed, surveying the gradually expanding throng of mourners. "I sure am enjoying myself so far."

"It's awful, isn't it?" I agreed. "Either Lock invited every hairstylist in town, or half of them, and they brought the other half along."

For the next few minutes, I was kept busy introducing him to acquaintances like Faylee Wilkins and Mimi Fontenot, who, drawn together over their mutual troubles, had become quite good friends. There was even talk of opening a new shop as partners, though Mimi still muttered darkly of murder.

Francesca Bacci popped over just in time to overhear Mimi's last words. "No, no! *Mia bella!*" she reproved, waving a glass of red wine with Mediterranean abandon. "Remember, it is the cut direct!" Francesca made a buzzing sound to accompany the circular sawing motion with her free hand, then giggled when she saw Dan's eyes widen.

Apparently, no man on earth can fail to understand such a gesture.

"Right nice company you keep," Dan drawled, when the three women, not yet three sheets to the wind but on their way, ambled off arm in arm.

At last our waiter returned, his tray practically sagging from the weight of the two large martinis which Dan, upon sampling, declared were exactly according to specs.

Gin really was medicinal, I decided. After two or three sips, I was feeling more crystalline by the moment. I mentioned this to Dan, who replied maybe we'd better eat something, just in case. He'd no sooner gotten the words out than our waiter reappeared with another tray, this one containing an hors d'ouevre which he identified as "golden doubloons." Spicy hot sausage, grilled and sliced into coin shapes, ready for dipping in a satiny, yellow mustard sauce.

"There's a lavish buffet just being laid out in the dining room, sir," the waiter confided.

"How much did you tip him, anyway?" I teased Dan.

He grinned. "Enough, evidently."

In contrast to his rather pristine, chrome and blond-wood hair salon, Lock's appetite for art deco was expressed throughout his home in the darker, more voluptuous curves of lacquer and velvet.

One entire wall of the den was occupied by an enormous colbalt glass showcase and hutch, with blue-lit mirrored shelves displaying Lock's incredible collection of cigarette and cigar holders and cigarette cases. Many were wrought of silver, gold and platinum, or carved from semiprecious materials such as amber, ebony, lapis, jade and ivory.

The remaining shelves were filled with vintage novelty cigarette lighters. Among these were several models of derringer pistols, a miniature Coca-Cola bottle, a tiny pack of Lucky Strike cigarettes, a fancy compact that ignited its wick when opened, and a fountain pen, ditto.

"This is almost enough to tempt a person into taking up smoking," I remarked to Dan, making a mental note that his eye was lingering upon an especially sexy-looking ivory cigar holder mellowed to the color of rich butterscotch.

I wondered who was handling the estate, and if they would be willing to let me buy one item from the collection.

We found Babs Hooper in the dining room, overseeing the arrangement of a sumptuous variety of foods upon the banquet-sized Chinese dining table, its lacquered cherry finish inlaid with intricate patterns in mother-of-pearl.

She looked flushed and quite lovely in a green-printed long silk dress that disguised her figure flaws and brought out her eyes.

Babs glanced up at our approach. "Oh! Hello, Claire," she said. "We're not quite ready to serve yet. So much to do—"

I introduced Dan to her, and she looked apprehensively over our shoulders, as if fearing the whole herd was about to thunder in.

"Don't worry, it's just us," I assured her. "Our waiter advised we should come grab a bite of something before the martinis grabbed us!"

Babs gave a relieved laugh. "Sure, help yourselves," she invited, saying that the duck pâté mini-sandwiches were excellent.

She was absolutely right.

"Oh, I was forgetting. Would you like to say hello to Lock?" Babs inquired, matter-of-factly, causing me to nearly swallow my third duck sandwich whole.

"Wh-where is . . . he?" I managed to stammer, after Dan had pounded me on the back a few times.

"In the next room."

Babs wiped her hands on a pink damask napkin and led the way into a glamorous burgundy and blue living room, where the ambience was so authentic, I almost expected Fred and Ginger to come dancing down the stairs and across the furniture at any moment.

Babs went over to an area that was swagged and draped in burgundy and blue striped silk like the tall windows facing the street, but she looped the curtains back to reveal an alcove containing a large television, VCR, and an elaborate sound system.

Atop the television sat a tall Roseville urn, in shades of blue and mauve, with a gardenia motif.

Well, of course. No ordinary funeral urn would have done for Lochner Smith. If he had to go, he was going out in style, in a fifteen-hundred-dollar piece of Roseville, by golly.

I raised my martini and said, feeling a little teary, "You still got your touch, Lock."

Babs nodded proudly. "Everything is exactly like he wanted it. And isn't that a pretty vase? He was thinking of starting another colletion but this one was as far as he got—" Her voice trailed off for a moment, then she resumed, "I would have chosen the mantlepiece, myself, but his instructions were very clear. On top of the television." She frowned. "I can't think why."

Dan smiled. "Maybe he just wanted to be on TV?" he suggested lightly, and a startled giggle escaped her.

"Thanks, I guess I needed to laugh," Babs said, dimpling at Dan appreciatively. "You know," she told him, "you look a whole lot like Tommy Lee Jones. I mean, you're bigger, and your face is much broader, but there's definitely a resemblance. You could almost be brothers."

"Well, thank you, Babs," Dan replied gallantly. "I'll bear that in mind in case the law business gets bad. Maybe Mr. Jones would let me be his stand-in."

The laughter died out of Babs's green eyes. "Oh, I doubt the law business will ever get that bad in this town. I'm sure I've paid off a mortgage or two in legal fees, all by myself."

The martini was loosening my tongue. "What you mean is, Babs, you've forked over a bunch of money to get Lamont out of his jams."

She started to protest, then shrugged. "What else can I do, Claire? I'm all he's got, really. If it weren't for me, my own family, and his . . . father's family, would have him locked up in an institution by now. I can't let that happen."

I shook her shoulder. "But, Babs. Lamont needs serious help. It's not okay to spike somebody's tea with tranquiliziers simply because you're mad at them, you know."

"That's not what killed her," she gasped painfully. "And he said he was sorry. You saw him, Claire. He really was sorry!"

"Babs, let's face it. Lamont didn't stop to wonder whether he was hurting her or not. The only important thing to him at the time was how *he* felt. It's always easy to be sorry afterwards."

I patted her arm compassionately. "Look, for true I'm no shrink. But can't you see, the more you cover up for him and protect him from facing the consequences of his own actions, the more he's going to just keep right on doing nasty things to people he gets mad at? But of course, he'll be sorry later, and that's supposed to make it all right."

Dan added gently, "Claire's right, you know. We're not just talking about pranks, here. The boy acted out his anger on someone else's body. If he did it once, he'll do it again. And one day, it just might be you he gets mad at."

Babs turned pale. "I-I don't want to talk about this anymore. Please."

"Okay," I said. "We're going to leave you alone and take a tour of the house now. But just tell me one thing. Did you get Lamont an attorney like Sergeant Savoy recommended?"

She hesitated, then nodded.

"Well, who is it?" Dan asked. "If you're not satisfied, I might be able to refer you to somebody reliable."

Babs avoided our eyes. "His father is an attorney. He's going to handle everything for Lamont from now on."

She gave me an imploring look. "Lamont's a sweetheart, Claire. He really is."

Just then, the sweetheart himself strolled past the living room, cracking his long "tail" into the air, black patent leather Doc Martens squeaking like little rodents against the highly polished wood floor.

I decided right then and there, if love is blind, a mother's love is probably the blindest of all.

Chapter 27

Lock's house wasn't that large, but he'd maximized his space. For instance, at the top of the stairs, a simple landing had been transformed into a tiny sunroom by placing a forties rattan settee beneath triple windows facing west. Its cushions were covered in what could easily have been the original fabric, only slightly faded red hibiscus strewn over a jade green background. Potted palms and a standing metal ashtray completed the picture.

"Quite a place," Dan observed. "It's practically like being in a museum. About the only thing missing here is the velvet ropes."

I nodded, having been thinking along much the same lines myself. This was not just somebody's house tarted up in art deco style. There was an eerie sensation of having actually stepped back in time, because all the furnishings seemed to exude both authenticity and master design.

Everything in Lock's house was indeed museum quality, and I wondered how on earth he'd gotten enough money to buy it. Not to mention those expensive, extensive collections displayed in the den.

Granted, I certainly wasn't privy to his financial affairs but I did know that he had not come from a wealthy background, nor could he have cleared more than a comfortable profit at best from his three salons.

Thinking back on our conversation (could it really only have been just over a week ago?) at Brennan's, I recalled Lock saying something about not giving up a life of "comparative luxury" to subsist in London squalor, but I'd assumed he'd meant exchanging a relatively higher standard of living for a lower one.

This, however, was not comparative luxury. This was luxury, period.

Therefore, Lock had had an outside source of income. And whatever it was, he couldn't have continued to access it from Great Britain.

On Sunday, he had declared to us he had no intention of relocating to London in anything but the top drawer.

On Tuesday night, he was dead.

But the following Monday, Babs told me he had been in the midst of preparing for a permanent move to London.

Something extraordinary, then, had happened to change his circumstances between our encounter with him on Sunday morning, and his death on Tuesday evening.

When I ran all this by Dan, he said approvingly, "Good thinking, Claire. And I hate to say this because I kinda liked the guy, evidently he was up to no good, because look what happened."

He thought for a moment, then added, "Remember, he said he was working on a scheme that could be his ticket to Knightsbridge?"

Yes, I remembered. Poor Lock, that ticket had taken him someplace else entirely.

When we'd viewed the guest room, a symphony in grey and dusty rose, Dan said, "Darlin', I see one more door down at the end of the hall, then I am ready for some food! How you doing with that drink?"

I slipped down the pink napkin the bartender had wrapped around our glasses to keep our hands dry, to check the level. "Over half left," I reported.

I was braced for Lock's master bedroom to be wallowing in tufted velvet, satin and mirrors. Instead, we found ourselves in the private quarters of an English gentlemen of great taste and means, a combination study and bedroom.

A double sleighbed covered with a tapestry spread completed the mahogany bedroom furnishings. There were brass lamps, a massive Aubusson rug, and a wall of well-stocked bookshelves adjacent to an Adam fireplace.

A plum silk paisley dressing gown was arranged precisely over the back of a big, tobacco brown leather chair, and there was brandy in the crystal decanter on a small table at its arm.

But what got to me was the large basket on the floor, piled high with copies of the London *Times*.

"Dan, let's get out of here," I choked.

Going downstairs, we had to step carefully around people who were busily polishing off plates of gorgeous-looking food, using the lower risers as tables.

"Hell, I hope they left us something!" Dan grumbled.

He needn't have worried; Lock had planned well. In no time at all, we were supplied with plates of our own, heaped high with broiled shrimp, oyster patties, jalapeño crabcakes and more of those divine duck pâté sandwiches.

Our feasting was frequently interrupted by greetings and introductions, but not seriously impaired.

"Clean plate club," Dan announced, a little later.

"Me, too. Mmm, that was good."

"May I bring you anything else?" Our waiter from earlier loomed suddenly at Dan's elbow.

"I think I'm okay for now, thanks," Dan told him. "You want more, Claire?"

I declined, and the waiter commented, as he transferred our plates to his tray, it would be wise to conserve space for the equally abundant dessert table. He also insisted on relieving us of our martini glasses, though they weren't yet empty.

"These have gone quite stale, sir," he said firmly to Dan, who displayed a marked tendency to cling to his. "You will be much happier with fresh ones."

Dan relinquished his glass and asked, "By the way, what's your name?"

"Max, sir," the waiter replied.

"Well, Max. I've got another question. How much *did* I tip you a while ago?"

The waiter smiled. "Enough, sir," he said gently, and disappeared.

By the time Max had returned with our drinks, a light rain had begun to fall, so people who'd been partying outside were making their way indoors now. I estimated there were at least a hundred people, maybe closer to a hundred and fifty, and nearly half were in some kind of costume.

Marzie Jones and Gino Gambara fit right in, because their regular clothes looked like costumes. Nobody who didn't know Gino would believe he would deliberately wear a moth-eaten green Irish heather hat, a wine-colored polyester leisure suit, yellow socks, and white patent leather loafers, out of sheer preference.

Marzie, in something long and black with flowing sleeves, was appropriately attired for either a funeral or a party, and in a sense, this was both.

Vince Platina pushed Gino's wheelchair to a spot where he would be out of the high traffic area, but could still observe the action.

Sal Romano was wandering restlessly around the room, drink in hand, as if looking for someone.

When Renee walked in, wearing a tight black crushed velvet pantsuit and zebra-patterned cowboy boots, his face lit up. Until he noticed that Harry Corvus had a proprietary hold on her arm, then he looked surprised.

So, for that matter, did Renee.

Surprise didn't even begin to cover what I felt. I nudged Dan, who turned to look, then drawled, "My, my. That boy sure knows how to worm his way into a party, don't he?"

I couldn't, or didn't, suppress a little bubble of glee, when Vince noticed the couple. He went into instant boil, and by the look on his face, Harry might find that elegant tweed jacket, which Lock would have coveted, turned into something only Gino Gambara could love before this night was through.

"Claire! My little *cucaracha* and her *mucho grande toro* of a husband!" somebody called out. "Why must it always be raining when I see you?"

It was Ricky Gomez, a hairdresser from Biloxi, who had shared in our adventures involving a beauty pageant and two murders during a hurricane a month ago.

Ricky, a gorgeous Mexican aristocrat from El Paso, affected a sarcastic, "Sí, Cisco," accent to distance himself from people at times, though he ordinarily spoke without even a hint of tongue roll to betray his origins.

The three of us exchanged greetings and I said, "It's good to see you, Ricky. But I didn't realize you and Lock were friends."

A shadow crossed his handsome face and he took a drink of his margarita before replying. "Long ago and far away, Claire," he said evasively, and I got the message.

The next instant, his mood had lightened, and he kept us laughing with his witty—and barbed—comments about various people in attendance.

Babs Hooper bustled up to us. "The oddest thing just happened!" she exclaimed. "I had a telephone call from Lochner's lawyer, who said he's on his way over here, as per his client's instructions!"

"Maybe you know him, Dan. It's—" she noticed Ricky and broke off. "Oh, good evening, Ricky."

I sensed she was uncomfortable and embarrassed around Ricky, for some reason.

"Hello, Babs," Ricky replied, with an undertone of amusement. "You just never know who's going to turn up at a funeral, do you?"

"Well, I hope this is everybody," she said, glancing around the room with a bewildered air.

But even as she spoke, another couple was making a rather spectacular entrance.

"My goodness!" Babs exclaimed, hastily pulling up her lower jaw. "Who in the world is that with Marcel?"

Ricky's aqua eyes danced. "*Ay yiyiyi!*" he yipped appreciatively, in a perfect imitation of Ricky Ricardo.

"Mercy!" Dan exclaimed with a laugh, even though I'd warned him ahead of time.

Marcel was in what I call his extremely French *comte* mode. You could almost smell the money woven into his custom-tailored wool suit, of a green so dark and rich it was nearly black. The cut of his jacket was exquisite, the mere fall of the pant legs a work of art.

At his side, wearing a white leather Versace suit, the skirt just an inch too short and the jacket just a tad too lowcut, was a tall, willowy woman with a Whitney Houston hairdo and earrings like chandeliers.

Her long, lovely legs were swathed in sheer black fishnet stockings, ending in a pair of Manola Blahnik high-heeled sandals that cost what it would take to feed a family of six for a week, and that tiny gold shoulder bag, elaborately chained and tasseled, was a Chanel.

Her jewelry was ostentatious and expensive, her makeup bright and perfect. She was a flashy, trashy, classy eyeful.

If I hadn't already known who it was, I might have wondered myself.

It was those brown contacts that did the trick, I thought.

"Oh," I informed Babs casually, "that's Honey Love."

Chapter 28

"If this was a movie, nobody would damn believe it!" Dan, his blue eyes brimming with mirth, indicated Marcel and "Honey." "And I can tell you one thing, he's loving every minute of this."

I agreed, watching Marcel and Nectarine work their way through the motley crew toward the buffet. He was the absolute picture of the wealthy dilettante, showing off his expensive party girl.

"This is the first chance that big old *jambon* has had to act since he did that walk-on in *The Client*," I said.

The pair's arrival caused something of a stir. Their progress was slow, because Marcel had to keep pausing to introduce Honey Love.

"Why, yayis!" I heard her squeal in response to somebody's question. "Ah'm from Baton Rouge, by way of Atlanta, Georgia? Currently, Ah'm working in a little bitty beauty shop over by LSU? But Mr. Barrineau here axed me to come to Nawlins to discuss a position in one of his salons, isn't that right, Mr. Barrineau?"

"A position flat on your back, sister," sneered Vince Platina, from where he was propped against a wall over to the left of Dan and me. He tossed off what looked like a half-inch of scotch in one gulp, and commented, to no one in particular, "Looks like old Marcel just loves that brown sugar. Can't remember when I last saw him with a real white girl."

It was clear Vince was on his way to getting ugly. Dan casually took my elbow and steered me away.

That's how I happened to see when, as Marcel was pulling Honey Love along behind him, Sal Romano caught her other arm and said something in her ear.

She jerked angrily away. "How dayuh you speak to me like thayut! Mr. Barrineau, would you puhleeze inform thiyus gentlemayun I do not wish hiyum to address me?"

"Is she good, or what?" I whispered to Dan.

Marcel turned around and faced Sal, who raised placating palms. "Hey, no offense intended. I'm sorry, okay?"

"Ha! Struck out, Salvatore!" Vince roared from his post.

Just then, Renee came up to me, glancing furtively behind her. "Claire, I need to talk to you, *chère*," she muttered.

In a wild-eyed, feverish kind of way, Renee looked beautiful tonight, if a bit consumptive. Frankly, anything was an improvement on how she'd been lately.

"Well, it's about time, Renee," I began, only to have Harry Corvus pop suddenly into our midst, carrying two glasses of red wine.

"Here you go, love," he said to Renee, handing her one, then raising his own to us.

"Well, cheers, and all that," he said, and sipped pleasurably. "Ahh, good bordeaux, this. Someone knows what they're doing."

"As I understand it, our absent host selected it himself," Dan informed Harry, who blanched a little at this information.

"What . . . remarkable forethought!" he managed to say. "By the way, Claire. Where have you been hiding this beautiful child?" Harry put a possessive arm around Renee's shoulders and gazed fatuously down at her, but she resolutely stared into her wineglass, clutching it tightly in both hands.

"Why," he went on, "when I looked down from my balcony tonight and saw her walking along all by herself up St. Ann, surrounded by ghosts and goblins, I said to myself, 'Surely that's Claire's lovely assistant. She shouldn't be out alone tonight, of all nights.' "

He went on to say that he'd called down to Renee, inviting her to come up, and then discovered she was en route to this party.

"And so," Harry concluded, "I offered to escort her, and here I am."

He beamed, inviting us to applaud his chivalry, but the whole thing seemed just a little too conveniently coincidental. Somehow, he'd gotten wind of this party. Maybe Charlotte, who'd heard about it from me, had mentioned it in passing.

Probably he'd decided right then to crash. After all, he'd been present when Nectarine broke the news to Marcel and me about Lock's murder, and that former tabloid reporter would relish the ghoul value of such a shindig.

In fact, it was amazing he hadn't trucked a camera crew over to shoot the whole thing, another first for WBGZ-TV.

Stumbling over Renee like that was just an unexpected ticket dropping into his lap. She wouldn't have known how to refuse his offer of a safe escort through the bedlam of a French Quarter Halloween.

But Renee wasn't looking any too thrilled about having a handsome man's arm around her. I saw her dart a longing glance in Sal Romano's direction, and a furtive one at Vince, who was still steadily chugging away at the Johnnie Walker.

He caught Renee's eye and glared. "Shit, it's frigging boring in here!" he announced loudly to the room at large. "Doesn't old Lock have any snapshots or maybe a few juicy videotapes we can look at?"

The sudden blare of his voice startled Renee so much, she shied like a spooked filly, and the wineglass slipped from her hands, crashing into a million pieces on the floor. Miraculously, the bordeaux didn't splatter onto anyone, maybe because all nearby immediately jumped back in such perfect synchronization, we could have been doing the bunny hop.

Like a genie, Max materialized upon the scene, producing a busboy armed with towels and a ShopVac.

"Not to worry, Miss," he murmured soothingly to Renee, extracting her from Harry's grasp with the dexterity of a magician.

"Now you come on out to the kitchen while I open a whole new bottle."

Lamb-like, Renee allowed herself to be led away by the ubiquitous and masterful Max. I could see her shoulders sag with relief.

I smiled when I saw Sal watch them go, then unobtrusively follow.

"Bloody cheek that fellow has!" Harry exclaimed, which I thought was pretty good, coming from him.

"Max is the best." Dan's tone was surly and challenging. I wondered if he was just putting Harry on, or whether he'd imbibed a drop more than he'd intended, until he winked at me.

But Harry spotted something that interested him far more than a macho hornlocking with Dan.

Honey Love had emerged from the crowd, momentarily Marcel-less.

Harry took one look and made a beeline, skidding to a comical halt when Marcel loomed imposingly behind her.

Honey moved away and over to us, which left Harry stuck with Marcel. She joined in our laughter, hooting, "This is the most fun I've had since the time Iman and I switched runway shows in Paris!"

Lowering her voice she added, "But these damn earrings are pulling my lobes down to my armpits, and I won't even mention what the shoes are doing to my arches. These heels are four and a half inches!"

"Guess you're just a flatfoot, for true, N—Honey," I teased. "You finding out anything, amid all this pain?"

Whatever she was going to say was drowned out by a voice singing out, "Trick or treat!"

Lamont sashayed through the room, throwing candy corn like confetti. At the sight of Honey, he halted for an instant, stared, then threw an entire handful of the stuff right in her face, and flounced off, cracking his tail.

Nectarine told us later that she was afraid her cover was blown, because, "It takes one to know one."

"What the hell—?" Dan began, but stopped when Babs came up, leading a pudgy, balding fellow with a mustache and a wary expression.

This was replaced by one of relief when he saw Dan. He grabbed his hand like a drowning man who's found a rope and pumped enthusiastically.

"Dan Claiborne! I certainly didn't expect to find you here tonight!"

"Well, I can truthfully say the same, Digby," Dan replied. "Digby Baker, I'd like you to meet my wife, Claire. Claire darlin', Digby is the competition from Baker, DeVille and Slaughter.

"This is Miss Honey Love," Dan continued, "and of course you know Marcel Barrineau, who has just joined us.

"Oh, yes. And Harry Corvus, of WBGZ Television."

"Well," Babs said, after the formalities were concluded. "Mr. Baker is Lochner's attorney I was telling you about earlier, Dan. I just found out what Lochner had instructed him to do, and I don't mind saying, I'm very disturbed."

Her hands fluttered nervously and I noticed she'd recently tidied her hair and freshened her makeup.

"What's this all about, Digby?" Dan inquired.

Digby fidgeted. "Dan, you know me. I don't much care for theatrics. But Lochner Smith was my client for nearly twenty years, and if this is what he wanted, it wasn't my place to object."

He indicated a large manila envelope, bound with cord and dramatically sealed with a large blob of red wax with a thumbprint in the middle. Lock's.

As Digby explained what was inside that envelope, we understood why Lock had insisted the Roseville urn containing his remains be placed on top of the television.

Chapter 29

By the time Lock's Chinese lacquer table was cleared of food and replenished with a panorama of desserts, it was around nine-fifteen.

From then on, the numbers dwindled rapidly as people went off to pursue their previously scheduled Halloween activities.

Dan and Digby Baker were huddled in intense discussion to one side, while I worked on a luscious piece of sweet potato pie, martini abandoned in favor of coffee. Digby's revelation had been as sobering as a bucket of cold water, and I wanted to be prepared for what was to come.

Ricky Gomez drifted up. "Claire, what's going on?" he asked.

I took a good look at him. His handsome face seemed a bit drawn, and there was not even a hint of laughter in those aqua eyes.

Tonight, Ricky wore his long, glossy brown hair pulled tightly back in a ponytail, and a beautiful, but somber, dark suit. All in all, a far cry from the usual self-absorbed, campy persona he turned toward the world.

"What makes you think something's going on?" I parried. "Incidentally, Ricky. If you haven't tried any of this pie, you should. It's delicious."

"Listen, Claire," he snapped through tight lips. "I didn't drive all the way over here from Biloxi for you to bullshit me."

I sighed, depositing my empty plate on the tray of a passing busboy. "I'm sorry, Ricky. Why did you drive all the way over here?"

He studied the floor. "Let's just say, for old times' sake, okay? I was . . . fond of him once, but it didn't work out. He had a few too many serious problems for me. Other than being homosexual, I mean."

Ricky gave a bitter laugh and started to say more, but I cut in.

"Ricky, please!" I begged. "If this is the speech about how, if only there was a pill you could take to lose the craving to sodomize, spare me. The last time you told me that you had me drowning in tears, then in the very next breath, you started babbling about the new voodoo love potion you'd just paid two hundred dollars for to use on that Swedish masseur."

He smiled sadly. "That's exactly my point, Claire, though there's no way you could understand it. Anyway, the problem with Lock was, he wasn't really a straight gay, if you'll allow the contradiction in terms. *Verdad!* Look at how they found him!" Tears sprang to his eyes. "I can't imagine anybody—" Words failed him.

Well, this was certainly proving an eyeopener for me. I had just taken it for granted that all homosexuals do all the same things. Apparently, there was an entire spectrum of attitudes and behavior involved, and I was beginning to get an idea.

"Ricky," I said thoughtfully, "talk to me about Lock. I have a feeling you may be able to shed some light on his death nobody else can."

He shrugged. "I don't see how, but . . . okay."

Ricky took a deep breath, searching for a place to begin. "First of all, I have to tell you, Lochner Smith was a walking contradiction, Claire. He was from a poor nothing family in Kenner, but he had visions of becoming an aristocrat. He loved money, all right, but he wasn't interested in hanging out with ordinary rich people. No, they had to have some sort of blueblood pedigree."

Ricky shook his head. "But also, for some weird reason, he was physically addicted to, and I'm quoting now, so don't be too shocked, 'mean little colored boys.' That's why he came after me in the beginning, you see.

"But when he found out who my family was, he completely flipped. I guess he thought he'd bagged the best of both worlds."

Ricky looked directly at me, pain in his eyes. "Only he immediately discovered I wasn't nearly mean enough for him. You wouldn't believe some of the things he wanted—" He stopped abruptly. "I don't see how this is helping any."

"But it is," I said, feeling sick at a hideous picture forming in my mind. "Tell me, Ricky. Why were you and Babs acting so skittish with each other?"

The question was just a formality. I was almost positive what his answer would be.

Ricky stared at me in troubled surprise, and I saw comprehension dawn. "Oh, my God, Claire!" he groaned.

"One night, Lock and I were having a drink at a certain club here in town, when Lamont Hooper walked in. When he saw us together, he came flying across the room in a jealous rage, yelling and screaming and stabbed me twice in the arm with—you won't believe this—a plastic swizzlestick!

"I was scared shitless, Claire. I'd never been around anything like that in my life. It took two bouncers to pull him off of me. I think he'd been doing PCP or something.

"Anyway, I lost about a half-pint of blood before they took me to Touro. Lamont nearly got an artery while he was at it.

"In the meantime, Lochner got hold of Babs, and she told him to offer me ten thousand dollars not to press charges. I said to tell her where she could shove her money. As long as she paid the hospital bills, I wouldn't prosecute Lamont. The less I had to do with him, the better, far as I concerned."

It explained so much. If ever there lived a "mean little colored boy" it was Lamont Hooper. Lamont, whose mother bailed him out of every scrape. Who knows how many others were bribed to drop charges?

Lamont, who knew he could get fired from any shop, and still be able to run back to LockSmith's. And here I'd always thought Lock had put up with him just for Babs's sake.

Ricky's perfect brow wrinkled. "But, Claire, that was over three years ago."

"Did you happen to see Lamont tonight?" I inquired.

He winced. "Yes."

"Do you honestly think he's changed for the better in the past three years?"

"Shit, Claire!" Ricky said miserably. "Obviously, they were both into that stuff, but I just don't think Lamont would kill him. Damn! This is awful."

"Horrible," I agreed. "But I got a couple more questions, Ricky. If you don't know the answers, maybe your guesses would be better than mine."

"What?" he asked dully.

"Do you have any idea how Lock got the money for"—I waved my arm around indicating the house and its contents—"all this?"

Ricky gave a genuine laugh. "Ask me something hard, Claire! Lock knew lots of naughty things about a lot of rich, important people. Just don't ask me how, because I don't know. Maybe some of his clients talked too much."

"You mean, blackmail?" Of all things, I hadn't expected this!

He nodded. "In fact, when we first met and romance was in the air, he told me the only way he could have ever afforded to go to Paris to train at Alexandre's was because he had a wealthy 'sponsor.' An Uptown man who would not care to have his wife and Carnival Crewe learn of his sordid little habits."

Ricky paused reflectively. "Come to think of it, he was amazingly indiscreet in the beginning. Infatuation with the brown *muchacho*, no doubt."

"Ricky, can we please bake that big old pity cake and have your pity party some other time? What I don't fully understand is how Lock was able to unearth enough people with sordid little habits to maintain this level of luxury."

"Yeah," Ricky agreed, sounding puzzled. "Hey, Claire. Maybe he had become some kind of Fagin character. And instead of orphans, he trained a bunch of 'mean little colored boys' to go out and get dirt on rich people!"

By creating such a ludicrous scenario, I knew Ricky was trying to lighten things up. Nevertheless, the basic concept appealed to me. Lock would have had to have a way of obtaining a high volume of negotiable information in order to sustain his lifestyle. But what had it been?

"I just remembered something else," Ricky said. "Did you know he lived in England for years after he finished studying in France?"

I nodded, and he went on, "Well, I'll bet you don't know he was being kept by some married lord or earl or some title, in a guesthouse on the estate, until they got in a big fight over a Pakistani cab driver. Oh, they had squabbled over everything from Hong Kong Chinese and India Indians, to jet black Rhodesian students with toff accents. But the Pakistani was the last straw, for some reason, and they broke up for good. It was just too *Upstairs, Downstairs*, for words."

So Lock had known whereof he spoke, living in the top drawer. Which hadn't stopped him from plundering through the bottom one.

"And now, Claire," Ricky wound up, "it's your turn to answer my original question: What the hell is going on?"

"Brace yourself, Ricky," I warned. "Lock taped a video the day before he died, and tonight is showtime."

Chapter 30

Ricky, declaring he was incapable of facing the prospect of viewing a posthumous Lock on one measly margarita, went off in search of more "Mexican courage."

Digby Baker, when he and Dan had adjourned their impromptu lawyer's confab, concurred heartily with Ricky's sentiments, and followed suit, still clutching the sealed video.

"No, Digby doesn't have a clue what's on the tape," Dan said, before I could ask. "I suspect he's more embarrassed about it than anything else. After all, Baker, Deville rarely finds itself smack in the middle of a lurid situation like this."

I had little sympathy to spare for Baker, DeVille's sensibilities. "Too bad, " I said, and rapidly plunged into a summary of Ricky's revelations, trying not to leave anything out.

Dan listened intently, his blue eyes narrowed in concentration. "Well, that explains a few things, anyway," he mused. "Now we know that Lochner Smith was a highrolling blackmailer, and the very worst kind of racist! We've also learned he had an ongoing relationship, for want of a better word, with Lamont, and that his death was most likely at the hands of somebody who didn't take kindly to being blackmailed."

"But that would let Lamont off the hook," I said. "He could hardly have had any secrets from Lock, or anybody else, for that matter."

"Hmm, that's true," Dan agreed. "Unless somebody used Lamont to do their dirty work. Anyway, we'd better impart this knowledge to, um, you know who, at the first opportunity. Where is she, anyway?"

"Behind you, Dan," I laughed. "And I don't think we'll be imparting knowledge anytime soon."

He turned to look at the corner where Honey Love was surrounded by men, thick as bees. At her side Marcel glowered possessively while his Honey flirted and cooed and the testosterone flowed.

It was quite a sight.

Harry Corvus gestured lavishly, flashing his pinky ring. "Are you quite sure we haven't met? You seem most awfully familiar."

"Yayis, Ah'm quite suah, Mr. Corvus," Honey purred, fluttering her lashes. "Ah know Ah would've remembered you. Ah just love a maayun with a sexy British ayeccent."

"Aw, now baby. That ain't too patriotic of you!"

Vince Platina, appearing to have gotten his second wind, swaggered up. I noticed he'd opened his shirt another two buttons to reveal plenty of cleavage. Some sort of religious medallion on a gold chain was tangled in his chest hair.

"Yeah, doilin'," he said. "You oughta be buying American. Italian-American, that is!"

Honey looked demure. "Oh, Mr. Platina. Ah'm afraid you Ahtalian meyun are way too hard for a girul lahk me to handle!"

Even Gino Gambara was about to get into the act, extending his cane like a scepter as Marzie reluctantly wheeled him over.

I was tickled to see him deftly use it like a billy club to prod Vince out of his path. "Hey, lady!" Gino greeted her, and then fell silent, content just to ogle appreciatively.

"Well, hey there yourself!" Honey trilled, bestowing a dazzling smile.

Marzie gazed at her with open displeasure. "Jus' where you say you be workin' in Baton Rouge, girl?" she asked.

Uh-oh. Gino's Emporium served the Baton Rouge area, and Marzie would probably get wise if she tried to make something up.

"Emergency!" I hissed to Dan, and moved quickly to join the group.

"Miss Love was telling me a while ago that she'd been working at Boose's over on Dalyrymple, Marzie," I burbled. "And excuse me for butting in everybody, but I forgot to ask earlier about Velma? I just had to find out if she doing okay after the operation?"

Surreptitiously, I flexed my hand a few times to alert Honey that Velma had recently undergone hand surgery.

"Oh, yayis! She's doing real good, Claire. Her fingers are stiyull a little bit stiyuff, but the doctor sayus not to worry, she'll be ayus good ayus new. Sheyull be so happy you ayusked about her!"

Mission accomplished, I returned to Dan. "When is the viewing?"

He checked his watch. "In ten minutes. Digby said Lochner set it for ten o'clock."

"I'm going to do a quick Renee check, then," I told him. "If she and Max didn't elope, I want to know where she is."

On the way to the kitchen, I passed Lamont, stuffing candy corn from the basket into his mouth. "You should've worn a costume," he reproved.

"I know, but there's no way I could've competed with yours, Lamont," I said truthfully. "I meant to ask you, are you portraying some specific breed of feline?"

Lamont stared at me like I was just too dense. "Well, duuh! A hellcat, of course."

Of course.

I found Max in the kitchen, but no Renee. "She went off with that nice young Italian man," Max informed me, but he didn't know where.

Well, at least wherever Renee was, I knew she was with Sal. Hopefully, that was good news.

When I returned to the party, there had been a new development.

Glowing happily, Babs was clinging to the arm of a big, handsome man who looked more like Billy Dee Williams than Billy Dee did.

After all these years, I had at last learned the identity of Babs's lover and the father of her demon seed.

I sensed Honey's sudden alertness when she became aware of the man, and knew Marcel was invoking every ounce of his considerable control to keep from blowing their cover.

Marzie drifted like a dark cloud to the couple, greeting him with a kiss. And why not? He was her son, and she'd met his father over the coffin of his previous wife, the mother of Duchess Crowe.

After a short conversation, Marzie returned to Gino and the group still clustered around Honey Love.

When Babs and her companion headed in our direction, Dan put his arm around me and murmured, "Yippee! Here comes more Halloween fun!"

"Oh, Claire!" Babs caroled, striving vainly for a casual tone. "Do you and Dan know Duke Abbidis?"

Chapter 31

On the stroke of ten, Lock's twenty or so remaining guests were herded into the Fred and Ginger living room.

Significantly, Harry Corvus didn't even seem to notice when Sal Romano walked in with his date, far more intent on getting that heartbreaker Honey Love to pay attention to him.

I was reminded of those lizards that frequently star in PBS nature documentaries, the ones that inflate some gland beneath their chins when they want to impress a female.

Vince Platina did react to the sight of Sal and Renee, but inertia had set in and he contented himself with directing an Italian hand gesture, involving a clenched fist, at Sal.

Both Babs Hooper and Marzipan Jones were disturbed by the fascinated glances Duke Abbidis was casting at Miss Honey Love, and I could imagine the discomfort the lady and her escort were feeling at his scrutiny. This was a real test of their masquerade.

Gino Gambara had drifted into an old man's light doze, emitting an occasional snore through his open mouth.

Among the handful of others, Ricky Gomez struck a grandee pose by the fireplace, determinedly working his way through another drink, while the hellcat Lamont perched on the back of a blue velvet sofa, his surprisingly large feet planted square in the middle of a seat cushion.

Digby Baker stood next to the alcove containing the television set presided over by Lochner Smith in Roseville.

He cleared his throat and began, "The day before Lochner Smith died, he came to my office with this sealed envelope." Digby held it aloft for all to see before continuing.

"His instructions to me were, in the event he met with an unnatural death, I was to play this video tape at ten o'clock of the evening of his 'farewell party,' which had already been arranged in advance, for the 'viewing pleasure,' as he put it, of everyone on the premises at that time."

He paused. "I am now about to execute Mr. Smith's final commission to me as his attorney. I have no idea what the tape contains, and you will note the wax seal, embossed with Mr. Smith's own thumbprint, is intact."

Digby reached into his pocket and withdrew a Swiss Army knife. As he selected a gadget suitable for breaking sealing wax from among many available options, I felt the room begin to throb with palpable apprehension.

Wedging something that looked like a cross between a butter knife and a corkscrew beneath the blob of wax, Digby heaved upward, and the thing popped like a champagne cork, releasing the tight strands of brown cord to dance in the air like live wires.

Without further ado, Digby extracted the tape, inserted it into the VCR, and punched PLAY.

And there was Lock, in death nearly as large as life on the big screen, seated behind a generic brown desk, against a generic blue backdrop, holding a sheet of paper.

He looked like a generic president, about to deliver a State of the Union address.

"Well, good evening, everyone. I hope I'm enjoying myself as much as you are, tonight."

This gave rise to too much uncomfortable speculation to elicit the laugh Lock had intended.

He leaned forward and raised his eyes as if trying to see the top of the television set. "Isn't that a lovely vase? I must say, I did not originally purchase it to fulfill such a mundane function. Then again, if anyone is going to get some use out of it, it might as well be me."

Everyone was staring at the screen as if hypnotized, hardly seeming to breathe.

"And now, let's get down to business, please," Lock said accusingly, as if we had been delaying him. How very like him.

"I have taken a calculated risk, which I have ample reason to believe has put my life in jeopardy. However, nothing ventured, nothing gained. Obviously, if you are watching this, it did not pay off.

"What is it? you are probably asking yourselves. I have always been amused at the dialogue that occurs at the place in the film where one character is assured by another they will be delighted to keep quiet about their guilty secrets . . . for a price.

"The character with the secret invariably exclaims, 'But—that's blackmail!' to which the other invariably replies, 'Oh, let's not call it *that!*'

"Well, tonight I am saying, 'Oh, let's *do* call it that!' Yes, I am now, and have always been, a blackmailer. No. I won't tell you how, or who, or where—any victims present may rest assured, your secrets have died with me."

Lock smiled wickedly and gazed directly into the camera. "Except for one. My murderer. I *do* draw the line at that! The reason I am fairly certain he—or she—will make an attempt on my life is that he—or she—has been getting away with murder for quite some time, and was not in the least pleased to be informed I had learned of it."

This was positively Hitchcockian. We were all on the edge of our seats. His next words were chilling.

"Oh, Duchess, dear. I mentioned that you were the one who originally discovered you had inadvertently acquired proof that murder had been done and who did it. And by now you have certainly deduced that I deceived you when I said that Lamont Hooper had stolen the items you so naively entrusted to my care and hidden them in a shop where he used to work, but refused to tell me where. The boy doesn't have a clue."

I stole a glance at Lamont, who was staring at Lock's image like a zombie. His cat ears were askew, and his whiskers had lost most of their sequins.

"I must say, I was taken aback when I heard on the news that Lamont's most recent place of employment had been destroyed, but felt quite certain you couldn't have managed such a feat with your own little hands. No doubt it was the work of that gorilla you sleep with, Vincent Platina."

Vince opened his mouth once or twice, but all that came out was a strangled sound. He didn't know how lucky he was that Francesca, Faylee and Mimi had gone on to another party and he was still attached to his *caglioni*.

"So, just in case you haven't figured it out yet, call off your goon before he wrecks every salon in town that Lamont has graced at one time or another.

"Really, darling. As a seasoned blackmailer yourself, you should have known not to trust another blackmailer."

Lock chuckled. "But, I digress. Now, I'm quite certain my killer is present among you tonight."

At that, everyone studiously avoided looking at each other.

"But, sir—or madam—don't panic! Surely if I intended to denounce you I would have already done so. I realize this tape will have come as something of a . . . shock, shall I say? And it wouldn't be playing the game, as someone back in England used to say.

"And so, I shall play the game of murder, my friend. I am going to read out some clues as to the location of the evidence you killed me to obtain, but have not yet succeeded in finding, as well as clues to your identity.

"Claire and Dan Claiborne!"

We jumped at the sound of our names.

"If you would schedule a brief pause in your bedroom gymnastics, and apply those fledgling sleuthing skills, I am confident you will discover the culprit.

"All right. Here are the clues. Listen carefully."

Lock consulted the sheet of paper before him, and began to read.

"Dan and Digby. As lawyers, this one's especially for you. *Avis avidus*.

"Next clue. It's not front page news, because it happens every day.

"Picture this! Rock and roll can be very shocking.

"Fergie must take good care of her special toy."

I saw Dan had his thin red leather notebook out and was scribbling hastily to keep up, as were one or two others, Harry among them. The whole thing was taking on the aspect of some macabre parlor game.

"Five. It's uncommonly dear at the price, but a fool, indeed, has great need of it.

"Six. *Sir* has a nice ring to it.

"And last, but not least. The first thing they look for after an airplane crash."

He crumpled the paper into a ball. "There! I think I've given a sporting chance to all concerned."

Lock glanced at his watch. "Oh, dear. I see time is running out. There are just one or two other things I want to say quickly.

"Digby, you may consider this an informal but definite codicil to my will. When you begin probate, you will make the terrible discovery that I have rather . . . overextended myself. However, I am certain that this house and its contents will bring in more than enough to cover what is owing, as well as your own fee, dear boy."

"Oh, great!" snarled Digby Baker.

Lock drummed his fingers on the desktop. "Let's see, what am I forgetting? Oh, yes! Remember earlier, when I said all my other victims' secrets would die with me? Well, I lied."

A collective gasp arose.

"I have never had any tolerance for drugs, or the people who purvey them. Yet I confess I have taken great pleasure over the past few years in collecting a great deal of money for not exposing those who where so engaged.

"However, I am no longer able to enjoy that privilege, and I abhor what drugs have done to dear Lamont, although much of his dilemma is certainly due to his parentage. And by the way, Barbara, Duke Abbidis will never marry you. Colored class beats white trash, every time. He is currently in ardent pursuit of a highfashion, highyellow policewoman."

Babs screeched, "What?" and half rose from her seat, resisting Duke's attempts to pull her back down beside him.

"Anyway," Lock continued, "as I was saying, Vincent Platina, Gino Gambara and Marzipan Jones are running drugs through Gino's Emporium, using various hairstylists as distributors. But by far, the biggest one-on-one traffic takes place at the Mirror Club—sorry again, Duchess—especially the very trendy concoction called grand slam.

"Which incidentally, is distilled by none other than that great little Italian cook, Vince's mother, Voncilla Platina."

"Stop the tape! Stop the tape!" roared Sal Romano. As he had a large gun in his hand, Digby Baker complied instantly.

Sal had something else in his other hand. A badge. "Police! Don't anybody move!" he shouted.

Renee watched adoringly as her hero, dodging the feeble flailings of Gino's cane, singlehandedly cuffed the aforementioned suspects who were ignoring their rights to remain silent. Gino and Vince were calling down a storm of Italian curses upon him, ably seconded by Marzie's own contribution which far surpassed even the original performance I'd witnessed.

Then Officer Sal Romano produced a wafer-thin cellular phone from the pocket of his tight jeans, and called for a squad car.

I noticed that Max had rushed in to investigate the commotion, but stopped just outside the doorway when he saw what was going on.

Suddenly, Lamont jumped off the sofa and began to scream at Honey Love. "You bitch! I know who you are and why you're here! You came to lock me up, didn't you? And now you're trying to take my daddy away from my mommy!"

He lunged at her, ripping the Whitney Houston wig from her head, then began to lash at her with his tail whip.

Caught off guard, it took the unmasked Nectarine a moment to extricate herself from the depths of the velvet sofa, during which time Lamont managed to lay a deep red welt onto her neck.

"No, darling! Get back!" she ordered Marcel, who was poised to hurl himself sacrificially between them.

Taking judicious aim at portions of Lamont's anatomy with those lethal Manola Blahniks, she quickly subdued him, and he collapsed onto the sofa, weeping.

"No don't take another step, Ms. Hooper!" she panted, as Babs started to run over to him.

"I'm sorry, I'm sorry!" wailed Lamont. "He was going to leave me and go away to England forever. Then he told me to get lost, he had a business appointment. But I knew he was lying, he had a date.

"So I tricked him into letting me tie him up, and I stuffed his mouth with cotton so he couldn't yell. And then I went off and left him! But I didn't kill him! I swear!"

Duke Abbidis called out to Lamont, "Don't say another word, son." He added to Nectarine, without meeting her eyes, "I'm speaking as his attorney now, not his father."

In the lull that followed, Dan asked Digby if the tape had finished running.

Digby shook his head as if to clear it, and said, "I don't think there could've been much more."

He pushed the button, and Lock's face reappeared.

"Well, I believe that's about it. Oh, wait! Barbara, did I mention that the person who came up with the idea of distributing drugs through Gino's to various salons and was using the Mirror Club to launder drug money, is your beloved Duke Abbidis?"

As the picture turned to static, Duke Abbidis reached swiftly for Nectarine, and jerked her in front of him. A small but nasty-looking gun had appeared in his right hand.

"Don't anybody move, or I'll blow her head off!" he stated flatly.

Sal Romano froze in the act of reaching for his own gun again.

Marcel's face was suffused with horror, and I saw the naked love in his eyes. In that instant, he was a loose cannon, capable of anything.

Nectarine saw it too, and gave him a look that plainly commanded, "No!" as Duke Abbidis backed out through the doorway, dragging her in front of him.

He was completely unprepared for the heavy metal tray that slammed down on top of his head, or the subsequent karate chop that broke his wrist and sent the gun spinning across the glossy wood floor.

Detective Sergeant Nectarine Savoy, aka Honey Love, barely had time to tell Max, "Thank you, Officer Maxwell," before she was swept into Marcel's arms.

Chapter 32

"Believe me, I never go into any situation like that without backup," Nectarine Savoy explained, adding that undercover officer Maxwell frequently worked the catering circuit.

It was nearly a week after the Halloween party to end all Halloween parties. Foley had just finished signing with a real estate agent to sell the enormous house on Newcomb he had shared with his ex-wife Belinda, and he and Charlotte were celebrating by serving wine and cheese one last time on the terrace to Nectarine and Marcel, Dan and me.

"Sounds like a mighty wild night," Foley commented, slapping at a mosquito. "Sorry we had to miss it."

"You're forgetting we weren't invited, Foley," Charlotte reminded him. "And are you saying you would have preferred to be there involved in some brawl, instead of where you were, with me in that dark, romantic edit bay?"

Foley blew her a kiss. "Not at all, darlin'," he denied cheerfully. "Only the romantic aspects of edit bays are starting to wear a little thin for me, if you want to know the truth.

"But I was trying to make the best of it, until that Harry Corvus oiled in and started breathing down our necks. More specifically, your neck, on the pretext of viewing the tape."

Charlotte laughed. "It wasn't a pretext, Foley-pie. He really did want to see the tape. After all, 'A Bad Hair Day' is a major project for the station. Especially now, let's admit it, since somebody was killed."

Foley went around the terrace, topping everyone's glass with Mouton Cadet.

Marcel stirred. "I was curious about that, Charlotte. Have you got some good things?"

"Plenty," Charlotte assured him. "More importantly though, you look simply marvelous."

"I'm sure you are far too kind," he murmured, pleased.

"I'm not kind at all, just ask Foley!" Charlotte said. "In fact, I just happen to have a very rough cut in my bag. We can stick it on the VCR right now!"

Foley groaned. "Oh, no. Please, not tonight! Forget 'A Bad Hair Day.' I've seen that tape so many times, I feel like Bill Murray in *Groundhog Day*! No matter when I look at the monitor, Charlie here is replaying that same scene of people going upstairs. Any minute I'm expecting to hear Sonny and Cher singing, 'I Got you, Babe'."

Charlotte joined the laughter, but said, "Honey, I can't help it. There's something strange I can't put my finger on. But you're right. I may as well throw it out because it doesn't really work at all."

Nectarine sipped her wine. "You know what, Charlotte? I'd like to see that tape myself. I haven't had a chance to look at all the raw footage Buddy sent over by Officer Cates."

Charlotte grinned. "That reminds me. I'm to tell you that Buddy wishes you would send Officer Cates to conduct an in-depth investigation into his private life!"

"Okay, we'll go in and watch the damn tape!" Foley capitulated. "But not until we get the official version of what's been going on."

Without removing his caressing fingers from the back of my neck, Dan concurred. "I don't mind admitting I'm still extremely unclear about the facts, Nectarine."

The problem, as Nectarine revealed, was there were far too many facts.

First of all, a few of the suspects were singing like canaries, particularly the Italian baritone.

Faced with the evidence he knew his *paisano* Sal Romano had against him, Vincent Platina admitted, based on the lie Lock told Duchess, he had wrecked the salons of Faylee Wilkins and Mimi Fontenot because those were the last two places Lamont had worked.

Duchess's instructions were to look for a leather case, which she said contained her marriage certificate to Teddy Boy Crowe, Tom's birth certificate, a ring, and another article she described as "a solid gold record." The literal-minded Vince naturally assumed she was referring to a lost recording by Teddy Boy Crowe and that he'd enjoy a share in the untold royalties Duchess would certainly reap from such a thing. Which explained Vince's ready willingness to conduct those crude search-and-destroy missions.

Failing to find anything, it occurred to them that Lamont always returned to the Prytania Street LockSmith's. By then, they were beginning to suspect that Lock was jerking them around, but they weren't sure.

In any case, armed with his trusty baseball bat, Vince had dutifully shown up at Prytania Street at 8:10, only to see that, though the blinds were drawn, all the lights were still on.

While he was trying to decide what to do next, he saw somebody run out the side door and around to the alley. A beat later, he heard a car start up and take off.

Curious, he let himself in through that same door, which had been left ajar, and that's when he'd discovered Lock, dead as dead.

Then he figured, what the hell, he'd give himself fifteen minutes to search for Duchess's things, then split.

He had to have enjoyed himself just a little bit, smashing up Lock's place. This was the guy who'd been blackmailing them over Mama Voncilla's homecooked drugs.

Vince had been the one to phone an anonymous tip to the cops, so he wasn't totally heartless. And he had recognized the man he'd seen running from the shop.

It was Duke Abbidis.

Duke, confronted with an eyewitness, readily admitted he'd gone to Lock's in response to a frantic phone call from Babs, at about ten minutes to eight, who had received her own panicky call from Lamont, telling her he'd left Lock tied up and helpless.

Duke had rushed over to release Lock, only to find him already dead.

Unless any or all of them were lying, the time frame for Lock's murder was between 7:15 when Lamont had left him bound and gagged, and around 8:05 when Duke claimed to have arrived. One ugly little detail that came to light was that the hairdryer was no longer running when Duke came onto the scene, having already burnt out after doing its dirty work.

There remained that mysterious 7:30 P.M. business appointment Lock allegedly told Lamont about, which would certainly fit in with what he'd called "a calculated risk."

But jealous Lamont hadn't believed him, and literally left Lock a sitting duck for his killer to cook. However Lock had expected to go, I'm sure it hadn't been that way.

Marzie, Gino and Voncilla weren't talking at all. They were busy trying to find themselves new lawyers, since their "staff attorney" was having legal problems of his own.

At least Marcel had been able to clear up one mystery, that of the relationship between Dominica Dolcevita and Gino Gambara. Gino was her uncle. Her father broke with his brother's business associates because he no longer wished to live a life of crime. They had gone him one better and relieved him of his life. Period.

That old strip of photos I'd seen on Gino's bulletin board was a teenage Dominica. Family is still family, no matter what.

The D.A. hadn't yet decided whether to bring murder charges against Lamont for Lock's death. Lamont swore up and down he hadn't stuck that blowdryer in his mouth. Presently, he was undergoing a battery of psychiatric testing to determine if he was fit to stand trial on any charges at all.

The autopsy of Duchess Crowe revealed massive amounts of grand slam and Quaaludes in her bloodstream, but that's not what killed her. She had died from sodium cyanide dissolved in dimethyl sulfoxide, otherwise known as DMSO, which enabled it to penetrate the skin, and kill within a very few minutes.

Since poison was suspected from the beginning, they had routinely looked for the classic signs of cyanide; a smell of almonds, blue fingernails when that bright red polish was removed, cherry-colored blood. But the DMSO part was admittedly a fluke.

DMSO is not poisonous in and of itself, and because it does penetrate the skin immediately, would ordinarily leave no trace of its presence. However, some sharp forensic person had noted a distinctive cabbagy odor coming from a slightly tacky stain on the front of her smock. When analyzed, that's what it turned out to be.

The examiner said there was absolutely no way to tell how it had been administered, but whoever had done it would have had to make certain that none of it touched their own skin, sourly pointing out that the place was crawling with latex gloves.

His best guess was that the point of contact was her nasal passages, completely raw from snorting grand slam and who knows was else. They would have acted like sponges to absorb the poison.

I remembered noticing a few dusty jars of DMSO in Gino's "natural remedies" section.

Savoy said yes, the police had discovered those when they got a search warrant for Gino's, but were far more excited about busting Voncilla, who'd been in her gourmet drug kitchen when they came, whipping up a batch of her secret recipe for grand slam on one burner, and pot of spaghetti sauce on the other.

As far as the time frame for Duchess' death, it had to have been that brief period between when I'd seen Vicky Su and Duchess talking, to when I'd witnessed Lamont lifting her dryer hood.

In one way, it let Tom Toy off the hook since he had left soon after returning from his junket to K&B. Unless they were able to prove he had somehow set the whole thing up before leaving, maybe collaborating with Vicky Su?

But what would Tom Toy have to gain by killing Lock to get hold of evidence proving his own legitimate birth and parentage? Lock had belatedly warned Duchess whoever got him would come after her, too.

The cops didn't really like either Tom or Vicky for one or both murders, but who else was left?

Unless it was Babs Hooper. But that didn't make sense. The only person Babs would kill for was Lamont, and neither Duchess or Lock had posed a threat to her baby, as far as anyone knew.

We discussed every variation on these themes we could think of, no matter how bizarre, but there was still a big piece missing.

At last, Foley stood up and stretched. "I guess we might as well go in and look at Charlotte's tape, now. The things I do for you, woman."

Charlotte moved close to him. "But just think about the things I'm going to do for you, Foley-pie."

He laughed. "I am rarely capable of thinking about anything else, baby. Come on inside, everybody. Try not to let any moths or mosquitos ride in on you. They'll lower the property value."

But all I could tell after watching the roughcut of 'A Bad Hair Day,' was that it was going to be thoroughly delightful when finished.

When Foley's famous recurring staircase scene came up, and he began to drone those immortal lyrics about love not paying the rent, I saw nothing that should have prompted Charlotte to keep going back over it.

There really wasn't much to see, unless you wanted to meditate on the poignancy of it being Duchess Crowe's last appearance on any earthly stage. The straggly little line of Duchess, Vicky Su, Tom Toy loaded like a pack mule with supplies, a sharp swerve of the camera when Buddy stepped on that hair roller, which caught the top of Charlotte's bright head as she followed behind with her microphone.

There were a few jerky frames of blurry faces watching from the foot of the stairs, mine among them.

According to the counter, it had taken all of three seconds for Buddy to regain his footing.

"Foley's right," Charlotte said, decisively, ejecting the tape. "That bit doesn't work at all. It's too abrupt to blend in, and not deliberate enough to be Felliniesque. I'm going to cut from when they just start up the stairs, to when Vicky Su puts her under the dryer."

Foley rose from his chair and began to circle a standing lamp, peering down at the floor.

Dan laughed. "You maniac! What the hell are you doing?"

"Look!" Foley pointed. "I see my shadow!"

Chapter 33

Thursday morning dawned with a November nip in the air, the perfect excuse to wear my new suit to lunch at Galatoire's with Dan. It was short and sassy, with a tassel belt, frogged jacket, and lots of gold buttons, in fuzzy mohair the color of ripe watermelons.

Juanita's sister, Bonita, more or less copied it right from a fashion magazine pictorial purporting to chronicle an average day in the life of Claudia Schiffer. And, without undue modesty, I felt it looked every bit as good on me as it did on Claudia. Not to mention, it had cost less than a tenth of hers.

The morning's appointments went unusually smoothly, largely thanks to Renee's return from the living dead.

On one hand, I was glad to see the sparkle back in those big brown Cajun eyes. On the other, I wanted to urge her to go slow with Sal, to get some inner healing for her wounded little spirit before getting too involved with another man.

I sighed, knowing I'd better just stay out of it. Anyway, Sal Romano had been the one who'd watched over Renee from afar as best he could without blowing his cover at the Mirror Club, and fallen in love with her in the process.

Chauvinistic Vince boasted to Sal, whom he believed to be part of the Gino/Mirror Club drug ring, that he had something on Renee guaranteed to turn her into a fine little mule, which I gathered was a slang term for someone who carried drugs.

When Renee finally poured out her story, I could almost look back and chart her spiritual, mental and physical spiral downward.

After her breakup with Beaudine Guidry, and his rebound engagement, Renee started hanging out regularly at the Mirror Club.

She was understandably depressed, and her self-esteem was so low, it left her easy prey for a carnivore like Vince Platina.

He persuaded her to try a little cocaine, something she'd never done in her life, to "cheer her up." But Renee's reaction to the drug was to unleash a flood of confidences to exactly the wrong person.

This is how Vince learned that Beaudine had persuaded her to let him take nude photographs of her, and videos of them together. Renee's shame over this had been festering so long, all it took was a snort of cocaine to expose it.

And Vince used Renee's own confidences against her. He stole the items from her apartment (the poor kid had never figured out how to effectively get rid of the stuff) threatening to mail copies to her parents and to me if she didn't start pushing drugs to clients in my shop.

Evidently, Gino's ring had been very successful in recruiting stylists for a little drug dealing on the side.

Renee, who had become Vince's sexual toy by then, was too frightened to refuse, and he'd assigned her a quota to sell within a certain period of time, at the expiration of which he required payment in cash.

In desperation, she accepted the goods, which were unobtrusively delivered along with legitimate supplies from Gino's. But instead of pushing, she'd merely stashed the stuff around her nail salon, and paid Vince from her own pocket.

But then he started increasing her quota, and she could barely keep up financially.

After Vince's arrest, Sal had slipped over to Eclaire and quietly removed twenty or so boxes, regardless of the risk to himself.

I hadn't scheduled any more clients for today, which would leave me a totally free afternoon, but Renee had several manicure-pedicure appointments.

Telling her to offer her hair services if anybody else wanted to come in today, I went upstairs to get dressed.

Dan called while I was debating whether to wear black or tan stockings, which would, of course, require completely different shoes and bags.

"Hey, darlin', guess what?"

"Well, I hope you don't have to cancel lunch, my big lovebucket, because I look good," I informed him.

"Not if you don't mind Digby Baker horning in," Dan responded.

"Digby? How'd he get into the act?" I inquired absently, deciding on the very sheerest black stockings and black suede Pancaldi pumps trimed in gold braid.

"Well, he just called a few minutes ago to invite me to lunch, on account of he was so damn glad I was there at Lochner's the other night. I protested I hadn't done anything but sit there like a lump while people were yelling and screaming and pulling guns and cracking whips and all. But Digby insisted before any of that drama unfolded, the minute he walked in the door and saw what kind of crowd it was, he'd felt a gibbering fit about to come upon him. And then he spotted me.

"But I told him I already had an unbreakable lunch date with my wife, and he said fine, we'll all go.

"I cautioned him we'd planned to go to Galatoire's, and he said perfect, because he had to be in the Quarter this afternoon anyhow, for a meeting at the Vieux Carré Commission. Then he's going to do a walk-through of Lochner's house."

"Sounds fine to me. I liked Digby," I assured Dan. The whole time we'd been talking, I'd been sliding on stockings and shoes. Perfect.

Now for hair and earrings.

"Dan, would you prefer I wear my hair up or down?"

"Up," he replied at once. "You haven't done that in awhile, and I like how those diamond pavé heart earrings I gave you look with a French twist or whatever."

In a lower voice he added, "Actually, you're my little Cajun twist, aren't you baby?"

"Mmm, Dan! I'm trying to put on my makeup and you're steaming up the mirror, here!" I laughed. "And you'd better promise to behave yourself at the table today, since we've got company," I advised.

"Now, darlin', you know I don't make promises I can't keep," Dan said huskily.

But he did make a few other promises that I knew he was fully capable of keeping, causing my face to grow so warm I saw I didn't need to bother putting on any blusher.

We hung up and I generously puffed myself here and there with a mist of Ivoire de Balmain, Dan's favorite perfume, in preparation for a lazy, carefree afternoon.

I dropped a small atomizer of the same fragrance into my bag for touchups later, little knowing that before this day was done, I'd be wishing it had been a can of pepper spray, instead.

Chapter 34

Galitoire's restaurant was established at the turn of the century, when Bourbon Street was still an elegant gaslit thoroughfare graced by stately homes and the French Opera House, where the likes of Sarah Bernhardt performed, and the name Rue de Bourbon evoked splendid imagery of France's royal family, instead of drunken lowlife.

Nevertheless, Galitoire's itself remains every bit as fashionable and in demand nearly a hundred years later as it was then. And, so I'm told, it looks almost exactly the same, too, from its green-curtained swinging entrance doors, white-tiled floors and ceiling fans, to the coatracks, the old clock and the reception desk.

And the food.

Since I was feeling particularly svelte, I'd already decided to order the sumptuous Trout Marguery, with shrimp and truffles, which I had been thinking sensuous thoughts about all morning. That is, if our waiter approved my choice. Sometimes those Galitoire waiters take matters into their own hands and if you're smart, you'll eat what they bring you.

When I arrived Digby Baker and Dan were already furnished with martinis on the rocks, and had their heads together over Dan's notebook, lying open to the page where he'd scrawled down Lock's clues.

I didn't know if the cops were even bothering to try to crack the code, but us amateurs were having no luck at all.

Both men stood politely as I approached and Dan said, "Well, I see what I want, but it ain't on this menu!"

"Thank you, darling. Hello, Digby," I added, shaking hands. "Have you recovered from our Halloween adventure?"

Digby's expensive lawyer pinstripes quivered slightly with his reminiscent shudder. "Yes, but it's left a scar," he said, with a hollow laugh. "I thought I knew Lochner Smith fairly well, but it turns out I didn't know the half of it."

After a delicate sip of my straight up Bombay martini, I indicated Dan's notebook. "You boys making any progress with that?"

Dan looked sheepish. "We've gotten about as far as deciding '*avis avidus*' is not a reference to car rentals."

"Oh, that's a brilliant deduction!" I scoffed. "I thought you lawyers could just flip your Latin switch and start spouting pro tems and corpuses and nolos all over the place."

Digby laughed. "Actually, we do know the literal translation, Claire. *Avis* means 'bird,' and *avidus* means 'greedy'."

"Hmm." I stared at the words. "It's almost like he's telling us his killer is a greedy bird."

"Okay, that's good," Dan said. He tore the clues out of the notebook so we could all look at them, and began a fresh page.

"*Avis avidus*. A greedy bird."

Digby raised a caveat. "But was he using bird as the British slang for woman? Or merely as a certain type of character who could be either sex?"

"Or, maybe the Latin name for a specific bird?" I suggested.

"What comes next?" Digby asked, buttering a piece of fragrant hot bread that had just been delivered to our table.

" 'Not front page news, because it happens every day'," I read out.

"Well, hell! That could be just about anything," Dan fretted, chewing at the cap of his aged Mont Blanc. "The sun comes up, politicians lie, hearts get broken."

Digby rattled the ice in his glass pensively. "You wake up, shave, eat breakfast, brush your teeth, go to work—" he broke off in mid-recital and unexpectedly sang the opening line to "Alfie."

"That's a tough one," I agreed. "You know, these almost sound like clues to a crossword puzzle. I wonder if he meant that whatever it is would be front page news if it *didn't* happen everyday?

"He didn't say it *wasn't* news," I realized suddenly, "just not *front page* news!"

Dan nodded. "That's got to be it, Claire. Which would leave us with stuff like, say, car accidents, suicides, homicides, domestic violence, robberies. What else is in the paper?

"Comic strips, Erma Bombeck, weather, sports, society, weddings, births and deaths," I ticked off on my fingers.

"Man. Woman. Birth. Death. Infinity." Digby intoned. "Remember Dan, that funny old doctor drawing those signs on the blackboad? Was it *Ben Casey*, or *Dr. Kildare?*"

Neither of them could recall for sure, but showed signs of being willing to debate the issue indefinitely.

I headed them off at the pass. "Anyway, Dan. Write down that it's something you could find in the paper every day."

"Yes'm Miss Claire," he murmured.

"That's telling her, Dan," chortled Digby.

We paused in this great intellectual exercise long enough to give the waiter our requests.

"Do you think he acted like I had a good chance of getting Oysters Rockerfeller?" Digby asked wistfully, and I said he'd seemed pretty noncommittal.

Dan consulted the clue list. "Picture this! 'Rock and roll can be very shocking'."

We kicked that one around without coming up with anything beyond maybe a particularly gross rock and roll group album cover, but that would be like trying to find a needle in a haystack.

The fourth clue, about Fergie taking good care of her special toy, was easy. Sarah Ferguson, Duchess of York, equalled a warning to Duchess Crowe that Tom Toy was in danger. But what, and from whom?

The arrival of Digby Baker's Oysters Rockerfeller inspired him to new heights on clue five. " 'It's uncommonly dear at the price, but a fool indeed has great need of it'," he repeated, his brows drawn together in puzzlement.

"I know that's a quotation, but something's wrong about it. I keep hearing a rhyme, or a song, but then . . ."

He trailed off, and seemed to concentrate entirely on his oysters, and I couldn't blame him because mine were delicious, too. Our waiter had decided we were all going to have them.

Digby looked up suddenly and laughed. "By George, I think I've got it! That first line is from some Gilbert and Sullivan thing, don't ask me which, but it goes, 'Tum-tum-tee, tum-tum-tee, tum-tum,tee, —quite nice, but a title's uncommonly dear at the price!' "

Rewarding himself with another oyster, he chewed blissfully, then went on. "But the rest is part of a quote about how a fool indeed has great need of a title, because it forces people to call him by something besides his proper title of fool."

Dan wrote, "Title."

I asked, "Do you think that means a title like a book, or a song? Or a title deed? A car title?"

Dan was staring at number six. " '*Sir* has a nice ring to it'," he read aloud. "I think Lock was talking about a British title." He made a notation.

We were served marvelous salads I didn't remember hearing anyone order. And then, finally, three sizzling plates of Trout Marguery. I took a bite and it tasted so good, tears came to my eyes.

"Well, this last one, the first thing they look for after an airplane crash, seems self-explanatory," Digby stated. "Obviously, it's the black box. Lochner is telling us, and warning his killer, that he had taken steps to record whatever happened between them."

Dan straightened attentively. "I think you're right, Digby," he said. "But if that's so, how come the cops didn't find it?"

Digby mopped his plate with a chunk of bread before replying. "Probably because they didn't know there was such a thing to be found. So why should they be looking for it? And if by chance they saw microphone wires, they might assume it was part of the sound system. The few times I was in there, he had speakers all over the place."

I'd thought of something else. "Now the killer knows what to look for."

"I think I'd better go phone Sergeant Savoy," Dan said, starting to push back his chair, but Digby pulled a cellular phone from his breast pocket.

"Use this," he said.

When Dan was put through to Savoy, his end of the conversation sounded a little diffident, since he didn't want her to think he was telling her how to do her job.

But she took his suggestion quite seriously, indicating she'd get somebody over to the Prytania LockSmith's right away.

Apparently she asked him what we were doing, and Dan explained we were just finishing lunch with Digby Baker.

He put his hand over the mouthpiece. "She says Marcel thought they'd come by the house for a drink later, okay?"

I reached for the phone. "Hey, Nectarine. What time were you thinking?"

"Oh, whatever's good for you. Marcel's picking me up here at seven."

I looked at my watch. Nearly four. I proceeded to rattle off our itinerary to Nectarine, not that she was particularly curious.

Dan was going to drop me off at WBGZ to hang around with Charlotte, while he made a trip to Rubenstein Brothers because Dave Louis required his wardrobe advice.

Then we would meet up with Digby at Lock's about five-thirty, because he insisted he needed us to hold his hand while he did the preliminary walk-through.

"That shouldn't take us more than an hour?" It was a statement to Savoy, and a question to Digby, who nodded.

"Okay, see you about seven-thirtyish," I told her. "By the way, how are things in the romance department?"

There was a long pause. "Scary," said Detective Sergeant Nectarine Savoy.

Chapter 35

Baroness Almonaster de Pontalba had been a lady of style and means, greatly involved in the design and construction of her two gracious apartment buildings flanking Jackson Square. Her many touches, such as the exquisite wrought-iron balconies displaying her flowing monogram at frequent intervals, have thankfully survived until the present day.

I entered the spanking new offices of WBGZ-TV and was directed to where Charlotte was editing by a costly bimbette seated behind a desk that looked as if it had been heisted from Versailles.

As I ascended the graceful curves of a spiral staircase leading to the upper reaches, I felt that the Baroness would be proud of the extensive restoration work on her Toulouse Street side building.

Buddy Gaines, who was just coming out of Edit Bay three as I approached, gave a long wolf whistle.

"Hot damn, Claire! You look like somebody's expensive girlfriend in that getup!"

"Oink, you chauvinist pig!" Charlo chastised, swiveling her chair around from the monitor she'd been hunched over. "Claire always looks like a kept woman because Dan Claiborne treats his wife like some adulterous husbands only treat their girlfriends. Nothing but the best. But when it comes to the women they're actually married to? Shoot, those dogs lay out more money on their cars than they'd ever dream of spending on a new dress or a day at the beauty parlor for their *wives!*"

Buddy raised his hands in mock surrenderr. "Geez! I meant it as a compliment!"

"Well, that's exactly my point," Charlo retorted. "And don't forget, Buddy Gaines. If you should ever be so fortunate as to find yourself a loving wife, I'll be watching to make sure you coddle her like a high-priced courtesan!"

"Gimme a break, I'm a good guy!" he whined.

"I'll be the judge of that!" Charlotte called after his hastily retreating back.

I was laughing as I slid into the chair next to hers at a long counter lined with complex rows and knobs, lights, switches and levers, beneath a bank of video monitors.

"One thing I know for true is Foley Callant's going to spoil his wife rotten."

She grinned. "And that's the way things ought to be, to paraphrase dear Rush. But seriously, Claire. What about all those guys who don't actually cheat on, or physically abuse their wives, but bascially neglect them, or make them feel like they don't deserve a little pampering and some good perfume, until spiritual and physical attrition sets in?"

"Hmm, I feel an investigative report coming on," I observed.

"You must admit, it's a different angle," Charlotte said. "Meanwhile, though, 'A Bad Hair Day' is lasting throughout all eternity, amen."

"What's the matter? I thought you were nearly finished."

"Well, I am, actually," she admitted. "It's just those special Charlotte Dalton brushstrokes I'm looking to add now. Just give me a minute to get this chunk out of the way."

She punched a few buttons and yards of tape fast-forwarded across the screen. Even at that speed, and without a soundtrack, I could see the comparative slickness of this version over the one she'd played for us the other night at Foley's.

From time to time, Charlotte would stop the tape and mark down something on a long sheet of paper, muttering things like, "room noise," or "music under," and "voice-over."

The process was mesmerizing, and I was a little startled when she froze on a closeup of my Reba-wannabe country singer (whose real name, believe it or not, turned out to be Gale Evans) and said, "So, what've you been getting up to, dressed in that fancy outfit, Claire? No good, I hope!"

"Well, not as no good as we'd originally planned." I told her about our Digby Baker lunch and how we'd so earnestly wrestled to solve Lock's final riddles.

"The CIA, we ain't!" I concluded, ruefully.

Charlo chuckled. "The CIA probably doesn't swill down martinis during decoding hours. Then again, maybe they do,"

Her eyes strayed to the monitors again. "I'd almost forgotten about those clues. Let me take a look at them,

Claire. Maybe a fresh, not to mention sober, perspective would help."

"Well, I don't have the clues themselves," I said, fishing through my black suede bag, "but I do have the list of what I will laughingly refer to as our answers. Maybe I can remember some of the questions, though." I waved the slightly crumpled sheet from Dan's notebook at her.

"Just a minute, Claire, while I start the B-roll running." Charlotte pushed a button which lit up the monitor next to the one emblazoned with Gale Evans's face, explaining that a B-roll consists of footage left over from the actual first rough cut.

"During the refining process, if we run short and need some filler, or want to put in additional shots for texture, we go to the B-roll," she elaborated. "But, on its own, it's just a mishmash of uninteresting stuff."

I soon saw what she meant, as scene after boring scene lumbered across the screen.

Charlotte glanced periodically at the monitor, while scanning the scrawled and food-spattered list, asking me an occasional question.

"Well, Claire," she said, finally, "I find this highly impressive. Perhaps the CIA should consider dosing their cryptologists with gin, after all."

"Why?" I asked.

She looked exasperated. "Why? Because you three drunken monkeys somehow managed to come up with a fairly coherent, albeit fuzzy, translation of what the late Lochner Smith was trying to say. Listen, while I put it into my own words." She squinted thoughtfully at the paper.

"His killer is a greedy bird, male or (British slang) female, with possibly a bird's first or last name. Whatever started this was in the newspaper, but not on the front page. Somewhere, there is a shocking rock and roll picture that ties into the whole thing. Duchess had better look out for Tom, because he's in danger from somebody. Plus, there is a British title that comes with lots of money and a very nice ring. Lochner knew he was risking death, so he made sure it was caught on tape."

"We figured out all that? Now I'm impressed!" I said. "But you got one thing wrong, Charlo. The clue said that the title 'sir' had a very nice ring. Not a ring, per se."

" 'Per se?' There you go with the Latin, lawyer's wife!" she teased. "Anyway, how do you know for sure?" Her eyes jumped to the B-roll monitor.

"Aha!" she exclaimed, and pounced on a button. "I knew there was something wrong about that shot!"

"What?" I asked.

"Look, Claire. Remember the scene Foley kept nagging me about running over and over? And I said it wasn't a question of whether I wanted to use it or not, but there was something wrong, or missing?"

Without waiting for my reply, she punched on the other monitor and the picture zipped forward on warp speed as Charlotte explained.

"When Buddy and I made the original rough, we included some of the random shots that little Filipino intern, Andy, had been darting around getting. The advantage is he's so small, hardly anybody notices him. Anyway, he'd shot some stuff from the back as that tacky parade was going up the stairs."

She stopped tape at the frame where Buddy had almost taken a tumble down the risers and pointed. "See? That's Andy there, over by that bench where Duchess and Tom were sitting. You can see him aiming his camera, right?"

"Right."

"Now, look over here. I swear we originally put this shot in, but here it is, mysteriously stuck onto the end of the B-roll, completely out of sequence."

She started the tape and I saw everything I'd seen before, only from behind.

Vicky Su leading Duchess up the stairs, wobbly from drugs and that extra dose of Quaaludes, courtesy of Lamont; Buddy's sudden swerve as he stepped on the roller; Charlotte dodging, and Harry, still at the foot of the stairs in the act of turning away from Andy's camera, bringing up the rear. He held Duchess's box of Kleenex at arm's length, as if fearing her germs would jump all over him, an expression of profound distaste on his face.

I noticed something flutter to the floor behind him.

"Charlotte, when may I expect to see a reasonably finished piece?" demanded a curt voice. "I'd rather hoped to take it along to our corporate meeting in Los Angeles next week."

She sighed. "Well, Harry. I do think I'd already be done by now if the gremlins hadn't tampered with my footage and had me thinking I'd lost my mind. And you might say hello to Claire, while you're at it?"

Harry looked at me with disfavor, obviously unaffected by my resemblance to a small Claudia Schiffer. "Oh. Good afternoon, Claire," he said perfunctorily, and immediately redirected his attention to Charlotte.

"And just what did these gremlins do?"

Charlotte explained, pointing to the missing link that had been bothering her, and Harry laughed.

"Silly girl!" he admonished. "Why didn't you come tell me? I took that bit out myself."

Charlotte stared at him. "You did what?"

Harry laughed again, in that boyish way I disliked so much. "Well, to be perfectly honest, my dear. I was so anxious to see if we'd managed to capture the look, the *feel*, we were after, that I just couldn't resist taking a peek. And then, quite without realizing it, I found myself actually making some creative decisions that were properly yours to make. You will forgive me, won't you?" He smiled winningly.

His profile, in the dim blue light pulsating from the monitors, reminded me of someone, but I couldn't think who.

"I guess so," Charlotte said grudgingly. "Although I wish you'd told me before I practically snatched myself baldheaded! Anyway, if you liked it with that part gone, you'll like it even better now. That whole scene is out."

Harry moved closer to get a better view of the monitors, and I saw him wince. His limp was more pronouced than usual.

I got up. "Sit down, Harry." I invited.

"Thanks, I don't mind if I do," he replied with a grimace.

"What's the matter, your superior British bone medicine not cutting the mustard?" Charlotte jibed.

"Not at all!" he said defensively. "My supply seems to have suddenly run short. I shall have to get my chemist to ship me a larger quantity."

His eye fell on our answer list. "What's this, may I ask?"

With a laugh, Charlotte explained Digby's, Dan's and my brilliant deductions of Lock's clues.

Harry listened, seeming interested for a change, and I was reminded he'd taken his own notes.

"Might I make a copy to compare with mine?" he requested. "Or wouldn't that be playing the game?"

I looked at my watch. "Sure, if you do it right now. Digby Baker wants Dan and me to meet him at Lock's house."

Harry rose painfully. "Whatever for?"

"Oh, I think he's still got the Halloween heebiejeebies about the place," I diagnosed. "Plus, he didn't plan on having to unload it right away to settle Lock's estate.

"If you make him a good offer, Harry, I'm sure he'd be willing to sell it to you, lock, stock and barrel, no pun intended."

"None taken," Harry said, limping away with the paper to the photocopy room.

He was back in a few moments. "This is certainly quite sporting of you, Claire," Harry said, returning my original to me.

I waved a magnanimous hand. "Think nothing of it, Harry. After all, it's not as if there's a prize for the winner or anything."

Harry Corvus tilted his head, and again I experienced a fleeting moment of recognition. "Oh, I rather think there is, don't you know!" he said.

Chapter 36

It was already ten past five and Decatur is not my favorite street after dark. I set a fast clip from WBGZ to the other side of Jackson Square, resolutely ignoring the denizens who seem to swarm up from the wharves at sundown.

Thinking of Harry Corvus, I smiled, knowing he was destined for Charlotte Dalton's wrath.

The more she'd stewed over his blithe admission that he hadn't considered it necessary to inform her he'd altered the tape, the madder she'd become. Loathe to miss the fireworks, I'd lingered while she stalked the studio in search of her target.

Failing to locate him (coincidentally, the bimbette from downstairs was also missing) she'd returned to Edit Bay three and I'd left her gazing moodily into monitors A and B, still fuming.

I turned left at the corner, heading past the opposite Pontalba building where Harry, the ingrate, had been so fortunate as to secure an apartment. Hearing my name, I looked up to see a party in progress, as usual, on local photographer Louis Sahuc's balcony.

Louis himself was waving a bottle of wine, calling down over the railing that Gerald and Delta and about thirty other people had just dropped by, and why didn't I come up and have a drink?

I yelled back, explaining why I couldn't, but thanks. In the French Quarter, many business and personal transactions are conducted in this fashion.

For example, Louis and I have a mutual friend who was out watering plants on her own balcony one morning, when a guy down on the sidewalk shouted up and asked if she wanted to be an extra in a movie being shot over on Dauphine Street.

She is now a television producer, living in Los Angeles.

Crossing Chartres, I stayed on St. Ann all the way up to Burgundy. As promised, Digby had the gate ajar for Dan and me so he wouldn't have to buzz us in.

I entered the passageway, struck by the difference in atmosphere from the night of Lock's going-away party. The twinkling trees had not yet been switched on, and the faint, murky glow cast by lights beneath the fountain's rippling surface served only to bathe the courtyard in shadows.

The only immediate illumination I could see on the ground floor emanated from blue bulbs in Lock's cobalt display case, which was doing precious little good out here.

Looking up, though, I saw Digby had the second floor blazing like Vegas. He had probably been prowling around up there when it got too dark to see, and hadn't been back downstairs yet.

My pump was well-primed by my earlier exchange with Louis Sahuc, and I had just opened my mouth to yell up to Digby, when someone grabbed me from behind.

They say when you're about to die, your entire life flashes before your eyes, but if mine did, I missed it. Instead, when I recognized my captor, all the pieces of the horrible puzzle begun by Lock's death fell into place while I watched the sequence unwind before me like a tape fast-forwarded on one of Charlotte's monitors.

Now, Lock's convoluted clues seemed to make perfect sense.

Nobody else's *real* name was that of a bird.

Nobody else ever had the same opportunity to kill Duchess.

Nobody else now stood alone to inherit the rock and roll "title" of Teddy Boy Crowe.

Lock hadn't been telling Duchess to take special care *of* him; he'd been warning her to take special care of herself *around* him.

I was vaguely aware I'd missed a point or two somewhere, but that's about the best I could do while staring up in terror at Tom Toy's shadowy face as he gripped my arms with fingers turned to steel by years of guitar playing.

He frowned down at me. "What the hell are you doing here?" he demanded, sounding more puzzled than threatening.

I've always admired those macho women in martial arts films who can deliver a snappy one-liner along with a perfect karate kick to the thorax without sustaining so much as a run in her pantyhose. Since I am not one of these, I wisely refrained, wondering instead if there was some way I could alert Digby before Tom eliminated me.

I decided my best bet would be to try and stall him as long as possible.

"You might consider letting go of my arms, Tom," I bluffed, trying to conceal the quaver in my voice.

To my surprise, Tom immediately released me, "Gosh, I'm sorry, Claire," he apologized sheepishly. "I guess I got a little spooked or something."

"Uh-huh," I said, realizing he wasn't exactly behaving like a desperate killer.

"What I'm doing here, Tom, is I was asked by the attorney in charge of Lock's estate to go through the house with him. My husband will also be here very soon," I added untruthfully. What Dan had said when he dropped me off at WBGZ was, "I'm probably going to run pretty late, darlin'. Dad likes to try on everything in the store."

Tom wandered to the fountain's edge and sat down, trailing a listless hand in the water. "I guess they're going to have to put it up for sale," he commented regretfully. "Old Lock was a big spender, you know. That's a real shame, I always loved this house."

I was getting more confused by the millisecond. With some hesitation, I sat down next to him. "You came here often?"

"Yeah. Him and Mom were pretty good friends, and all. They liked to have Sunday brunch a lot together, said it reminded them of England."

Sunday brunch. Brennan's. Lock with the London *Times*. Duchess Crowe in the powder room.

Tom tossed his glamorous mane, the one his mother had died trying to duplicate. "They used to talk about people I didn't know, things I didn't understand. One time, I heard Mom say she sure hoped I didn't turn out to be like Humphrey, and Lock said I might be the next in line, but there'd never be another Humph."

"Tom, why did you come here tonight?" I asked.

He shrugged. "Well, Vicky Su totally refused to go to the Halloween thing, so I didn't go, either. But, boy, did we hear plenty about it!

"Anyway, somebody wrote down those clues Lock left, and showed them to me. And I finally figured out, they were mostly about *me!*"

So far, we were in agreement.

"And then I figured out, whatever there was to find had to be right here." He waved at the property. "Lock gave Mom a gate key, so I decided to come over and take a look around. But the gate was already open. I'd just gotten here when you showed up."

I swallowed hard and took a big chance. "Tom, did you kill Lock and your mother?"

He looked bewildered. "No way, Claire! I don't know who did Mom, but Lock, well, I thought Lamont . . ." He trailed off.

"Did she ever explain both of you might be in danger from somebody?"

He nodded. "Yeah. That's one reason she didn't want anybody besides the Toys to know who my real father was. You know he got fritzed right onstage at the London Palladium? Well, she said she had proof it wasn't an accident."

Picture this! Rock and roll can be very shocking!

Duchess Crowe, in addition to cutting hair and singing backup, had been an inveterate shutterbug. She would have been onstage at various intervals that night, doo-wahing for her Teddy Boy.

But what about when she was backstage? Had she actually snapped a picture at the exact moment someone did something to make it look as if Teddy Boy had been electrocuted by accident?

I bet she had.

My heart began to pound faster. "Tom, do you know what we're looking for?"

"Oh, sure." He sounded surprised I had to ask. "My mother's marriage license, my birth certificate, and a ring."

"Her wedding ring, you mean?"

He frowned. "I don't know. Could be, I guess. I never actually saw any of this stuff, you know?" A thought occurred to him. "Hey, Claire! I betcha it's one of my dad's rings that he used to wear onstage. Boy, that would be cool!"

It would also be worth a fortune.

I felt like I was groping blindly though a dark tunnel. Way down at the end was a tiny dot of light. The problem was, I could break quite a few bones trying to get there.

"Did your mother ever give you any clue as to the identity of the person who was a potential threat?" I grasped a straw. "Could it be this Humphrey you mentioned?"

Tom laughed. "You mean Humph? Lock always called him Humph. Nah, that was somebody he shacked up with in England in the Year One. Anyway, I know it couldn't be Humph, because he just died a few weeks back."

He paused. "You know what? I heard Mom arguing with Lock about something to do with Humph's death the day before Lock was . . . you know."

The courtyard started to tilt.

Not on the front page. In the *obituaries!*

Plain as day, I could see Lock reading the obituaries at our table, while pretending to listen to my prattle about Charlotte's new job. I'd been offended when he'd commented, "Hmph!"

What he'd really said was "Humph!"

He'd been exclaiming over the obituary of his former lover. And somehow, this Humphrey had had something to do, not only with Lock, but with Duchess and Tom Toy.

What had Lock told Ricky? That he'd been living in a house on the estate of some lord or earl or some title . . .

I stood up stiffly. "Tom, I think I know where those things are."

"No shit? Where?"

"In the London *Times*," I said.

Chapter 37

"Digby!" I shouted, pulling Tom Toy into the house behind me.

"Oh, Claire!" came a groggy voice after some delay. "I'm up here. Can you see? Wait a minute."

The downstairs area suddenly filled with light, then Digby Baker, rumpled and puffy faced, started hesitantly down the stairs.

"Don't bother, we're coming up," I called.

Wearing the expression of a little boy caught with his hand in the cookie jar, Digby admitted the lunchtime martinis had clobbered him, and he'd fallen asleep in Lock's big leather chair.

I introduced Digby and Tom, who, odd couple though they were, seemed to hit it off immediately. Tom Toy would certainly be in need of a lawyer to prove his identity and collect Teddy Boy's millions, and he could do a whole lot worse than Digby Baker.

And, in fact, had, during his brief representation by good old Uncle Duke Abbidis.

When we reached Lock's retreat, I explained to Digby what I'd deduced since lunchtime.

He grew excited. "You mean, the stuff has been sitting right there all the time, in the *Times*?"

The two men joined me as I knelt down by the big basket of back issues poor Lock couldn't bear to throw away. I was thankful to see they were chronologically arranged, since I remembered noticing the exact date of the paper as it lay on the table at Brennan's—Sunday, 30 September. So it should be right on top.

Yes, here it was. And sure enough, here was a long, slim leather case, tucked between the pages of the obituary section.

A sudden cheeping noise startled us all, and then Digby remembered his tiny cellular phone.

"Oh, hey, Dan," he said genially. "Guess what! Claire just"—he broke off. "What? Yes, now that you remind me. Hang on, I'll tell her."

I'd been scanning the obituaries on the two pages Lock had concealed the case between, looking for a Humphrey. Finally, I found him, but my eyes refused to accept what they saw.

"Hey, Claire," Digby was saying, "Dan wants me to tell you D.L. says that the Latin word for crow is—"

"Corvus!"

Everybody in the room but Tom Toy, who looked bewildered, spoke at exactly the same moment.

Which left Digby, myself, and . . . Harry, pointing the gun.

Chapter 38

He took the leather case from my limp fingers.

"All right, everyone. Hands up, on your feet, and turn very slowly to face me," Harry Corvus commanded.

The angles of his face seemed strangely exaggerated, and I finally realized who he resembled. It was Teddy Boy Crowe. I looked at Tom Toy's profile and saw the same fine bone structure.

Harry correctly interpreted my gaze. "Right!" he gave a bitter laugh. "Theodore flushed nine hundred years of meticulous breeding down the loo to produce this . . . mongrel. The very thing I tried to prevent."

"How? By pouring beer into his amplifier or something?" Tom suggested nastily.

"Actually, it was pure Glenfiddich, but I wouldn't expect someone like you to appreciate the difference." Harry smirked. "Dear Cousin Theo would have, however, had he but known."

And with that, Harry launched into an account of how clever he'd been at depriving the music world of one of its legends in such a way that it seemed like an accident.

In every concert, midway through the second set, the stage would be plunged into total black, except for one spotlight beaming down on Teddy as he sat on a metal stool and sang a solo, accompanying himself on his electric guitar.

The number had been, Harry sneered, a slow, sweet, sad ballad called, "What Is Real?" Teddy always introduced it by saying, as Mick Jagger had said about "As Tears Go By," he couldn't believe he had actually written this one himself.

Cloaked in darkness, none of the band could see Harry slip behind the curtain to stage left, and pour the pricy whiskey into the ventilation grill on the head amp.

He hadn't long to wait for the Glenfiddich to flow over all those red-hot tubes in the tube amp, which then shorted out to the cord of Teddy's guitar, into the metal strings, and into his hands, while the metal stool acted like an electric chair and turned the barefoot singer into "fish and chips," as Harry charmingly put it.

During the resulting pandemonium, Harry quickly wiped the amp, just in case there were any stray drops of liquor not evaporated by the heat, then expertly diddled Teddy's guitar cord just as he'd planned, to make it look like the indisputable cause of the "accident." If there had been lingering fumes of Glenfiddich, no one would have thought it odd; Teddy Boy and his band were famous for heavy drinking on and offstage. And at any rate, Harry knew he could count on the odor of charred flesh and burnt metal to overpower everything else.

"Somehow, I can't believe maintaining the purity of the line was all you hand in mind when you went to such great lengths, Harry," I remarked. "That's a mighty altruistic motive for murder, and you certainly don't strike me that way."

In a quite leisurely manner, Harry reached out and slapped me across the face with the leather case. I could feel something heavy connect with my cheekbone. The mysterious ring, no doubt.

"Indeed? And how do I strike you now?"

I glared at him defiantly, resisting the urge to spit in his face. "Like an *avis avidus.*"

Harry thoughtfully weighed the case in his hand, and I braced myself, but then he shrugged. "Well, you're right, of course. Uncle Humphrey, that's Sir Humphrey to you, was a disgusting old pouf who rather miraculously begot one stalwart son, Theodore.

"My father, his brother, was the second son, which, if you know anything about British entailment laws, means he really shouldn't have bothered to be born. But he was the one who really loved the family history. And all he ever got for his trouble was a lousy ring with the Corvus crest." He waggled his right hand, the one holding the gun, displaying the pinky ring, and I swear, that bird's wings seemed to flap.

"He died without a bean, of course, while Uncle Humphrey, well, I shan't bore you.

"At any rate, Theodore took on the name of Teddy Boy Crowe, and became incredibly successful and wealthy. He was even so kind as to offer his poor cousin employment with his band."

"A *roadie.*" Tom Toy achieved a sneer every bit as aristocratic as Harry's.

Harry's face darkened. "As you say. But then, the son of a second son really has no choice, does he?

"It was actually quite fun for a while," he went on reminiscently. "Eventually I was promoted to a managerial position. It was only then I realized the magnitude of the wealth Theodore was amassing.

"Also, around that time, I became aware that chink nigger bint he'd taken up with was not just a passing fancy, but actually quite serious."

Harry was terrifyingly candid about what followed, no doubt because we wouldn't be around to repeat it.

Even if he could drive a wedge between Duchess and Teddy, he'd reasoned, there would always be another woman. So, no point in killing Duchess. Inevitably there would be a marriage and, most likely, children. Even if there weren't, Harry would lose out because all the money would automatically go to his wife.

And Harry Corvus had decided that not only Teddy's huge fortune, but the title, was going to come to him after Sir Humphrey died.

But after he'd gone to all that trouble to remove Teddy, Harry was irked when Duchess swore she could prove she was his wife.

Acting through his lawyers, Sir Humphrey arranged to pay hush money to Duchess all these years, never knowing that Teddy had left behind a legitimate grandson, heir to both the Corvus title and the Crowe millions.

Somehow, Duchess had learned of Sir Humphrey's death right away, and notified the British lawyers. They in turn had contacted Harry, informing him both she and the boy were now living in New Orleans.

Humphrey's widow had authorized Harry to offer her any amount of money she wished to abdicate all claims, and he had anticipated very little trouble, being convinced of his own powers of persuasion.

Someone else from Pinwheel had already relocated to New Orleans to manage WBGZ, but Harry pulled rank and took over the job himself.

He hadn't even dreamed Duchess was in possession of hard evidence that he'd murdered his cousin until Lock, intent on his own agenda, jumped the gun and started blackmailing him.

"How did you manage to kill Mom?" demanded Tom Toy in a choked voice.

Harry shifted his weight and winced. "Nothing easier, if you must know," he grunted, ignoring the furious surge of blood to Tom's face. "And rather ingenious, if I do say so, myself."

"And of course, you do," Digby drawled sarcastically, the first words he'd spoken since Harry had walked in on us. I'd thought he'd gone catatonic.

Harry sailed right on. "Actually, it was a spur-of-the-moment decision. You see, I'd always rather fancied her myself, and I decided if she didn't recognize me, I simply wouldn't bother.

"I had every confidence I could find the proofs Lochner Smith had so stubbornly refused to yield, and after that, the only thing remaining would be to eliminate—*you!* He pointed the gun suddenly at Tom and laughed when he flinched.

"Perhaps you noticed, Claire," he suggested, "that I made a great fuss over her?"

Unwillingly, I nodded.

"The object, of course, was to give her every opportunity to recognize me. But she didn't because I have undergone a quite radical transformation since our mutual rock and roll days of yore. I even made a dinner date with her.

"And then, that wretched little twat Lamont stuck a long wig on my head, and that tore it."

I recalled the moment exactly, although I hadn't realized I was witnessing Duchess Crowe sign her own death warrant as she saw how a head of long hair transformed a sleek television producer named Harry into Teddy Boy's murderous cousin, Hardy Crowe, as he'd been known at the time.

Just to make sure, she'd even asked me his last name.

From then on, she'd withdrawn into a shell, sniffing more grand slam, and downing more tranquilizers, aided and abetted by Lamont, who was angry because she wouldn't share her drugs with him.

I wondered whether she'd guessed Harry would manage to kill her before the day was over, and that was why she'd made peace with Vicky Su, and sent Tom off with her blessing to buy a ring.

"You still didn't answer my question, *Cousin* Harry," Tom snarled, baring his teeth.

To my right, I saw Digby Baker's eyes widen in surprise. He was facing more toward the door than I, and seemed to be staring in disbelief at something out in the hallway.

Before I could turn my head to look, something black whistled through the air past my face, followed by a noise like a bundle of firecrackers exploding in the room.

It all happened so fast.

Harry screamed in pain as the first blow knocked the gun from his hand. He dropped the leather case and was nursing his injured wrist when the second blow cracked across his face, and blood started to spurt from his nose.

I don't believe I'll ever forget the sight of Lamont Hooper, roller skating full-tilt into Lock's own private British Museum, swinging his whip and delivering lash after stinging lash with surgical precision onto the face and neck of Harry Corvus.

How Babs had ever managed to bail him out this time was way beyond me, but the hellcat was back, and on wheels.

"Yes, why don't we tell them how you killed my auntie Duchess?" Lamont shrieked at Harry.

"I saw what you did and I figured it out because I'm *smart!*" Now he was skating a circle around Harry, like Indians surrounding a Conestoga wagon, that deadly whip flaying Harry's tweed jacket to ribbons, and slicing gushing new wounds across the backs of Harry's hands as he sank to the floor, futilely attempting to protect himself.

For the first time, I noticed that Lamont was carrying a large box of Kleenex under his left arm.

"Here's what he did, Tom," Lamont said in an entirely new voice that was chilling in its very masculine lack of affectation.

"He opened that new box of Kleenex you almost dropped, and poured something inside."

Lamont pivoted gracefully and applied a judicious stroke alongside Harry's ribcage.

"It smelled all yucky, like cabbage or somebody farted or something, and I thought he was playing a joke on her like I did. But it wasn't a joke."

Lamont cracked the whip again, and a vertical line of blood divided Harry's face neatly down the center.

Which side was washed in ordinary soap, and which side was washed in Dove?

"Fee, fi, fo, fum!" Lamont squealed, back in character. "I smell the blood of an Englishman!"

He pulled a wad of Kleenex from the box and dropped to his knees on the floor next to Harry. "Oh, poor, poor, Mr. Englishman. Here are some nice Kleenex to wipe that nasty old blood away."

"No, no!" Harry cringed back in horror. "Don't touch me with those!"

"What's the matter, Mr. Englishman? Nice Kleenex. Soft Kleenex," cooed Lamont.

Suddenly, he lunged straight at Harry's face with the handful of tissues, and Harry let out a bloodcurdling yell.

"My God, no! They're full of cyanide!"

"Actually, they're not, Mr. Corvus," said Nectarine Savoy as she stepped into the room. "Thanks to Lamont and Charlotte, we've got those."

Lamont blew his nose theatrically on the tissues he was holding and stuck out his tongue as Savoy snapped the handcuffs around Harry's bloody wrists.

"Gotcha, Mr. Englishman!" purred the hellcat.

Chapter 39

It was two weeks later, getting close to Thanksgiving, and everybody gathered for cocktails at the State Street home of Dan's parents, had much to be thankful for.

A lot of the dust surrounding the murders of Lochner Smith and Duchess Crowe had settled, though the tricky issue of venue raised by Harry Corvus's citizenship was still being negotiated between the British and American legal authorities.

On one hand, no Louisiana jury, confronted with the mountain of hard evidence Nectarine Savoy and her NOPD team delivered to the district attorney, could fail to convict Harry Corvus of murdering Lochner Smith and Duchess Crowe. I actually caught myself wishing there were some way to send him to the electric chair twice.

Maybe even three times. Right after he'd murdered Lock so horribly, Harry had beeped Charlotte from his car phone, then crashed our party, cool as you please. And we'd all actually shaken hands with him!

On the other hand, concerning Teddy Boy Crowe's death, what Duchess had called "a solid gold record" turned out to be the record of the singer's murder.

Inside that leather case, along with ample proof of Tom's legitimacy—including Sir Theodore's Corvus family crest ring, which would now go to his son—were a snapshot and negative, carefully wrapped in plastic. When the British tabloids got wind of the photograph's existence, there was an outcry for Harry's extradition and a movement to reinstitute public hanging—just this once.

Though the original print was artistically shadowed because Teddy always sang "What is Real?" sitting beneath only one overhead spotlight, after the negative had been enhanced by modern technology, the resulting image was all too clear: a long-maned Harry pouring something from a bottle into Teddy's backstage amp while behind him, Teddy's silhouette faced his adoring audience for the last time.

Naturally, there remained a number of questions, and Nectarine was endeavoring to answer those now.

"What I still don't understand," complained Foley, "is why you decided to send in that character on roller skates!"

"Hey, you use the right tool for the right job, no matter what it is," Nectarine replied breezily. "And Lamont was the right tool. Thanks to that tip Dan phoned in from Galatoire's about Mr. Smith's version of a black box, we retrieved the tape Mr. Smith left for us. There was a microcassette recorder concealed in the space between a station mirror and its frame. I'll come back to that point a little later.

"In addition to the actual murder, which was indisputably committed by Mr. Corvus, the tape also records what actually transpired between Mr. Smith and Lamont Hooper.

"As Lamont claimed all along, his motive was pure jealousy, and there was clearly no intent to kill."

She selected a cube of marinated chicken from the platter offered by Rae Ellen and popped it into her mouth.

"I knew I had more that enough to indict Mr. Corvus for the murder of Lochner Smith," she said.

Charlotte interjected, "And then I called and told you what I spotted on the tape after Claire left."

Harry had aggravated her so badly, Charlotte said, she'd paid more attention to those few frames than she ordinarily would have.

When Buddy Gaines returned, she told him what Harry had done.

Naturally, he'd gone over the tape a few times, more to watch himself almost fall than anything else. But then, Buddy noticed something which made him curious.

Using an electronic blowup process combined with slow motion, Charlotte and Buddy saw that Harry had turned toward the wall at the foot of the stairs, pulled the cardboard from the opening of the Kleenex box, and seemed to be shaking his hand over the slot.

The he'd quickly slipped his hand in and out of the pocket of his bomber jacket, and carried the Kleenex at arm's length before him. No wonder he'd put on driving gloves to make a two-minute trip across the street to Billy's!

The camera also plainly revealed that only one person, nearly concealed by the wall dividing the staircase from one half of the classroom, was watching Harry at the time.

Lamont Hooper.

After Nectarine had rushed over to WBGZ to view the tape, she realized that it wasn't good enough evidence.

"No amount of technical enhancement was going to show us what he'd sprinkled into that box, or what he'd put into his pocket," she explained. "And by then, I wanted to nail him for Duchess in the worst way."

She'd immediately alerted Marcel to evacuate the classroom, telling him to warn everybody not to so much as touch a Kleenex, because she was dispatching an officer to confiscate any and all boxes on the premises.

Miraculously, the tainted tissues were still on one of the built-in shelves crammed with back issues of magazines around the corner from the dryer area, where somebody had stuck them out of the way in the confusion following Duchess's death.

By the grace of God, that innocent-looking box of Softique had not turned Harry Corvus into a mass murderer.

Savoy had then visited Lamont in his cell. After questioning him about the incident, she was satisfied he had indeed witnessed everything.

That's when she'd gotten the idea to use him to extract a confession from Harry.

"When I told him we had proof that Mr. Corvus murdered Mr. Smith, he was more than willing to help," Savoy wound up. "The roller skates were his own idea," she added, with a slight smile.

D.L. removed his cigar and boomed proudly, "The reason they knew where to find the bastard was because when I told Dan that *corvus* was Latin for crow, he got worried about Claire and called up Digby on his cellular phone."

Dan's arm was stretched along the back of the sofa behind me. Now he reached down and squeezed me tightly against him. "Little knowing I was about to be an earwitness to that asshole holding a gun on my wife."

Thank God, that telephone was so weensy, Harry hadn't even realized Digby was using it when he'd caught us by surprise. Clever Digby had managed to slide it into his breast pocket still switched on. That's why he'd been standing there like a plastic plant, to keep from interfering with the reception.

While Dan was glued to the receiver at Rubenstein's counter, D.L. got on a pay phone and told the cops what was happening. They were able to tap into the signal, so Savoy and Lamont got an earful on the way over to Lock's.

Savoy had defended her decision to use Lamont Hooper, a civilian, because he truly was the only person on earth who could have done what he did, "the right tool for the right job."

As she'd pointed out to her superiors, if a police officer had elicited a confession by slashing a person with a whip, and offered to stanch the blood with allegedly poisoned tissues, where would they be?

When asked whether she didn't feel she had allowed the whipping to continue too long, she'd simply said no.

"Now, as to that tape recorder Mr. Smith had planted inside his mirror? Well, we did some more checking, and there are itty bitty tape recorders behind every single mirror in every single LockSmith salon."

So that's how Lock supplemented his income so abundantly.

People told their hairdressers *everything*.

Lamont Hooper had resumed his psychiatric testing, and based on his invaluable assistance in capturing a murderer and saving three lives, there was a chance that a judge would order him confined to a private institution for a number of years.

Tom Toy, rather, Sir Theodore Thomas Corvus, had obligated himself to foot the bill for the best therapy available to his distant cousin, for as long as necessary.

Administration of the Crowe and Corvus estates would be divided between Digby Baker of Baker, DeVille and Slaughter, and Dan Claiborne of Blanchard, Smithson, Callant and Claiborne.

Digby was to oversee all financial arrangements, as well as work with the British attorneys, while Dan was going to stretch out into entertainment law, dealing with Teddy Boy's copyrights and Tom's contracts.

And Tom had made one of his new lawyers very happy indeed by purchasing Lock's house and the entire contents (except for a certain cigar holder) as a home for himself and new bride Vicky Su.

The subject exhausted at last, we gradually fell into a contented silence, accented by the occasional clink of ice against glass and the cheery crackle of logs burning in the fireplace.

I looked around Rae Ellen's lovely Victorian parlor at the seven people I cared most about in this world, and felt on the verge of tears when I remembered that two would soon be leaving us.

Dan noticed and stroked my hair comfortingly.

Earlier, Dave Louis and Rae Ellen announced they were moving to Austin, Texas, where D.L. would be doing legal work for Dr. Miguel Jesus, who was constantly harassed by everyone from the insurance companies to the AMA, not to mention the government.

"The man saved my life, and . . . more," D.L. stated simply. "Now maybe I can save his ass."

D.L. had already met with some of the city's leading attorneys, and several had committed to advocacy for practitioners of alternative medicine. They were going to draft a charter laying out guidelines, qualifications, ethics and standards for the field, and present it at a congressional hearing.

Nectarine, who was curled up decoratively on the Aubusson rug at Marcel's feet, reached absently for her glass, which contained the dregs of Rhum Negrita Bardinet on the rocks.

I noticed Marcel raise a questioning eyebrow at Dave Louis, who nodded slightly and grinned.

"Hey, Nectarine," D.L. said, reaching for the bottle of Negrita, "drink up and I'll make you a fresh one. That is, unless you're fixing to go on duty."

Nectarine smiled. "You got yourself a deal, partner. I'm free as a bird for forty-eight hours and this is good stuff."

Foley hoisted his own glass. "Yessir, they sure know how to make rum down there in the Caribbean."

Charlotte laughed and kissed him. "As opposed to where else, you nut?"

As Savoy raised the glass to her lips, Marcel leaned forward with a strange expression. So did D.L.

What was going on?

"Down the hatch!" she declared, and started to take a swallow. Then she stopped abruptly.

From where I was sitting, I could see her eyes practically cross as she reached into the glass and pulled out the biggest, greenest emerald ring I'd ever seen in my life.

And then it happened.

Marcel Barrineau got down on one knee beside her and said, "My darling, surely you must know by now, I love you with all my heart and soul.

"Will you do me the richly undeserved honor of becoming my wife . . . Nectarine?"

Watch for the exciting fourth book in Sophie Dunbar's acclaimed Eclaire series, coming Spring 1999!

Shiveree

Read on for a taste of this delicious new mystery . . .

Shiveree, *alt.* shivaree *n.* Uproarious serenade with pie pans, horns, cowbells, musical instruments and various noisemakers to celebrate the union of a newly married couple. (F. *charivari*)

From the Atlanta *Journal Constitution*, Sunday, October 6

Dalton-Callant

Mr. and Mrs. Emory Meredith Dalton of Buckhead, announce the engagement of their daughter, Amalie Charlotte, to Foley Preston Callant, Jr., a native of New Orleans, Louisiana.

Miss Dalton and Mr. Callant are to wed in a formal ceremony on Christmas Eve at the Peachtree First Baptist Church, after which transportation will be provided for guests attending the reception and dinner dance to be held at the Peachtree Chateau Hotel.

Miss Dalton, who graduated from Sweetbriar College with a degree in Journalism, was recently appointed Executive News Story Director of WBGZ Television in New Orleans. Mr. Callant, a graduate of Tulane University School of Law, is senior partner in the firm of Blanchard, Smithson, Callant and Claiborne.

The bride's mother is the former Daphne Lambert of Marietta. Her father, Emory M. Dalton, currently serves as Chairman of the Board for Peach Island Textiles. Parents of the groom, Foley Preston Callant, Sr. and the former Opal Key, are both deceased.

Following a wedding trip to Italy, the couple plans to make their home in New Orleans.

From the Atlanta *Journal Constitution*, Sunday, November 17

Dalton-Callant

Due to unforseen circumstances, Miss Charlotte Dalton and Mr. Foley P. Callant, Jr. will not be married at the Peachtree First Baptist Church as originally announced. Invited guests will be notified of the ceremony's New Orleans location at the first opportunity. The date, December 24, has not been changed.

The Dalton and Callant families regret any inconvenience.

Mr. and Mrs. Emory Meredith Dalton

request the honor of your presence

at the marriage of their daughter

Amalie Charlotte

to

Foley Preston Callant, Jr.

in

The Crystal Ballroom

of

Riverside Manor Hotel

New Orleans, Louisiana

on

the twenty-fourth of December

at

seven o'clock in the evening.

RSVP

Black Tie

Reception immediately following the ceremony at the River Queen Club

Don't miss these titles by some other terrific mystery writers!

The Charlie Parker series by Connie Shelton

Deadly Gamble
Vacations Can Be Murder
Partnerships Can Kill
Small Towns Can Be Murder

Albuquerque's Charlie Parker doesn't want to be a private eye. As CPA and partner with her brother Ron in their investigation agency, she's only supposed to handle financial matters. But when trouble walks in the door, Charlie can't say no. Against her better judgement, she finds herself in danger on many fronts.

Join Charlie and her lovable dog, Rusty, along with helicopter pilot Drake Langston and the rest of Charlie's family in this critically acclaimed series. Optioned by Tri-Laurel Productions for a series of television movies.

"Charlie is slick, appealing, and nobody's fool—just what readers want." —*Booklist*

"Charlie is a fabulous amateur sleuth!"

—*Midwest Book Review*

Ask for them at your favorite bookstore or call 1-800-99-MYSTERY to order.